MW00880126

CAPTURED

AMAZON BESTSELLING AUTHOR
JORDAN MARIE

DEVIL'S BLAZE
MOTORCYCLE CLUB

Copyright © 2016 by Jordan Marie
All rights reserved.

No part of this publication may be used or reproduced in any
manner whatsoever, including but not limited to being stored in a
retrieval system or transmitted in any form or by any means,
electronic, mechanical, photocopying, recording or otherwise,
without the written permission of the author.

This book is a work of fiction. Names, characters, groups,
businesses, and incidents either are the product of the author's
imagination or are used fictitiously. Any resemblance to actual
places or persons, living or dead, is entirely coincidental.

Cover Design by Vicki Jones Portraiture
Cover Art by LJ Anderson of Mayhem Cover Creations
Model: Jared Caldwell

Interior Design & Editing by Daryl Banner

CAPTURED by JORDAN MARIE
DEDICATION

I'm kind of wordy and my dedications tend to be way too long. Now, if I try and list everyone, I know I would leave people out and feel miserable. So with that in mind I'll try and keep it quick and clean (hah you know better right?)

1. Thank you to Stephanie Puterbaugh and Rosemarie Crespin for allowing me to use your names and play with your pretty toes. Michelle McGinty, I used Michelle in here and thought of you the whole time, but I just need you to know how special you are to me!

2. Thank you to my Badass Bitches #BB4Life

3. Thank you to my Dirty Girls. You know who you are I have no words for the support you've given me.

4. To Daryl Banner, thank you so much for the awesome formatting and editing. You did so much to help me and I will love you forever!

5. Thank you to Dessure Hutchins for being my friend and for petting my hair when I need it the most.

6. Thank you to Fran Owens and Tammie Smith for everything you've done for being my friend and for working tirelessly to help me live my dream. People these ladies are releasing books in February and March and you DO NOT want to miss it. I'm so incredibly excited.

7. Teena Torres my Princess. THANK YOU. That is all.

8. Danielle Palumbo, thank you for helping me to fine tune my self-editing!

Finally, thank you to each and every reader who took a chance on me a year ago and have stuck with me. I love you more than words.

Xoxo
J

CAPTURED BY JORDAN MARIE
CONTENTS

FOREWORD

This book was a labor of love. I put so much into it and though I know most hate cliffhangers, I couldn't find a way around it that wouldn't cheat Beth and Skull. I will get Book 2 in the Devil's Blaze Trilogy out on February 25th and then Book 3 will conclude with Conquered in March. I hope you stick with the books and learn to love these characters as much as I do.

Please note this book is a whirlwind of emotions and may contain sensitive material that could trigger problems for some people. It's not intended for readers under the age of eighteen, as it does contain extreme violence, sexual situations, sensitive topics and death.

Please let me know how you like it! I love to hear from readers!

Xoxo
J
www.jordanmarieauthor.com

CAPTURED

AMAZON BESTSELLING AUTHOR
JORDAN MARIE

DEVIL'S BLAZE
MOTORCYCLE CLUB

CHAPTER 1
SKULL

> **" I get what I want. If I have to work a little harder for it? . . . then it'll be that much sweeter. "**

Three Years ago
Raven Hills, Georgia

I don't know what it is about her. I fuck a lot of women. I'm serious, I fuck *a lot* of women. As president of the Devil's Blaze MC, I have a stable of them. I don't even have a type. Skinny, curvy, firm asses, asses with some cushion to slap, big tits, a handful, small... doesn't matter. I fuck them all, and enjoy them all. Still, when I see her standing on the street in that summer-white sundress with her shoulders bare and that white-gold, blonde hair laying gently on her pale skin, I'm bowled over. It's like something out of a damned movie. The wind blows just right, her hair dances across her face landing against those pale pink lips, and just like that I'm mesmerized.

I have shit I need to be doing. The club has a major arms deal that is trying to go south. I need to have my head in the game, but one fucking look and I have to have her. So, instead of working, I find myself following her into a small coffee shop on the corner of Main Street.

Raven Hills, Georgia is a small town, barely a blip on the radar, and that's what makes it great for Devil's Fire. Nothing comes in or out of this town that we don't know about... with the small exception of this woman I've never seen before.

I stand by the door, ignoring the hush that comes over the room when I enter. I'm used to it. Every person here knows who

I am, and they're smart to fear me. I'm a twisted asshole. Empires are built on fear, and I revel in it.

She orders coffee and a cinnamon roll, takes her order, then sits in the back of the room. My eyes never leave her body. She fails to notice me. Then again, I don't think she realizes the whole damn room is watching her. There are a few men here I may have to kill. I don't care if I haven't spoken one word to her yet. For now, she's my property.

I let her get settled, watching as her eyes clench shut in response to that first luscious taste of coffee. I want to see that same look on her face when it's my lips she's tasting. I watch her take a bite of her hot cinnamon roll and can almost hear the small sigh of pleasure escape her lips. She's found heaven in just one little taste.

I want that look on her face when it's my dick she's putting past her lips.

I cross the room because I can't *not* do it. When I stand by the table, she looks up, giving me her eyes. Hot damn, I didn't know they made eyes that color. Gray, but no gray I've seen before. Warm, crystal clear, breathtaking gray... and I want them to *stay* on me.

Her eyes move slowly up my body. I know what she sees. Scarred, inked, pierced... I have miles on me, miles that have hardened and jaded me. I'm a cold bastard who hides behind an easygoing persona. My men see the real me. Some respect me, but all fear me, and I'm good with that.

She's a princess and I'm no one's Prince Charming, so a part of me feels like I shouldn't touch her. She's pure, sweet, and innocent. I watch as she uses a finger to slide a small dollop of white icing that escaped to the corner of her lips. My dick throbs, imagining my cum on her lips instead. I reach down and adjust the raging hard-on I have while continuing to watch her.

She is not small. Her curves move in all the right places and her breasts are heavy. I have the urge to slide my dick into the valley that shows at the top of her dress.

Yeah, I'm not walking away from her.

"Hello," she murmurs, her voice soft and nearly a whisper. My eyes are drawn to the icing that sits on the pad of her index finger.

"*Querida*," I reply, sliding into the seat across from her.

She looks confused for a minute, then a small smile breaks on her lips.

"Have a seat," she mocks, as I lean back and watch her. We're quiet for a few minutes before she finally shakes her head and asks, "Can I help you?"

"Just taking in the view."

"I see," she says with a frown. I don't like her looking unhappy, though I gotta admit, that little indentation she gets in her forehead is cute.

"Is something wrong?"

"I was enjoying my breakfast," she tells me. "No offense, but I don't really want company."

"None taken," I return as easily, sitting up a little straighter and putting my arms on the table. I lean in so our faces are close together. I smile as her eyes dilate.

"This means... you should leave...?" She says it like a question, and I grin.

"I'm not just *company*."

"You're not?" I watch as she takes a finger and twirls it in the glazed icing of her roll. Her forehead creases again, showing her irritation. I was right; it *is* cute.

"Of course not."

"Then what are you?"

"I'm your future," I tell her honestly, bringing her finger to my mouth. My eyes lock with hers as I let my tongue slide around to lick off the creamy confection. I use just the tip of my tongue, dragging it slowly and teasingly along the tip and then further to her knuckle. My eyes watch hers the entire time before I finally put the digit completely in my mouth, letting out a moan of appreciation.

She bites into her lip. I can tell through the thin white dress she's wearing that her breathing has picked up. She's not immune to me and that pretty much decides her fate.

"Do you mind?" she grumbles, pulling her finger away. She tries to sound pissed, but in her voice, I detect a note of excitement. It's that sound that calls to the beast hidden in me.

"I can give you something else to eat," I tell her, and we both know I'm not talking about anything on this table. I can see the moment recognition flares in her eyes because she blushes. Fuck me sideways. Have I ever known a woman who blushes that sweet?

"Do you know who I am?" she asks, her face tilting to the side.

"Not yet, but I will."

"Be careful what you ask for," she says cryptically, and it makes me smile. She's a sweet little lamb teasing the big bad wolf and she doesn't even know.

"I think I can handle anything you send my way."

"Are you always so…."

"Asombroso?"

"Asombroso?" she repeats, butchering the Spanish word with her sweet, southern accent.

Mi madre was Spanish. I look nothing like her or her family, with the exception of my dark hair. I am my father… the fucking bastard. Still, having been raised by my mother, words slip out from time to time. The woman in front of me inspires them. Spanish words are more lyrical, more soothing, and that is what she reminds me of. She triggers the poetry inside me.

"The man of your dreams," I paraphrase.

"I hate to rain on your parade Casanova, but I have to leave. I'm late," she says, getting up and reaching to gather her trash. I'm quicker, taking it first; I'm no gentleman, but I have my moments.

"And where are you off to?" I ask. "Is there a man I should know about?"

4

"A man?" She smiles. "And if there were…?"

"I'd have to have him taken care of," I tell her honestly. I leave it to her to wonder what that means. If I tell her that no one gets in the way of what I want, I wonder what her reaction would be?

"You're just a tad over-the-top creepy, aren't you?" She says, moving away from me. I let her go, enjoying the curve of her ass as it sways under her dress.

I follow her out to the street. "Same time tomorrow, *querida*?" I ask when it becomes apparent she's intent on ignoring me. My question makes her stop, and she turns around to look at me.

She studies me and those damned gray eyes are sparkling with laughter. I'd like to keep that look on her. A second later, I decide I really want to know what those eyes are like when I'm slipping myself deep inside her, her legs wrapped around me.

"Sure. Knock yourself out." She turns to walk off again.

"You better be here," I tell her, and there's no mistaking the order in my voice.

She turns to fully face me. Confusion and defiance war in her eyes and broadcast on her face. We're having a showdown and I'm going to win. She just needs to accept it.

"And if I'm not?" she asks. I like the spunk she's showing. A woman with fire will warm a man at night.

"I'll come find you," I answer, deadly serious.

"You don't even know who I am."

"Doesn't matter."

"You could be asking for trouble."

"I like excitement."

"I don't know your name."

"You will," I tell her with a grin. I can already hear her screaming it out when she comes on my cock.

She studies me for a moment. Much to my surprise, she gives in. "I'll be here."

I like that she gave in, but am not happy with the note of

sadness in her voice. I'll trade that sadness for moans of excitement soon enough. I watch her walk away until she's out of sight, then head for my bike. She's going to be a challenge. I can't wait.

CHAPTER 2
BETH

*" Just for the promise of him ...
just for the promise. "*

I walk away wondering what exactly just happened. Was that sexy biker really hitting on me?

My body feels like it's been energized with electricity as I make my way back to the bus stop at the end of town. I'll catch the bus, then get off at a stop just a block away from my prison— better known as the Sacred and Pure Hearts Learning Academy of Bantam, Georgia. Bantam is in the next county over from Raven Hills, and there's really nothing there. In fact, the only thing in that place is the private Catholic high school that my stepbrothers Matthew and Colin sent me to when our parents died. I *hate* it. Then again, I don't guess anyone actually likes being shipped off to boarding school, especially an all-female one. It's a failsafe way for the board to make sure the sacred and pure part of their school stays that way.

My life has never been one where I could truly enjoy dating and have a normal teenage lifestyle. The other girls gripe about it constantly. With no boys around, there's a lot of girl-on-girl experimentation. It's either that or Ryan, the school's janitor. I'm not going to say having a little "experiment" hasn't passed my mind, but then again, I've never really had time to think about sex with males *or* females.

Until now.

The guy at the coffee shop was unlike anyone I've ever met. Covered in piercings and tattoos, he looked sexy and deadly at the same time... the ultimate forbidden fruit for a girl who hasn't had much time to think about any of it.

Will he really be there tomorrow? Or was he toying with me? I saw his buddies waiting for him outside the shop. I can't help but wonder if they're all just laughing at the stupid schoolgirl. The guy didn't seem like that type, but I don't know many men to gage him by. He's older than me, and he's definitely a man who knows more than I will ever know about… life. I doubt a high school student who's been sheltered her entire life could keep his interest. Then again, I doubt he realizes I'm even in high school. I look older for my age, plus I'm wearing makeup today. We're not allowed to wear it at school, and when I paid Ryan to help me sneak out today, I insisted that I'd wear real clothes and makeup—*no uniform*. I even had my hair fixed. It's been one of the best days I can ever remember having. It was a big risk, I knew that much, but it was well worth it… even before I met the biker.

And to top it all off: today's my birthday. Not my *actual* birthday, because I won't be twenty for three more months. Today makes eighteen months that I am cancer free. I don't know how to describe what happens when a doctor looks at you and delivers the words that you won't ever be able to truly wrap your mind around: *I'm very sorry, Beth, but you have cancer.* I still wake up in a cold sweat at night hearing those words.

They're not something you can forget.

But I beat the odds, and here I am. No one remembered what today is. Not that I thought they would. I don't really have anyone who cares. My mom married Edmund and that gave me an instant family, but I don't really know my stepbrothers. Last Christmas, mom and Edmund were in a plane crash coming back from the Cayman Islands. I wasn't really close to my mom, but she was probably the only person left in the world who cared—*at least a little* about me. Matthew and Colin? To them, I'm just a responsibility, since they pay for my education and give me a monthly allowance. I guess there are worse things in life, even if I am a bit lonely.

Then, the biker showed up and disrupted my coffee, and the part of me that's filled with loneliness and isolation morphed into something else. I feel excitement. I feel happiness. I feel... *pretty.*

That's another thing you take for granted, you know. *Feeling pretty.* Where you might have thought that about yourself once, cancer finds a way to steal that from you. It ravages your body, leaving you with black bruises, flesh that sags from your bones, and eyes that are so dark and shadowed, you wonder if they'll ever go away. You lose your hair. I'm not a vain person, not really. But each morning, waking up to another small clump on my pillow, or brushing my hair and seeing more in my brush than what was left on my head, killed me. It killed something inside of me that made me feel young and carefree. It killed something that made me feel... *pretty.* Trust me: no amount of wigs or pep talks make it better.

Late at night when I was alone in bed... late at night when I was cramping from the medicine and the hunger, knowing that there was no way I could eat—and not wanting to anyways... that's when I really felt it: *ugly.* All the way through. *Ugly.* I hated the way I looked. I hated the disease inside of me that I had no control of.

I hated... *me.*

The nights were the worst. They were so much worse than the day, because that's when the fear and the doubts crept in. I would get weak and go into the bathroom, stare into the mirror, and cry. I'd cry for losing parts of myself, cry for not knowing what would happen next, and cry because I felt completely and utterly alone.

With memories like that hanging on you, feeling beautiful even eighteen months later is not an easy feat. You grow your hair back, and it's thicker and a slightly different shade than before. Though you like it, you're afraid to trust it, because somewhere in the back of your mind, you're afraid it will leave you again. Even as you watch your body heal and the medication

work its magic, and after you're no longer a rack of bones...
even then, rarely do you feel beautiful.

Today in that coffee shop, I felt beautiful. I felt that way
because this large, scarred, tattooed and pierced biker looked at
me in a way that made me feel like my skin was on fire. I felt
beautiful because *he* made me feel that way.

That's why I am determined to find a way to sneak out again
and return to the coffee shop. That's the real reason I will risk the
wrath of Sister Margaret, because today, a man who was unique
and gorgeous in his own right made me feel beautiful.

As I board the bus to go back to school, I do the one thing
that might even make Sister Margaret proud of me: *I pray*. I pray
that the biker is there tomorrow and I'm not just being naïve.

CHAPTER 3
BETH

"A small taste of freedom is intoxicating. It seduces you. It makes you drunk. Soon, you convince yourself you can have whatever you want. How stupid is that?"

Three days. Three days straight I've thrown caution to the wind and had breakfast with the man known only to me as Skull.

I don't know much about him other than he is sexy as hell, dangerous, sweet, scary, and the first man I've ever met who makes me want... *more*. Which is crazy, because he's the last man in the world who should get that reaction from me. *He's a biker.* Not only is he a biker—if that patch on the cut he wears is to be believed—but he is the *president* of the Devil's Blaze MC. I should be running away from a man like this, not sneaking off to have breakfast with him.

If Matthew or Colin knew I was even in Raven Hills, there would be hell to pay. If they knew I was having breakfast with the president of Devil's Blaze...? Skull or I would be *dead*, maybe even both of us. There would be no in-between.

But even knowing what could happen, I still got Ryan to help me break out of school for the third day straight. I'm still sitting beside the smoothest, filthiest-talking man I've ever met—and loving every minute of it. He makes me laugh. He gives me a taste of... life. For so long, I've just gone through the motions, never knowing what real life was like. I've been, in some ways, afraid to experience it or test the strict boundaries that my family has on me. I know it's foolish, but I want to savor these stolen moments because I know they can't last. *They just can't.*

"You're looking sexy as usual," Skull whispers into my ear. He doesn't bother sitting across from me now. He's right beside me and he has my hand in his, resting them on his lap. His large inked hand swallows my much smaller pale one, and the contrast is beautiful. He's so much bigger than me and he's covered in ink. I see it everywhere on him, and all of it is dark and foreboding—but at the same time captivating. I want to trace every mark and learn why he chose it. His voice rakes across my skin and sends shivers of awareness through my body.

"I shouldn't be here," I tell him honestly.

"You should be in my bed," he growls, nibbling down my neck.

It's ten a.m., the café is pretty empty, and yet still there are eyes on us. That should bother me. It should at the very least *worry* me, but it doesn't, and *that* terrifies me. I could lose myself in his seduction.

"We've only known each other four days. I don't see that happening. Besides, I don't even know your name."

"*Nombre*? Is this what stops you, lovely Beth? My name is Andre. Now, let's get out of here." He growls.

Andre? Okay, that wasn't a name I expected, so I laugh. He stops nibbling on my neck, which makes me sad, but it's for the best. Even though he brings out inner-whore tendencies in me, I can't sleep with him. I won't.

"You find my name funny, Beth?"

"I'm sorry, I just do not see you as an Andre. It doesn't fit," I tell him, choosing to be honest. Skull may have a sweet side when talking, but he's also gritty and dirty and... *Andre* just doesn't quite give that impression.

"Does this mean you will not call me Andre?" He asks, but there's a semi-smile on his face.

"Nope. Sorry, it just doesn't fit. I'll stick to Skull."

"I like the idea of you sticking to me. A coincidence, *si?*"

I shake my head at him. "You're horrible. Stop already. I told you, I'm not falling into your bed."

"It does not have to be a bed. We could use a wall, a table, shower... or perhaps you'd enjoy a hot tub? That can be arranged, no bed required."

"You should get an A in effort."

"You have no idea. Wait until I show you what else I deserve A's in."

I shake my head no. "Do you ever talk about anything other than sex?" I ask, exasperated.

"Of course, though it's not as fun. What would you like to talk about?"

I study his dark face. A few small scars are imbedded in the hardened features, and there's a piercing on his lip with tattoos all the way up to the top of his neck. He's got one of those things in his ear that admittedly I hate, but somehow he pulls it off. Perhaps all the hotness that is him drowns that part out? Who knows? All I know is he makes me weak in the knees.

"What's your favorite color?" I ask.

He leans back and studies me. "Out of all the questions you could ask, the one that comes to mind is what my favorite color is?"

I shrug. It wasn't, but it seemed the safest to go with.

"Black," he answers.

"Black isn't a color."

"What color is that dress you're wearing?"

I frown at him. "Okay, well, black is a *kind* of a color. It absorbs light. It's like the absence of color."

"You make my brain hurt. But I do find myself wishing that the dress you are wearing is absent, so I'll agree with you on that."

I sigh heavily, but it's more to stop the giggle that bubbles up at his hound dog expression. "Your turn," I tell him, glad he's giving me a little room to breathe.

"Are you wet?"

I was taking a sip of my coffee, but at his words I stop mid-drink and nearly choke. "I said no sex talk!"

He winks at me and leans back in the chair. "Where are you from?"

My heart speeds up, but I breathe evenly and relax. There's nothing he can find out if I do this right.

"Montana."

"That fits," he answers cryptically. "How did you end up in Georgia?"

"That's two questions. It's supposed to be my turn."

"I'll owe you one."

"My mother remarried."

"You don't sound happy about it. Who's your stepdad?"

"Ah, ah, ah. It's my turn. Umm… What made you decide to join a motorcycle gang?"

"Club, not gang." He grumbles. I can tell the question irritates him.

"Club," I amend, waiting.

"That is a question for another time," he says, getting up and reaching out his hand to me.

"Time to go?" I ask stupidly, because I don't really want him to leave yet. I enjoy our time together. In fact, spending the mornings with Skull has become the highlight of my day.

"I'm afraid so, *querida*. I have a meeting I can't reschedule."

I get up and let him lead me outside. He always holds me close and puts his hand on my lower back. I like the feeling. It feels as if he has to have me near. I don't think I've ever had that.

"Thank you for breakfast. I've really enjoyed talking with you this week," I tell him lamely as we come to a stop outside the café. Then he does something that I've been admittedly wanting from the first time he spoke to me. His hand slides around the side of my neck and he pulls me to him. The texture of his skin is rough, and a shiver runs through me at the way he grabs and demands I follow his lead. At the same time he pulls me into him, his thumb applies pressure under my chin, so I raise my lips towards him. I don't really need the encouragement. I want his kiss.

At first, his lips against mine scare me. His taste is intense and I want to drink from it. I may never want to stop. But the

cold metal of the hoop in his lip touches me and it feels...
strange. Does it hurt him? How do I kiss him?

"Run your tongue over it and tug gently," he coaches, reading
my mind, and I do as he instructed. It feels different, but erotic...
especially when he groans and shifts my head so he can delve
into my mouth. I guess he likes my fumbling. That's the last sane
thought I have before I get completely lost in his kiss and the
way his tongue seeks out every inch of my mouth.

When we break away, I say the only word I can think of at
the moment: "Wow."

He lets out a snort of laughter, and his fingers wrap into the
hair at the back of my neck. The pressure is enough to cause a
small sting of pain. He rests his forehead against mine. I'm not
sure how long we stay like that, but I like it. Eventually, he pulls
away and his dark eyes look dangerous, intense. They are
predatory.

"I think my knees are weak," I tell him before I can stop
myself.

"Come with me, Beth. You can wait for me at the club, then I
will most definitely fuck you until your knees are weak. You
won't be able to stand for days," he promises, and I'm
completely positive he could make good on that promise.

But I need to go back to reality. "You keep bringing up sex. I
feel it only fair to tell you, I've taken a vow of chastity," I tell
him, avoiding eye contact.

"Chastity? *Mujer loca!* What the fuck for?"

"My life is complicated. This is a way to simplify it."

"So, you are saving yourself for marriage?" he asks
incredulously. It annoys me because, although it's not a popular
decision in the biker world, it is *not* completely unheard of in the
rest of the world.

"Not exactly. I just don't need anything or anyone making
my life more difficult right now."

"I'll change your mind," he says, and he sounds so cocky and
sure of himself that it annoys me further.

"That's not possible," I huff, pulling away from him. I turn around, intent on getting away. I'm not even sure why I'm upset. Part of it is because he's not taking me seriously. The other part, and it is considerably larger, is the fact that I kind of want him to talk me out of it, and that *cannot* happen, *will not* happen.

He slaps me on the ass. It stuns me and I turn around to look at him.

"Be at breakfast tomorrow, Beth. Do not make me come find you."

I don't answer because there's not much to say. I want to tell him I won't be there, but we both know I'd be lying. I'll be there because I can't stop myself. I can't stay away from Skull, and that's bad—*for both of us.*

CHAPTER 4
BETH

" Dreams die hard
and their death can be brutal. "

"There's no way you can sneak out again today," says Michelle, one of my friends from school. "The sisters are already upset that you've missed classes two days straight. They're not buying that you're *that* sick. Mother Margaret already brought up that you were missing Sunday, too. Three days, Beth! If Tiffany hadn't been covered up in your bed pretending to be you at curfew check, you'd already be screwed!"

"I know, *I know*... but I just need one more day. Then, I'll make an excuse to Skull on why I can't be there for a few days. Please? I just need your help to make it happen today."

"I can't believe you're dating a guy named Skull," she says. "When you decide to taste the wild side, you go all out, woman."

"Yeah, I know. Will you do this for me, Michelle? Please?"

"Okay, but if you get caught, you are on your own. I'm not having nuns up my ass because you're looking to get dick in yours."

"That is *not* happening. You're just nasty," I tell her, though the thought of Skull in that moment makes my stomach flutter nervously—and not entirely because I'm turned off.

She laughs and shakes her head. "You'll see. I've heard about those Bikers in Raven. You're in for a wild freaking ride."

I bite my tongue to keep from asking what she's heard. I can't help myself. I want to know everything about Skull and his friends. The days we've met, he's talked about them, and I can tell he really cares about them. They're all close. What would it be like to have people care about you like that? Like... a real *family?*

"I've got to run. Ryan's watching the door so I can sneak out. Thanks, Michelle. I owe you!" I call over my shoulder, intent on making it before my chance is gone. I run down the stairs to the basement. Once there, I use my cellphone as a flashlight and make it to the small door that opens to the backyard on the outside. Once through, I turn around to make sure it's locked with the key Ryan gave me. I'm unprepared for the large hand that claps down on my shoulder. I scream before I can stop myself. He claps a hand over my mouth, muffling my cry and jerking me around hard. My eyes grow large as I look up into the eyes of Gerald, my stepbrothers' chauffeur and lead henchman. This is *not* good. And, from the look on Gerald's face, it may be much worse than I fear.

He doesn't talk. His scarred hand wraps around my wrist and he drags me along behind him. We make it to the limo and he all but throws me in the back of it. As the car door slams, disappointment and fear settle in my stomach.

Some people wait their whole lives to ride in a limo. Some people would kill to have the kind of life I could have, but I don't want it. I never have. I hate everything about being a member of the Donahue family. I might be young and even naïve, but *everyone* knows who the Donahues are and how they've made their fortune. If people find out that I'm a member of the family, reactions invariably go from shock to fear, and for the extremely stupid: *interest.*

The ride back to the house Colin and Matthew live in feels like it lasts forever. In reality, it's a mere forty-minute drive. Still, with each minute that passes, my fear amplifies. I don't know what this is about, but the fact that Gerald was there when I snuck out means bad things.

Shit! I should have been more careful.

When the car comes to a stop, I wait. The Donahue estate is huge. Its large stone pillars and brick façade look cold and regal.

It reminds me of a large funeral home—and just as cold. Gerald opens the door and pulls me out. He didn't need to, I was getting out; I know better than to refuse my stepbrothers. Gerald doesn't care, but then again, I've seen him inflict pain on command. He enjoys it. Even now, his hand is making a horrible bruise on my wrist. I ignore the stinging pain and just follow. There's not much else I can do.

We make it to Colin's office and Gerald shoves me into a chair. Part of me is relieved it's Colin's office. Between him and Matthew, Colin is the one who's been the softest with me. I suspect that's because he wants more from me than he should—especially since I'm his sister by marriage.

"Beth."

Colin's dark voice rings loud in the room. I jerk my head to the patio door to my left. I didn't realize it was open and Colin was there. I swallow because suddenly I'm having trouble finding my voice.

"Col…" I say, using the nickname I gave him when I first came to live with Edmund and my mother. I was foolishly excited to be part of a family and wanted to have big brothers. I soon learned that being a part of the Donahue family wasn't anything like I envisioned. Colin, however, liked the name I tagged him with. He insists I use it now—*just me*. He enjoys it. I hate it, but I don't dare disappoint him. I've also seen what happens when people do that.

"Did you really think my protection would be so lapse that I wouldn't find out what you've been up to?"

I take a breath, trying to figure out the best way to respond.

"Don't bother denying things, Beth. You will only make it worse for yourself. Gerald has been following you to the café the last few days. I know you have been meeting that *biker*."

My stomach churns at both the discovery that Colin knows and at the way he says the word "biker". You can hear the disgust in his voice, as if Skull is so far beneath him. In Colin's eyes, he probably is. He makes me sick with his holier-than-thou

CAPTURED

attitude. Does he think I don't know what the family does to secure their place and fortune? I don't know anything about the biker world, but I know that Skull is heads and shoulders above Colin in being a real man. I've seen it in the way he treats me and in the way he talks about his club and the men he considers his brothers. Colin and Matthew have never cared for anyone but themselves.

"He's just a friend," I tell him, deciding to go with the truth.

"Do not lie to me, Beth."

"I'm not."

"Do you always kiss your friends like you are dying for them to fuck you?"

I flinch in reaction to his question. Colin doesn't talk to me like that. In fact, I can't ever remember him using coarse words at all around me. The fact that they are laced in anger scares me. The very last thing I need is to have Colin displeased with me. Most people never survive that.

"It was just a kiss, Colin. I'm almost twenty now," I tell him, doing my best to sound defensive and not scared or guilty. I'm not sure I achieve my goal.

He grabs my hair, wrapping it around his fist and pulling it tight. Tears sting my eyes and he forces my face up to look at him.

"Have you given him your body, Beth?"

My heart pounds against my chest. Cold, clammy beads of sweat pop out of my skin. I feel the tears leak down the side of my fear-stricken face.

"No… of course not."

"Has anyone got in this body, Beth?" He asks, his voice so cold it amplifies my fear. Before, I only *suspected* Colin thought of me in a way that was not sisterly. Now, I see ownership in his eyes. I see… jealousy.

"No, Colin. No. I was just curious. All the girls talk about kissing, and I wanted to… see what it was like. It wasn't even that good. I think, maybe…"

20

His hold on me loosens, but the venom is there in his eyes and I know, like a snake, it wouldn't take much for him to strike. I find my fear isn't anything to do with me. No… I'm scared of what Colin might do to Skull now.

"Think what?" he asks, his eyes moving down my body. My stomach churns in revolt.

"I… didn't see what they're all so curious about. I… didn't enjoy it," I lie. "I think maybe I'm cold."

"Cold?" Colin asks, and there's something in his eyes I can't describe. I'm lying through my teeth here, but I need something to discourage him, something to diffuse his anger. I'm scared for me, sure. But more importantly, I'm scared of what he might do if he gets Skull in his sights. I can't let that happen. Skull doesn't even know about my family. I haven't wanted to tell him.

"Sister Puterbaugh says that some women are saved from earthly desires… that God has a higher purpose for them."

Colin lets go of my hair and steps back. His eyes never leave mine and I do my best not to show fear while trying to inject sincerity in my lies. Maybe if Colin thinks I want to be a nun, then he will leave me alone. Maybe…

"Dear Beth, no one with a body like yours is made to be a nun."

"If your faith—"

Before I can form a complete sentence, he pulls me from the chair and pushes me against his desk, his hand tight around my throat. I can't get air. My fingers claw into his and panic threatens to engulf me. There will be more bruises there—if I live. I'm beginning to wonder if I will.

"You do not give your body to anyone, Beth. Not even your lips. Do I make myself clear?"

I can't agree or disagree; the tight grip he has on my throat doesn't allow it. Black spots are swimming in front of my eyes and I think I might pass out. Whether it's from fear or lack of oxygen, I can't say.

"I've been gentle with you because of your illness.

Apparently too gentle. You are mine, Beth. No one will touch you except me. No one will stick his goddamn tongue in your mouth but me, and no one will get inside of your body except me. Do I make myself clear?"

His words make disgust boil inside of me. My eyes close, finally the panic and lack of oxygen combining to put me out of my misery. His hold on me loosens and I gasp for air, coughing and sputtering as my lungs try to take it in all at once. My legs are too weak to support myself and I sink to the floor.

"You will stay here the remainder of the week until I see that you have learned your lesson. Gerald, take her to her room."

I hate having Gerald carry me. I want to argue, but I can't, my whole body shaking at this point.

"Beth?"

Gerald stops and spins us around, my head lolling back, but I do my best to hold it up and look at the monster in front of me. We stand like that for a couple of minutes until finally I try to respond. "Yes?" I ask, my voice hoarse and raw. It sounds like I've screamed until I've lost a vocal cord.

Colin's smile makes me shiver. "You will be dressed and down for dinner at six. Do I make myself clear?"

"Yes," I tell him, managing to hold my tears in until Gerald deposits me on the bed and leaves me alone in my room.

I cry until I can't anymore. Exhausted, I fall asleep on the bed. My last thoughts are of Skull and what he must have thought when I didn't show at the coffee shop... or when I never show again.

CHAPTER 5
SKULL

❝ Shit has a way of going from bad to worse in the blink of a fucking eye. ❞

She's late.

It's an unusual feeling, waiting on a woman. It's not something I can remember doing in all of my thirty years. I glance at the clock again. She's exactly twenty minutes late. Each time the door opens, I feel tension coil inside of me, and each time it's someone else, my anger spikes.

I can't tell you if the anger is directed at her or at myself. I was stupid, playing the tease with her. I beat down the feelings inside of me that said to just take what I wanted. She just seemed so innocent. I wanted to give her time. Truthfully, it never occurred to me that she wouldn't be here today. Women don't usually turn me away. They *never* stand me the fuck up. As the door opens again, and it's not her that walks through the door, I realize that I was way too smug.

It's disappointing. I wanted to learn more about this woman, and I most definitely wanted to get lost inside of her. I pull away from the wall I've been leaning on. I'm standing outside the damn coffee shop waiting like a fucking loser.

Screw this shit. Torch is over on his bike talking to some wanna-be muffler bunny, but he looks up and points to the fucking watch he wears. *Mother-fucking-loser.* What kind of fucking moron wears a watch these days? He wants to be a fucking smartass? I'll remind him I'm his president the hard fucking way.

I walk towards my bike which is parked next to him.

"You stay here and don't move. She shows up, you call my ass," I growl, climbing on my girl.

"What?"

"You heard me, fucker," I yell over the purr of my bike. Then I take off and don't stop until I get to my damn club.

* * *

I stare at the empty shot glass. How many have I had? I can't remember. It doesn't fucking matter.

"Thanks for leaving me in town all day, Boss. Real fucking classy," Torch says, coming to sit beside me at the bar. I glance at him before motioning for another drink. I down the shot and let the burn connect all the way down and then flip him off.

"Life's a bitch," I tell him.

"Yo, Skull man. Latch and Sabre just pulled up outside. They're back from patrol," Beast says, grabbing my attention. I'm a little buzzed, but still alert.

"Who told you to come home?" I ask Torch. I've been a bastard to him today and I shouldn't have. I was upset over Beth and he got the brunt of it. Torch is a good brother. He's the man I wish I could make my second. Unfortunately, Pistol was voted into that position before I even made president.

And I hate Pistol. He's a sorry motherfucker, but I tolerate him. He challenged me when I first took over, replacing my *tío*. I beat him down and enjoyed every fucking moment of it. That was six years ago—a lifetime in the club world. Lately, he's been making waves again. I don't know what makes him think he can overtake me, but that shit isn't about to happen. I beat his ass down once, and it appears I'm going to have to revisit that crap.

"No one," answers Torch, "but I figured after three fucking hours, it was okay to give up the ghost and call her a no-show."

Jesus. Three hours? I've been here drinking that long? I look at the still half-full bottle in front of me. *I guess not.* I apparently have just been staring at my drink and mooning over a fucking woman like a damn pussy.

"It's about time we talk about club business instead of having our president sniffing after a piece of ass and ignoring shit that needs to be done," Pistol barks.

Yeah, it's time I visit that shit again. He's asking for it. *Not today though.* Today, I've had more than enough, so I just give him a warning. It's a warning I hope he heeds, but I'm not holding my damned breath.

"Sostenga la lengua or te la vas encontrar cortada," I growl at him, using words only he and I will get the full effect of. I basically tell him to hold his tongue or else he'll find it no longer there. He gives me a look filled with hatred, then walks off. I motion to Latch who just came in with Sabre. Latch nods and, after a few minutes, follows behind Pistol.

Pistol has a brother who is the leader of our Florida chapter. I may hate Pistol, but I do have respect for his brother, so I'm trying to contain this. Still, I'd be stupid to let Pistol out of my sight. A fight is coming, but if the motherfucker is trying to cut my neck or shoot me in the back before then, I want to know.

"You're gonna have to handle that soon," Torch echoes my thoughts. I don't comment. We both know that he is right. Instead, I give him a look of impatience and that is completely on the up and up. I don't want to deal with business. I want to sit here and nurse my drink while remembering how soft Beth's sweet lips were. Jesus Christ, I feel like I'm missing a hit from my favorite drug just thinking about her.

"Visor and a few others from the Chrome Saints have been in our town," Sabre says when it becomes clear I'm not going to talk about the issues with Pistol.

This new piece of news does nothing to improve my mood. I'm going to have to blow that motherfucker off the face of the Earth. I would have already done it, but Visor's a distant cousin to the Irish faction in the area—Matthew and Colin Donahue. In that fucking group, family is family. I have no wish to piss them off. The Donahues are not a group I want in my business. I've had to have a few dealings with them when their pipeline got too close to my territory. Since then, there has been a tentative truce with me overlooking the fact that they run their wares in the county over. I don't want to get in a pissing match with them. I have big guns at my disposal, but so do they. Sometimes, the smartest thing to do is back away and keep an eye on the situation. So, Visor lives... *for motherfucking now.*

"Did they leave?" I ask.

"They're held up in a ratty motel on the outskirts of town, the one beside the Flamingo."

"We need to load up," I growl. "I'm getting too old for this fucking shit."

"Already ahead of you, Boss. I had some of the prospects fill our bikes up. We're ready to head out anytime," Torch says.

"I must be getting old if you already know what I'm going to do," I grumble, getting up and walking towards the garage. I won't be yanking my cock to the memory of Beth today. *Damn it all to hell!*

"Just being prepared, Boss, just being prepared," says Torch, and I flip him the finger as we head out to our bikes. Maybe I'm wrong and this shit won't take long.

We pull into the Flamingo an hour later. We went to the hotel first and found it deserted, so I decided to try the bar. There's not a bike in the parking lot, so it's probably worthless at this point. The roar of our bikes can be heard easily. We're not trying to hide our presence. The bar is not club owned, but the owner and I have an understanding. Therefore, the fact the owner didn't call and tell me the Chrome Saints were in town is something I need to address. I lead the way with Sabre on my right, and on my left is Beast. They're two of the scariest motherfuckers on this side of the Mason-Dixon Line. Behind them is Torch, Briar, and K-Rex. It's not all my firepower, but enough to show we're not about to be fucked with.

What I see when opening the door sends my bad day from bad to fucking shit in about two point four seconds. Big Ray, the owner, is trussed up above the bar hanging from a chain, field dressed like a fucking side of beef in a meat locker awaiting a butcher. The other five customers have all been killed and the two waitresses have their throats slit.

It's a fucking blood bath.

It's all been done for a day or so because the rotting stench is already overwhelming. There's nothing quite like the smell of death. It's an odor that, once you've smelled it, you will never forget.

"Jesus H. Christ," Sabre rumbles behind me.

"Do you think the Saints did this?" Torch asks, and he has a right to be skeptical. Visor and his crew are fucking bastards, but even they wouldn't be this messy, unless he had a reason. That would mean the Chrome Saints' presence here isn't just an annoyance. It means something else, something else entirely.

"Fuck, this smells of Donahues," Beast says, and he's not wrong. The Donahue Gang are famous for leaving scenes like this.

Fuck me sideways. What caused them to do this? They're bastards, sure, but to start a war and send a message this big without reason? It just doesn't ring right. There's more going on here.

I look around and my hand curls into a fist as I think of a way to deal with this shit. I'm going to have to meet with the Donahues. First, I need to clean this fucking mess up before my area comes under scrutiny from sources I can't contain. *Christ on crutches!* I did not need this headache.

"Call Martinez," I tell Torch, naming our main guy with the Calloway County police force. "Make sure this shit gets contained."

"This isn't exactly going to be easy to sweep under the rug, Boss," Sabre speaks up, and I flip him off. I'm not stupid, and Sabre knows it. Martinez will know with one look who is responsible for this shit. He'll know who to contact and where to sweep it.

I walk out of the bar and drink in the fresh air. This shit is going to get ugly. I can feel it. The only good point is, it might keep me from dreaming about Beth. I've got enough on my plate. This was a message tonight, and the message is clear. For whatever reason, my truce with the Donahues has ended. I need to keep my mind focused and my wits about me. There's no time for Beth in my life. I need to keep remembering that.

CHAPTER 6
BETH

" Is lying by omission the same as lying? I never wanted to be the kind of person who lied to get what she wants, but I think I might be when it comes to Skull. "

It's been a week since I've been under house arrest. One week with no one for company but Colin, Matthew, and the staff. One week in which Colin has been watching me like a hawk. He hasn't laid hands on me again, but he has touched the bruises he inflicted, petting them and warning me that I should not make him do that again. The thing that has become clear though is, he *likes* the bruises. I get the feeling he wants more of them. Looking at him across the table makes my skin crawl.

"You will go back to school today, Beth."

Joy spreads through me at the announcement. I was beginning to think he wouldn't ever let me go back.

"Thank you, Col," I say, hoping I sound suitably remorseful. My time here has been hell. I have this plan slowly percolating in the back of my mind. I think I might try to run away on a bus, if I can make it to the Greyhound station. I'll just start riding until Georgia is nothing but a bad, bad memory. I won't miss anyone unless you count Skull. Then again, I can't have him anyway.

"Gerald will drive you. Do not disappoint me again, Beth. There will be consequences if you do."

"I understand."

"I will also expect you back home every weekend. We need to start getting to know each other."

"We do?"

"We do. You have a future and a place in our family. The biker does not fit into that. Do not forget, or I'll show you in a

29

way you won't be able to forget."

I can't answer. My voice has fled once again. I just nod in agreement and walk towards the front door. My body stiffens when Gerald's hand touches my back, and he guides me to the car.

* * *

I never thought I'd be glad to see SPH, but as it comes into my line of sight, I'm nearly jumping for joy. When the limo comes to a stop, I don't wait. I open the door and jump outside. I don't turn around when I hear Gerald call my name—I just keep going. I don't take a breath until I make it behind the locked gate. Even then, I keep going. Friends try to stop and talk to me, but I don't answer them. I walk past everyone, my mind on only one thing. I walk down the stairs and into the basement. I don't have my cell because Colin took it, and even though I got it back, I left it in the hall when I first entered the building. I don't know if he did anything to it, but I wouldn't be surprised if he put some kind of tracker on it.

I go through to the door that Ryan always leaves unlocked for us girls to sneak out of. It's probably sacrilege, but I offer up a prayer of thanks when the door pushes open. The backyard is more like a thin strip of land; if I lay flat in it, one hand could touch the building and the other could touch the fence. Because it's so small and fenced off from the front, the nuns apparently don't think us girls use it. The back fence is nothing like the cold black iron bars of the front. The back is cement blocks and, while definitely tall, they still are only about four and a half feet. Ryan has brought out some more blocks for us to stand on, and once I climb on those, I can jump over the fence.

It's crazy, and I shouldn't be tempting fate this soon, but I'm not running away to Bantam. I won't see Skull again. I don't want to put his life in danger. No. This time, I'm just having a meltdown. So I go to the one place that makes me feel real.

Gethsemane Gardens Cemetery. It's a huge local cemetery that you can't walk by without seeing several tents up of people that have passed on and are being buried. I go here once a week, but not to visit my mom or Edmund. Their plots are on the other end far away from the small grave I visit. I walk by the manmade pond, which has swans swimming in it, then go to the third grave on the left. It's a seemingly unimportant grave marked only by a small nondescript gravestone, yet it means everything to me.

Katie Benson. Daughter and Sister.

"Bethie? Do you ever wonder if we'll marry someone like our dad someday?"

"Not me. I'm never going to marry someone like our dad. The guy I marry will be kind and sweet. He'll have pretty green eyes that sparkle and he will laugh. He'll like rainbows and ponies and, most of all, he'll like me. And when he has a little girl, he'll make sure he hugs her and plays with her. What about you, Katie?"

"I'm not getting married. I'll use a man for sex and that's it."

"Katie!"

"What? That's what mom says men are only good for."

"What's sex?"

"I think it's where you hug and kiss and watch movies together."

"Oh. Well, then... I'm just using a man for sex, too!"

"It's a deal then. Let's pinky swear..."

I play over the memories in my mind, hearing our voices just like it was yesterday. God, I miss her. Would she be disappointed in the person I am now? We were so close when we were younger. Then our parents divorced. Somehow they got it in their heads that, because we were twins, dad would take one of us and mom would take the other. I still wonder which of us got the better deal. In truth, neither Katie nor I won the parent lottery on either side. The last time I saw my sister, we were ten years old and Roger, my dad, let Katie come visit for a week before he took her to Scotland to visit his relatives there.

"What happened to your sister?"

It's Skull. I look up, startled to find him standing right there beside me, staring down at Katie's grave. There's a hundred questions that form on my lips. I look around to make sure I'm still without Gerald. All I need is for Colin to think I've already disobeyed him.

"What are you doing here?"

"Tracking you down," he answers simply. "You've not been at school all week. You didn't tell me you were in high school."

His voice sounds accusatory. I've already had about all I can handle.

"It didn't matter," I tell him, resenting the fact that he's here and taking my time with my sister and angry because he's within touching range after a whole week without him—and I can't touch him.

"It matters very much, *querida*. Men go to jail for fucking kids. Hell, I feel dirty for even talking to you."

"I'm not a kid."

"You're in fucking high school. You're a kid."

"I'll be twenty in just a little over a month now."

"I know. It's the only reason I'm allowing myself to chase you down," he says, crouching down beside me.

My eyes follow his movements, drinking him in. I've missed him. I'm dying to touch him and I can't.

"How did you know to look here?"

"It turns out, Beth, it's hard to track a woman down with just her name."

"Did you ever think that might be a sign that you shouldn't?"

"I did. Especially after finding out you were in high school. Why are you, anyway? Your records said you took a year and a half off on personal leave. Why?"

"You went through my records? Aren't those things supposed to be confidential?"

"Unfortunately, I've not been able to go through all of them yet," he says, ignoring her question. "Who knew a damn school would have such great security? But I will, eventually, so you might as well tell me."

"I was sick," I tell him, getting up and dusting myself off. I really need to get back to the school. The last thing in the world I need is to be seen with Skull now. Colin would kill him. I don't have any doubts.

"Sick, how?" Skull asks, standing.

"You know, that's a personal question I don't choose to answer. I stopped meeting you. I may be the young one here, but even I know what that means, Skull."

"What does it mean, *querida*?"

"That I've moved on...? That I don't want to see you again...?"

I tried to make my voice sound hard. I know I failed. It sounded weak and unsure because it's not what I want. I should just tell him about Colin and Matthew. If I do that, then he'll leave me alone. He'll see why he *must* leave me alone. I can't bring myself to do that. I don't want to shut the door completely. *Not yet.* I have to work up the courage for that.

His hand goes around my throat. He's the second guy in a week to do that. Skull's hold is much different, though. It's strong but gentle at the same time. His hold makes my heart beat faster, but not in fear. His thumb brushes back and forth on the pulse point there and he holds me so my gaze locks on his and I can't look away.

"You're young, *querida*, so I will explain this to you one time. *I* will tell you when we are through. *I* will tell you when it is done, *not* the other way around."

"That's crazy. You can't just make those decisions about my life."

"Aw, but that's what you were doing to me, *si?*"

"No! I just decided I didn't want to date you. You're all wrong for me."

"I've decided I don't want to date you, either," Skull says, and I feel like I've been sucker punched. All of the air lodges in my chest and I do my best to hide my reaction.

"You don't?" I ask, confused and feeling like I want to cry. What I should be doing is celebrating, right?

"No, Beth, I don't. I want to fuck you. And I'm going to."

His words leave me speechless... and aroused.

"Skull..." I trail off, because I can't think of what to say. Not one word.

"I'm going to fuck you hard," he tells me, and my knees threaten to buckle. "I'm going to fuck you slow." My nipples harden and my body heats as he continues. "I'm going to fuck you so many times and in so many ways, you won't remember the name of any of the men who came before me. And woman, any that come after will pale in comparison."

I should run away now, or call him out on being a conceited bastard... but I do neither of those.

"There hasn't been anyone else," I whisper mindlessly, hypnotized by the sweet mixture of his words and the look in his dark eyes. When I tell him I'm a virgin, his look changes. I can almost feel an electric current pass between us.

His hand moves up from my throat to my chin. He drags his thumb along the corner of my mouth and then sweeps under my bottom lip and back again. I try to concentrate on the movement because my heart is hammering like crazy and I feel like I might float away, all because I have somehow captured this man's attention. I've made him... *happy.* That's what I see in his face right now: happiness.

I've been alone most of my life. I've had a lot of reasons to be unhappy. So, I'm familiar with that look. And Skull from the coffee shop? Despite his teasing flirting, he had *that* look. To see the change in this moment and know that I was the cause, for whatever reason, hits me, and it hits me hard.

"*Cristo!* You are something else," he finally says, and then he leans into the side of my neck and whispers softly in my ear. "You've stopped breathing, Beth."

He's right. But, as I feel the soft trace of his breath against my skin, I still can't make my lungs drag in air. His hand slides to my side and holds it. His touch seems to brand me and heat me from the inside out. My pulse is hammering in my body, the sound of it echoing in my ears.

"My sweet, delectable Beth... I will fuck you gentle the first time. Exciting you until you scream my name and come over my fingers, and then I will feed your hungry body my cock one slow inch at a time."

"My house mother says making love out of wedlock is a sin," I tell him, trying to ignore the dampness in my panties. I'm kind of amazed they haven't melted yet.

"Are you Catholic, Beth?" he whispers again, and his lips touch the side of my neck placing soft, teasing kisses.

"My family is." I gasp as I feel his teeth pinch the skin, then his tongue brushes away the sting.

"Were you raised by nuns?" he asks, sucking on the skin he's been toying with. I go to the tips of my toes and lean into him, wanting more. My hands find his thick, muscled arms to cling to.

"What? No. Sister Puterbaugh is a teacher..."

His tongue slides to my ear, tasting my skin and sending pleasure through my system. He sucks the lobe of my ear into his mouth next, using his tongue to tease me further. My eyes close as my head falls back, giving him more access. My fingers bite desperately into his arms now because without that hold, I fear my legs will give out.

"Do you remember everything you are taught in school?"

I try to concentrate on his words, but his other hand has pulled on the fabric of my dress. Cool air hits my thighs and his fingers dance over the rim of my lace panties. Chills explode over my skin.

"What?" I ask again, losing myself in the feel of his fingers against my skin.

They slide under my panties. His fingers dive into my center and the wet heat that has pooled. He doesn't do anything else. He just keeps his hand there, cupping me. It feels as if he's claiming

35

that part of me. Branding it as his... with just his solid touch. I never let anyone touch me there before. Right now, I think I might die if he stops. His fingers slide through my lips, separating them and gathering the moisture he finds there. I can feel my cheeks heat up in reaction and I finally release a breath, my nails biting into his skin. The sound is ragged and winded. My heart beats harder against my chest and my entire body feels flushed.

"You're wet for me, Beth."

I swallow and bite my lip to keep from moaning. "We shouldn't do this," I tell him even when I don't want him to stop.

"We're going to do this and much more, Beth. I'm going to teach you how much fun sinning can be, *querida...*"

"I can't... I have to be back at school before... before lunch is over..." I moan as one of his fingers pushes into me.

"I'm going to have *you* for lunch," he says, and then his lips take over mine.

Before Skull, I've kissed a total of two people in my life. When I was nine, Thomas Slone pulled my pigtails on the playground and chased me. When he caught up with me, he shoved me down on the ground and kissed me. The other was before I got sick. I was a sophomore in high school and my roommate had a date with Ted, a boy who went to a reform facility. Our school invited several over for a coed dance. Well, when I say she had a date, I really mean they were going to sneak under the gym bleachers away from the ever-watchful eyes of the sisters. He was experienced. Rose wasn't. That's where I came in. She and I were each other's first real French kiss. It did nothing for me. Rose apparently liked it because she's had four girlfriends since then.

This kiss from Skull is different than our first. The first was good, but this one is meant to seduce and destroy my defenses. It's also totally doing the job. I never want him to stop what he is doing to me. *Ever.*

His tongue pushes into my mouth at the same time his finger

slides through my wet depths. He hones in on my swollen clit and I moan into his mouth. My body feels weightless. Skull's tongue swirls in my mouth, dancing with mine in the same sweet movements with which he's teasing between my legs. I've touched myself a few times, mostly before I got sick, but nothing I ever did made me feel like this.

When he pulls away from me, my lips follow him, still needing his. He ignores my silent plea, instead going back to nibble on my shoulder and neck.

"You kiss much better than Rose," I whisper inanely.

Skull's body tenses for a minute and then I can feel his lips curl into a smile against my neck.

"Rose, *querida?*"

"Rosemarie Crespin. She was my roommate at SPH," I explain, trying to position my body to get his fingers to move back where I want them. He, unfortunately, ignores *that* silent plea too.

"Odd," he whispers, finally bringing his fingers back to my pussy, petting me gently. I clamp down tight over his hand and moan at the friction that vibrates from my clit. My hips buck as I try to ride his hand, needing the orgasm he's begun inside of me.

"Odd?" I question, trying to keep up with the conversation, but my word ends with a frustrated growl as his hand latches onto my hip and he stops me from moving.

"From any other woman, the idea of you kissing another female would have me hard and demanding I watch. I find my jealousy will not even allow another woman to touch your lips. They are mine now, sweet Beth. Just as the rest of you is. I'll show you when we get back to my club and then, and only then, will I allow you to come. So stop trying to ride my hand before I have to spank you."

An image of me bent over with Skull spanking me flashes in my mind and my body betrays me by getting… *wetter*. I know Skull can feel it slide out onto his hand. His smile widens.

"Perfect, Beth. I believe you might just be *perfect*," he

groans, taking my mouth again, harder this time, and I can feel a fine tremor run through his body as he pushes against me. "Let's get out of here so I can fuck you the way you deserve," he growls, taking his hand away from my pussy and letting my dress fall back down my legs. My heart stutters as I watch him take his fingers in his mouth, tasting me. I'm frozen, so lost in my excitement that I can't think. Skull pulls on my hand to lead me away and that's when I begin to come out of the sex-induced haze that he put me in.

What am I doing? What was I thinking? My eyes dart around our surroundings and I'm thankful everything seems to be deserted.

"I can't, Skull. I have to be back at the school. I'm already in trouble for missing." Again, I omit who I'm in trouble with. It's foolish. I need to give Skull a reason to leave and not come back. Colin Donahue would definitely do that and more. Why do I keep skirting around that?

"It doesn't matter. I'll bring you back tonight," Skull says impatiently. I want to agree with him and forget all about my obligations. I want to open myself up to anything and everything he wants to give me, but if I do that, it could mean his death.

"It does, Skull. I have responsibilities here and I need to graduate," I tell him, only half lying. Right now I don't give a damn about graduating. But I do care about Skull. I have to get him to leave... *I have to.*

CHAPTER 7
SKULL

> **It's time Beth learns who is in charge.**

I stop at Beth's words. Not because I fully agree, but because I'd like to make sure she's graduated high school before chaining her to my bed. I have a feeling that when I get her, that's exactly what I'm doing.

But for fuck's sake, I've gone a week without her. I don't know why I'm so addicted to this woman, but I am. And I felt how wet she was for me. She feels the same. She's too inexperienced to hide it from me. Hell, maybe that's part of the draw. She's innocent and that innocence lures me in. I've never had that in my life. She's like light in a dark room. Shit, just seeing her smile makes me feel younger, less jaded and beat down from the world. I shouldn't touch her, but I want to. I shouldn't want to claim her, but I do. I'm enough of a cynic to know that once I've had her a few times, I'll probably grow bored. It might hurt her, but she has to learn about the world from someone, and why shouldn't it be me?

"When can I see you again?" I ask her now, conceding only because it's not practical for me either. The Donahues aren't taking my calls. They are purposely ignoring me. I had Torch send them a message today. I need to get back and see if things get... *ugly*.

She pales at my question and pulls her hand away. Her body goes into a defensive position and, as she opens her mouth, I know she's just going to deny me, so I stop her before another sound's uttered.

"Don't bother saying no, Beth. This will happen. You need to get used to it. You let me in. I'm not fucking leaving until I grow tired or bored."

"Oh my God! You did not just say that!"

"Why not? It's the truth."

"You're a jerk... a conceited jerk!"

I shrug off her answer. She really has no idea who she's dealing with.

"Just tell me when and where, and you can go back to the school."

Fuck, I feel like a dirty old man just saying that. Apparently I *am* a fucking pervert because my dick jerks at the mention of her being in school. I wonder if she has a school uniform. Does she have a sexy little plaid skirt?

"I... Skull, I... well, there are things you don't know. It's just—"

"What don't I know?" I ask, thinking it might be best just to cart her over my shoulder and be done with it. I'm getting tired of hearing her challenge me.

"Well... I mean, I just don't think it's a good idea for us to see each other."

"You're wrong. Now, you have about two minutes to give me a time, or I'll just drag you back to my place and make sure you're there when I want you," I tell her calmly, crossing my arms and appraising her.

"You're kidding me! You just said you could break it off when you grew bored! Well, I don't want this. You're a jerk. I don't want to give my virginity to someone who tells me he'll grow tired of me eventually. It's over!" Beth announces, then twirls around and begins marching away.

She's cute. Damn cute. I can't deny that what she says makes a certain amount of sense, if you're young, naïve, and still believed in relationships that lasted a lifetime. I don't. *Never have, never will.* And, as much as I like watching her ass twist as she walks away...

It takes two large steps and, being the bastard that I am, I wrap my arm around her waist, pull her hard against me, and wrap my hand in her hair, pulling her head back tight so she stops squirming. I'd enjoy the fuck out of her squirming, but if she keeps it up, I'm going to take her virginity here in the cemetery—and there's not a fucking thing that'll be gentle about it.

"It's not ending yet, *querida*," I say. "Not by a long shot."

"I don't... want you," she whispers.

Maybe I'm a bastard for not listening to her denials. I lean down and run my tongue up the salty skin of her neck, stopping when I'm at her ear.

"You may say no, but your body says something else entirely," I tell her. "Even now, your sweet little cunt is filled with your desire. I bet it's running down your legs because your body is weeping for me, readying itself... *for me*. I could fuck you up against the tombstone right now, Beth, and do you know what? You'd not only let me—you'd *beg* for it by the time I was done. So name a fucking time for us to meet, or I'll prove you a liar right now. The choice is yours."

Her breaths are coming in ragged gasps. Her nipples are pebbled hard against the white cotton dress she has on. She's close to the edge and I've done very little compared to what I want to do. She licks her lips and her gray eyes search for mine, but it's impossible for her at this angle.

"My guardians know I've been sneaking out. It will be hard to get away," she reasons.

I kiss her temple and carefully release her, knowing I've won. The thrill of victory is not there. It's a sad consolation gift because what I really want is to fuck her—and fuck her *hard*.

"Tomorrow, meet me here at this same time. Do not be late, *querida*. I am not above coming to your school to get you, and I'm pretty sure that is *not* what you want."

She pulls away from me. She looks back briefly, and her eyes are large with shock.

"Skull…"

"Go, while I'm still of a mind to let you, Beth. *Tomorrow*."

She swallows, her hand coming up to her throat.

"Tomorrow," she repeats, then backs away from me. Once we are about ten feet apart, she turns and runs the way she'd come.

Me? I adjust my dick and promise myself to make it better tomorrow. *Damn…*

CHAPTER 8
SKULL

I like fucking -- not being fucked with. Some assholes need to know the difference.

"Hey, Boss," Latch calls out.

He's getting ready to re-up. They'll be shipping his ass out to Kandahar next month. I'm going to miss the bastard. It's been nice having him home, but he gets bored when he's not deployed. Sabre has tried to talk him into sticking around, but he's not having it. Latch and Sabre are closer than brothers. They fought alongside each other for five years in that hell. When their platoon got cornered and was taking fire, they lost every friend and squad member they had. The two of them worked to save each other. They survived being POW's together—and I figure a hell of a lot more. I don't ask. Some shit a man never wants to talk about. I know I have crap I don't want to rehash ever again.

"Hey, man. Sabre and Torch back yet?"

"No, not yet, but Sabre checked in about twenty minutes ago and said the package was delivered."

I nod. Well, that's one good thing for the day. Let's see if the Donahues can ignore that shit. *Bastards.* Scarlett, one of the club girls, comes over and my body goes tight.

"Skull," she purrs, setting my nerves on end. Her body pushes up against mine, her breasts against my arm. My dick doesn't even move. It's like the damn thing is broken. I know the truth, though. I only want Beth. No other pussy will do. It's a temporary thing. I've always had a healthy appetite for sex. I just need to fuck Beth out of my system and get back to normal.

That begins tomorrow. "Hey, Scarlett."

"I've been a bad girl. I need to be punished."

And the dick… *still doesn't move.*

"Tell me you're *not* that big of a fucking idiot!" Pistol yells from across the room, marching in and slamming the door. He strides over to me and, as much as I want to kill him, I'm grateful he gets me out of the mess with Scarlett.

"Another time, pet. Another time," I tell her before turning all of my attention to the man I'm going to kill before the month is out. I just know it in my gut. He's pushing me too far. I turn around and face him like I'm bored, then wait.

"You had Torch tell the Donahues that unless they agree to meet with us, you're confiscating their next delivery? Are you loco or just fucking stupid?"

"I do not like being ignored. I needed to get a message across."

"Oh, you'll achieve that. You'll get every fucking one of us killed!"

That's when I snap. I strike so fast he doesn't see me. A quick kick with my steel-toed boots knocks him to the ground, giving me time to get up. While he's holding his damn dick, I stomp his ribs—I'm not sure how many times. Could be three, maybe four… it's so fun that I lost count. I have a lot of anger inside of me right now, and this motherfucker just tipped me over. I grab him by his damn cut and slam my fist into his nose, the same fist which happens to have my rings on each finger— skulls, of course. Blood splatters out and Pistol groans, but I've been so fast and hard on beating him down that he honestly can't do much by this point.

"Has ido a hermano ahora," I tell him, my voice laced with disgust. *You've gone too far, brother.* Even the words annoy the fuck out of me. He's not my brother, but he sure as hell went way beyond too far. I slam his head hard against the thick wooden bar. The bottles and glasses rattle in response. Any resistance left in Pistol is gone as he loses consciousness. I drop him to the ground. "Beast?" I call, looking at the pathetic pile on the ground.

"Yeah, Boss?" Beast lifts his bitch of an old lady off his lap. She must need money again; it's the only time we see her around here. Why Beast keeps fooling with her fucking ass, I don't know. Ain't no pussy worth the shit he's gone through with her.

"Lock him in his room. Have the prospects guard him. He doesn't go for a shit, unless I know about it. Then, contact Spike in Florida and tell him I need to talk to him. We'll have Church after I talk with the fucker's brother."

"Damn… Gone so long without war and now we have two," Beast mumbles, dragging Pistol away.

"You got a problem with it?" I ask Beast because I respect him. This wasn't something I could bring before the Church. I'm president. This is *my* club. I'm not asking anybody for permission and I won't tolerate disrespect. I've tolerated it for too long with Pistol. That ends tonight.

"Been a long time coming, Boss. I'm just thinking shit might get a little *too* interesting around here."

He's probably not wrong. I'll have to call in a few markers from our other chapters and talk with some of my allies. It's time to circle the damn wagons. My taste for the drink gone, I leave the bar and head off to my room. I lock the door and make it to my bed. This place is like an apartment of sorts. It has my office and two doors. One is a regular door, which leads to my bedroom with a connected bath, and the other is a steel-reinforced door that is the back exit of the club. Both stay bolted, and I'm the only motherfucker with the key.

I'm too fucking keyed up. I yank off my cut and shirt and throw them into the chair by my bed. I undo my pants and zipper, leaving them hanging low on my hips. I'll need to go back out and deal with shit once I know the response to my message. Right now, I just want to be by myself and drink. I grab a half-empty bottle of vodka on the nightstand and open it before taking a swig and falling back on the pillows.

My mind should be anywhere but on Beth right now—but

she's all I can think of. Even now, I can remember the feel of her sweet cunt. Hot and wet, sucking my fingers in so eagerly. My cock swells with need, and I regret not forcing her to come back with me. I try to tell my body: *tomorrow, just twenty-four hours.* Then I remember the way her cream felt clinging to my fingers, and fuck, her sweet taste.

Being a man who has always enjoyed sex—perhaps too much—you would think that the taste of pussy would all be the same. That's not the way it is, though. Each one has a special essence, a special flavor. But Beth... Beth is unlike any woman I have ever tasted. She's indescribable, and something I must have over and over. My balls ache from the need to come. I slide my hand around my cock, choking it tightly in my hand, trying to stem the need inside of me. Instead, translucent strands of pre-cum slide from the head, trailing down the shaft and onto my hand. I lean back on my pillow and close my eyes. Beth's face immediately comes to mind. Her lips swollen from my kisses, her sweet pink tongue coming out to tempt me, and her hair tangled around her face because I've held it tight in my hands... I can hear her sweet voice whisper my name... *Skull...*

My hand glides up and down my shaft, my pre-cum bathing my cock. Up and down I move, squeezing, imagining it's her sweet pussy I'm tunneling inside of. *Skull...* Again, her voice haunts me and I imagine she's moaning my name before she comes, tightening the muscles of her pussy and clamping down on my cock, squeezing it tighter and tighter. I growl out her name when I can feel my climax racing forward. The electric zing flashes up my spine and then cum is streaming from my cock, shooting in the air, and falling down on my stomach and against the headboard of my bed. I pump my dick until my orgasm is finished then squeeze the head tight, draining the last of my cum.

When it's over, I lie there... *unsatisfied.* She's going to make this up to me. I'll fuck her face so hard she won't be able to close her mouth for a week. Disgusted, I go to the shower. She'll definitely make this up to me.

CHAPTER 9
BETH

> *Fear overwhelms you,*
> *but apparently it doesn't stop you*
> *from making stupid decisions.*

What am I doing? I'm so stupid. I'm an idiot, really. It's the only thing that's certain in my life. My mental tirade has repeated over and over in my head from the time I left Skull yesterday until right now at this very moment, standing in front of Katie's stone, waiting for the one man in the world I should stay completely away from. I don't, though. I choose to ignore common sense. I ignore my overpowering fear... and end up here instead of back at school.

The only excuse I have is that after Colin's text this morning, I have a bigger fear. Colin has ordered me home this weekend. We're going out to dinner together. Like a fool, I thought it was just another family dinner, and I asked if everything was alright.

His response made my blood run cold. He thinks it's time to announce to the family that we're a couple. "You ought to get accustomed to what I expect of you." That's what he said. I have no idea what that means, but the implications chill me.

I can't let it happen. I just can't let my life be one in which I'm... *Colin's.*

That means I have to run away before Friday evening when Gerald comes to pick me up. I'm scared to death, but I'm more afraid of what will happen if I don't try. It also means I have three days... *three days...* with Skull. It may be selfish of me, but I'm going to ignore everything inside of me that screams this is a bad idea. I'm ignoring the part of me that's enraged and hurt because Skull's already planning on moving on to another woman before we've even begun. I'm going to ignore everything and just live.

Skull is the only man to make me feel like a woman. I almost died, and one of my biggest regrets was that I would never feel what it felt like to make love... *to be in love.* Skull is that chance for me.

There's a very big chance that my escape will fail and I won't be able to get away from Colin. If I do, then he's not going to be the only memory I have of sex... of being with a man. I'm going to give my body to Skull, except I'm doing it on *my* terms. What Skull doesn't know hopefully won't get him killed.

And that is the real reason I'm standing here. I expected Skull to show up by now. I glance at my watch. If he doesn't show in the next ten minutes...

"*Cristo...* you're in a uniform."

"What?" I ask, taking in a breath after he scared me. He's standing behind me. How long has he been there? I'm going to have to be more alert if I am really going on the run from my family. I turn around to look at Skull.

"I don't usually engage in games," he tells me. "I like my fucking straight forward. But... Christ, Beth. I wondered yesterday and now seeing you in a school uniform with that damn skirt... I suddenly see the appeal of role-play."

His words warm me with heat—not embarrassment, but desire. I like knowing I get a response out of him that he hasn't had before. Suddenly I find myself, the virgin who is slightly scared of going all the way, liking the idea of role-play, too.

"I didn't have time to change," I lie. I was afraid to change. "I brought some clothes in my pack," I tell him, holding up the large backpack I'm carrying on my shoulder.

"Good girl, but you forgot one thing," Skull says, stepping closer to me until our bodies are almost touching.

"What's that?" I whisper, loving the look he has in his inky dark eyes.

"I've been almost twenty-four hours without your lips,

querida," he tells me, his hand sliding along my neck, adjusting me the way he wants before he takes my mouth.

I've spent all night remembering how it felt when he touched me... the way his fingers felt inside of me. Add that to the fact I know in my heart that I only have a few days with him and I'm dying for him. So, as his tongue dives into my mouth, I don't wait for him to coax me this time. I let the taste of him invade my system and moan at how delicious it is. My tongue seeks his out, fighting with it, warring with it and demanding more. Skull's arms come under my ass to pull me up on his body. I steady myself on his shoulders, our lips never parting as I wrap my legs around his thick body. We're moving, but I don't care. I want more of his taste, more of his kiss, more of... *him*.

I feel something hard hit my back. He has me against a tree. His mouth pulls away from mine and I let out a growl of protest; I'm not ready to stop yet.

"Christ. You've turned into a she-cat," he says, his voice hoarse. One of his hands reaches under my shirt to palm my breast. I look at him, listening to the sounds of our ragged breath mixing with each other.

"I need you," I tell him, saying the one fully honest thing to him I can.

"Are you horny, sweet Beth?" he asks, his thumb brushing against the fabric of my bra, teasing a puckered nipple that begs for his attention.

When I said I needed him, I wasn't just talking about sex. I knew that's where Skull would take it. I'm okay with that. He doesn't have to know that he's everything I've ever wanted in the world. Just like he will never know that he won't be in control of when this ends. It's just as well. I need to be the one to walk away from Skull, because if I have to watch him walk away from me, I know I'd never survive. Skull would laugh. I'm not so young and stupid that I don't get that he doesn't believe in love, but I know that I could love him. *I could love him completely.*

"Did you think about me last night, Beth?" he asks and I

force my mind back to the here and now because that's all I have… *all I may ever have.*

"Yes," I tell him, and it's the truth. That's just one more complete truth between us.

"Did you need to come? Did your body remember what it felt like to have me touching it, exciting it?" He growls, freeing my breast from the bra, again torturing my nipple by pressing it firmly between his thumb and forefinger and pulling.

"Skull…" I complain, trying to grind myself against him, needing more than what he's allowing.

"What is it, *querida?*"he asks like he doesn't have a clue.

"Stop torturing me!"

"Aww, but torture can be so much fun, *querida…* So. Much. Fun." He looks down at me commandingly. "Unbutton your shirt, now."

His order grabs my attention and I don't argue. I do exactly what he says, unbuttoning the white dress shirt. My fingers are shaking, whether from nerves or need, I can't decipher. My fingers brush the back of his hand as I work, but my eyes never leave his. I watch his face, his attention glued to my breasts, and as the cool air hits my chest, I see that familiar heat zap into his eyes… and I feel *beautiful.* I feel like a woman… *his woman.* It takes some work, but I shrug out of the blazer and shirt, letting them fall to the ground. I don't want them between us. I want to be bared to him—*for him.*

His head goes down. I expect more of his soft kisses, but on my neck or stomach, while his fingers keep up their magic. I don't get that. Instead, I'm shocked as he sucks one of my aching nipples into his mouth. My body goes still for a minute as a wave of sensation barrages me. Then, *need* explodes through my body.

This. This is what I knew only Skull could give me. This is what is worth Colin's wrath. *This.*

My hands go into Skull's hair, urging his mouth on, and I cry out when he releases my breast with a wet *pop.* The sound echoes, but I don't have time to voice my frustration because he instantly moves to my other breast, which for some reason is even more sensitive.

"Skull... oh, God. That feels so good," I moan, wanting more, but wishing our positions were different so I could touch him too.

He looks up at me, and I don't even complain that he's left my breast alone. It doesn't even occur to me, because he has this look in his eyes that hypnotizes me.

"Just wait, *querida*. I plan on making you feel much, much better."

I swallow at his dark smile and darker promise. Fear is not there this time. Now, it's all *need*.

CHAPTER 10
SKULL

❝ She's a hit straight to the gut, taking away my oxygen and leaving me without defenses. ❞

I told myself I was going to get her back to the club and savor her… that I'd coax her and tease her until she gave me what I wanted. I wasn't expecting her to *demand* I give her more. It's a welcome surprise. Still, I might be a bastard, but I don't want to take her virginity in a fucking cemetery.

Well, I do… but she deserves better.

I claim her mouth again. Her taste has seeped down inside of me and changed something. I have to have it now. A drug? I think it may be more powerful. I'm starting to think I may never be free—*and I don't really give a damn.*

As my tongue tangles with hers and I take another hit, I slowly let her down on the ground, holding her close to me. We break apart and those beautiful gray eyes of hers are clouded with need. Her body trembles and I feel like a fucking king. She's completely mine and, though she might deny it, I know she wants anything I give her. My hand slides along the side of her neck and I raise her head up to place a gentle kiss on her lips.

"Button up, *querida*. I want to get you back to my home," I tell her. It's fucking hard to turn down what she's freely offering me right now.

She swallows, her face heating and her eyes breaking from mine as she starts buttoning her shirt. Something about the move bothers me. I bring her face back up and see the embarrassment there and… something else. Vulnerability? I don't think I've ever met a woman who has had that quality. The women I usually deal with are just as jaded and hardened as I am. I need to remember to take into consideration that she's different. She's unlike anyone I've ever encountered.

"What?" she asks, her face reddening even more.

"You're beautiful, *mi cielo.*" The endearment slips out. I should take that as a warning. Again, it seems I don't care.

"Skull," she whispers, and those fucking eyes of hers are glowing. My chest grows tight, but I ignore it and help her button up her shirt. It's a shame to cover her up; she was made for a man to gaze upon.

"Let's get out of here," I tell her, my voice gruff.

"I… I could be—I mean, there's a chance they're… looking for me," she stammers, and her face flushes worse.

Something about the way she says that troubles me. Is she *that* afraid of being expelled from school? I know she wants to graduate, but can she be so innocent that she thinks she is the first woman to get in trouble for skipping school? Maybe it's her Catholic upbringing. Did she mention parents? No. Guardians? Fuck, why didn't I find out more about her? Even as my brain asks that question, I already know the answer: I just wanted to fuck her all along. I still do, but… fuck me sideways, she's tying me in knots.

"We'll go out the entrance that leads to the back street. That's where my bike is," I tell her, frustrated with myself. I lead her down the path that will go to the small gate at the back of the fence for this section.

"Can I change into my pants? I brought jeans so I could ride…"

I watch her lips, already swollen from my attention, say just that one word: ride. My dick pushes against the zipper of my pants and the poor fucker is begging me to come.

"Go ahead," I tell her, standing back to wait on her.

"You aren't going to… you know… turn around?" she asks, and I smile at the rosiness in her cheeks. How many times a day can a woman blush? I have the urge to find out.

"Why?"

"Uh, because I'm going to put on clothes…?"

"Only if you hurry. You can't kiss a man like you just did me and expect me to be patient long, *querida*."

"But—"

"Okay, let's go," I tell her, reaching for her hand.

"No, I mean… don't you think people will notice a girl on the back of a bike in a school uniform? I need to change."

I shake my head at her. Does she not realize that people will notice her no matter what the fuck she is wearing? I give her a heavy sigh and turn around. I can hear sounds behind me and know she's digging through her bag for her pants. I'm a bastard and eventually Beth will realize that, but I turn back around and watch as she pulls her skirt up her hips and steps into her blue jeans. I catch a glimpse of small, white cotton fabric and have to adjust my cock. How much bare pussy have I seen? How many thongs or scraps of lace have I seen? Yet Beth in fucking white briefs, which not only cover her pussy but her hips and part of her fucking stomach, makes my dick hard enough to pound rocks into dust. It's fucking ridiculous. I'm being owned by her damn pussy and I haven't even been inside of it yet.

Beth looks up as she buttons her pants. She pulls her skirt over the top of the jeans and kicks it off.

"You looked!"

"I'm going to do a hell of a lot more than looking. You ready?"

"I'm starting to not trust you," she grumbles, but she follows me when I take her hand.

"That's probably your smartest move yet, *querida*," I tell her, even if the fact that she said it annoys me.

CHAPTER 11
BETH

> **"** *He makes me someone I don't recognize,*
> *someone I never got the chance to be... someone I like.* **"**

I hold onto Skull the whole ride. He said we were headed "home", but as we pull up to the huge building surrounded by a high chain-link fence with electrified barbwire running along the top punctuated by electronic gates and guards, I assume we've gone to his club. Even being in the family I'm in, I haven't seen security this tight, or at least not this loudly broadcasted. No, Colin is much more understated.

My hands tighten around Skull's stomach as I hold onto him tighter. I'm only going to get a few days with him. I want to enjoy them.

He pulls his bike into the garage and I slide off to my feet. He joins me, wrapping his arm around my waist and leading me into the attached building. The man who's been with him in town is here. He's a tall man with dirty blond hair that's all mussed and choppy looking. It looks like a woman just ran her fingers through it and spent hours touching it. He's got a look on his face that makes me want to blush and I don't even know why. I think it's the dirty promises that even *I* can read in his eyes. He's wearing a leather cut like Skull's with a white t-shirt under it and tight jeans molded to his lean body.

"Quit looking at my woman, motherfucker," Skull growls at him, and I stop staring to look up at Skull. He's shooting the guy a look like he could kill him.

The man shrugs and says, "I'm only human."

"Which means I can kill you, so back the fuck off," Skull

growls back.

"Hey, honey. I'm Torch," he says with a wink, totally ignoring Skull's warning. When I hear Skull's growl, I have to conclude that Torch might not be very smart. I sure wouldn't want to piss Skull off.

"Hi," I whisper, cursing myself for blushing.

Skull all but yanks me away from Torch as we delve deeper into the room. This might have been a mistake. There's obviously a party going on in here. There's women. Naked women. They're dancing and... *Oh. My. God.* There's one woman having sex with two men in the back—*at the same time.* I stop dead in my tracks. Skull tries to tug on me again, but I'm not ready to go anywhere near that.

"Beth?"

I drag my eyes away from the woman who is... well... "Skull," I finally manage to say, "I don't think I belong here." I pull my arm from him, ready to run back outside.

"Where do you think you're going?"

"I... I don't think I'm what you're looking for, Skull. I don't think I'm anywhere close. I need to go."

"What's wrong with you now?"

We're starting to attract attention—and that's the last thing I want. I stand up on my tiptoes and try to reach his ear. "They're having *sex!*" I whisper, though it comes out more like a hiss because... really, I mean, he can *see* it. I shouldn't have to explain it to him.

His eyes go back to the threesome. I just saw a *threesome.* A real life threesome! His lips move to a full grin and the light catches the glint on his lip ring. I've gotten used to kissing him. I even kind of like it now. In this light, with that look on his face, he looks like every woman's fantasy.

I expect him to turn me around and help me get out of here. He doesn't. Instead, he turns me around so I'm facing them. He imprisons me with his arm, holding me against his chest. His hot breath slides along my neck as he whispers into my ear.

"What's wrong, *querida?* Does it not turn you on? Watch how Sabre holds her head while he thrusts his cock into her mouth. She likes it. Do you see how she pulls against his hold when he slides back out?"

"Skull, please... I don't..."

"Watch how she thrusts her ass back against Latch every time he plunges his cock into her. She's on fire for both of them."

His words are dark and forbidden, just like what I'm seeing right now. I shouldn't be watching this. I shouldn't be... *aroused.* I am, even if I don't want to be. I'm completely aroused. So much so that I can feel moisture gathering in my panties. I try to turn my head because watching this goes against everything I've ever been told. Skull doesn't even allow me that comfort. He nibbles along the side of my neck, pulling on the skin, then lets his tongue brush away the sting to keep us so connected that I can't turn away.

"Sabre and Latch are close, sweet Beth. They do this often. They work as a team. They love pushing one woman to her brink. Working together until the woman doesn't know anything or anyone is around. All she can do is take what they decide to give her. Fuck her harder and harder until they give her what she really wants."

"Skull, please..."

"Sabre is getting ready to shoot his load in her mouth," he points out, ignoring my plea. "You can tell by the way he's driving faster and faster into her. Do you think she'll drink his cum down that sweet little throat? Or will it be too much and run out of her mouth...?"

"Skull..." I all but cry, because as his hand comes around to cup my breast and he teases it much like he did earlier in the cemetery, I know that he could make me come. Just like this, doing nothing more than teasing me and uttering his filthy dark words while we watch these *three* people do what I can only *wish* he was doing to me. Does it make me horrible for enjoying it? Why do I feel horrible—*and* excited? I'm so confused, and I really do want to run away.

Skull doesn't let me. Instead, we stand there in the middle of his club. His hand moves from my breast and slips into my jeans. It shocks me, and I struggle, trying to move and peering around to see if anyone is watching us. No one is; they're all laughing and talking as if this kind of thing happens all the time. I'm starting to believe maybe it does. Skull's arm around me tightens to the point of near pain as he bites the juncture between my shoulder and neck—in warning. I instantly go still. In reward, his fingers pet my pussy, and I know it's a reward because he kisses my ear, sucking it into his mouth and using his tongue to taste the skin there.

"Good girl. We'll stay like this only until they make her scream in pleasure. We won't stick around for the second show. By then, *querida*, I'll have you back in my room and eating that sweet, wet cunt out."

His words make my body tremble. I know I should be protesting, but I can't. It's a forbidden fantasy that I seem to be trapped inside of and my body feels like it's on the edge of a cliff. I need this. That's exactly what it comes down to. I am nothing more than a woman in need of everything Skull is doing. I'll worry about anything else later. I'd be lying if I said it wasn't exciting and arousing to watch the three of them having sex.

"Are you imagining what it'd feel like to be the plaything for two men, Beth?" he asks. "To have one man feed you his cock in this sweet wet pussy… while another stretches that tight little ass of yours?" His dark words continue to torture me. My face heats up with a mixture of embarrassment and excitement. I bite my lip to stop sound from escaping as he slides his fingers against my clit. My hands, which have been useless, bite into the sides of his legs because I feel like I might fall.

"You're so wet, *querida*. Tell me, do you want me to make you come right here? Let your sweet cream run all over my hands while I finger fuck you, so you can watch Sabre and Latch give Tiffany their cum?"

My skin feels hot, flushed... I'm on a razor's edge. I want to tell him yes because I *do* want to come. But not here. *Not like this.* Maybe this is what Skull is used to, what he enjoys. It's hot. It's exciting, but...

"Too late, *querida*. Watch," his dark voice whispers.

My eyes are glued to his hand and where it disappeared in the waistband of my jeans and panties. I automatically bring them back to Sabre and his friends. Sabre has his cock in his hand jerking it over and over, holding it over the woman's face. Then, he covers her mouth and face with his cum. He's holding her head tightly by the hair, slapping his cock against her mouth as he ejaculates hard, leaving a white streak of fluid scattered over her.

At the same time, the other man slams into her so hard from behind that you can physically see the way it jars her body. His yell rings out in the room. I don't know if anyone else is listening because I can't look away. I watch as his hand moves under him and disappears between her legs. She cries out and thrusts back against him, all the while trying to lick up Sabre's cum.

I forget to breathe as I watch the three of them finish. The girl falls down because her hands and knees refuse to hold her up anymore. I would have thought that'd be the end of it, but it's like they don't even take a breath. Sabre rolls a condom on. Latch does the same, and I know they're getting ready to go for a second round. I watch Sabre gather his own cum from the woman's chest and face. He covers his condom, then positions himself behind her.

"He's getting ready to take her ass," whispers Skull. "I'm gonna fuck you like that. Stretch your little ass so tight, you'll think I've split you in two."

His words work to bring me out of my haze with their shocking claim while at the same time setting me on fire. It's then that I catch sight of a man at a table across from us watching everything Skull is doing to me. I'm on fire. I need to come, but not like this. I don't want it to be like this.

"Skull, please…" I whimper, looking up at him and trying to turn my body away from the stranger.

"What is it, Beth?" he asks, his voice dancing across every nerve ending in my body.

"Take me to your room, please?" I ask him.

He doesn't even pause. He takes his hand away and picks me up in his arms to carry me off. I bury my face into his neck and hold on, desperate to be alone with him.

CHAPTER 12
SKULL

It's a war inside me, wanting to dirty Beth up while wanting to savor her innocence.

I battle with myself. It was a risk to push her so far, but *fuck* it was fun. She's so young, so untainted by the world. I can take her and make her mine completely. The idea has settled inside my brain and I can't get rid of it. Why would I need to move on? I want to own her. I want her to be mine to do with as I want. It's not rational, but it's fucking real. When Torch kept looking at her, I wanted to end the motherfucker. "Mine" was the one word my brain kept repeating. I felt like a fucking caveman, and the only word I could form was... *mine*.

I take her to my room, help her stand, then lock the door behind her. The silence in the room is thick, and I wait for her to tell me what's on her mind. It doesn't take long.

"I'm not that person," she whispers like she has something to be ashamed of.

"*Qué?*"

"I'm never going to be someone who could ever be comfortable doing what we just watched," she says, and as if she's still seeing it, her face flushes blood red. Something about it pleases me, but I still want her to admit she liked it.

I lean back against the door, watching her. My eyes travel up and down her body. I can still see signs of arousal in her body and her breathing, not to mention she's having trouble meeting my eyes.

"You enjoyed it, *querida*. Even now, you're dying to come," I tell her, crossing my arms and waiting for her to admit it to me.

"It was…"

"It was fucking hot as hell," I tell her, and somehow, her face grows a darker pink.

"If I have sex with you…" she starts.

But I don't let her finish. "There is no 'if', Beth. I'm gonna have you. Before you leave this room, I will have you over and over," I promise her.

"In this room," she says, nerves making her voice shaky.

"Do you have a problem with that?"

"In this room, *not* out there," she says, and perhaps I'm stupid, but it smacks me in the face when she tells me that.

I push off the wall and stride over to her. She takes a step back, but I don't let her retreat from me. I let my hand cup the side of her neck. Her gray eyes are large and I stare straight into them, so she sees that what I'm about to say to her is the truth.

"No one will see me bringing you pleasure but me, if that's what you want. Being with another means it must be enjoyable for both of us, *mi cielo.*"

"Do you—Do you enjoy… what *they* did?" Beth asks. "Is that what you do?"

"Are you asking if I like to share women? *Sí,* I do sometimes."

"And in front of people?"

"No. I like to give my partner my complete attention. I have no need for others to enjoy that with me."

"Oh."

"But, Beth, there is nothing wrong with people who need that kind of pleasure in their life."

"I guess. Listen, Skull, I really like you and all, but I don't think I can do this. I don't want it."

"You're a liar. Do you want me to prove it?"

"No, I'm really not. I'm serious. I want to be honest with you," she says, backing away from me. Since she's going to the bed and sitting down and not trying to leave the room, I let her.

"I'm listening," I prompt her when she goes quiet.

"It was taking all of my courage to give myself to you. Until I met you, I never really thought about sex much at all. So... this is kind of new to me."

The jaded part in me wants to call her a liar, but I can't deny the shy honesty on her face right now. My chest tightens in reaction, and that fucking word blasts through my brain again: *mine.*

"There is no 'was', Beth... We've come too far to turn back now."

"That's just it. I can't be that woman out there. I just can't..."

"I told you I don't do public shows. There's no one in this room but me and you, *querida.*"

"It was... interesting to watch," she fumbles.

"Interesting?" I ask, thick with disbelief.

"It was arousing..."

"It was fucking *hot,*" I correct her, then kick myself as she physically jerks as if I hit her. Fuck, I keep forgetting how young she is and, hell, how *innocent* she is... even if that's the reason for this conversation. I've never dealt with this before. I wonder if it's worth it, but it doesn't matter. I'm not going to be satisfied until I have her. *Mine.*

"But I can't do that. I don't want to do that."

I sigh, tired of talking.

"Tell me exactly what it is you *can't* do, Beth, so we can end this conversation."

"I can't be her!"

This time, my sigh come out more like a growl because, Jesus, I know she's young, but since when did it get this fucking hard to understand a woman?

" *Who?*"

"I don't want to have sex with more than one person—more than *you.* I can't do that, Skull. I can't and... I won't." She takes a breath. "So, I think it's best if you just... take me back now."

"Do you see anyone else in this room, Beth?"

"Well, no, but... All of that was obviously normal for—"

63

"For them, yes. I didn't bring you here to share you with any fucking person. Did you not hear me threaten my own man outside for just looking at you?"

"Well, yeah, but I didn't think you were serious."

"I was dead serious."

"You're very confusing, Skull."

"Jesus, woman, look in the fucking mirror. Now, are we done with this damn discussion?"

"I guess."

"Thank fuck. Now strip."

"Strip?"

"Yes. Take off those clothes. *Now.*"

Her face gets more color in it, but it has nothing to do with embarrassment anymore. Now, she's just pissed at me. I like it. I like it when she shows me spirit.

"You do realize I haven't done this before, right?"

"*Sı*, and it's driving me crazy."

"Aren't you supposed to be understanding? Or... maybe even considerate?"

"No. I'm just supposed to make sure you come over and over and can't walk when I'm done—which I will do. And, as an added bonus, I'll make your body crave what only I can give it, so you will always want more... even when I have made you come so hard you pass out from the pleasure. Now, *mi cielo... strip.*"

CHAPTER 13
BETH

" *What have I gotten myself into?* **"**

Strip, he says. Like that's so easy.

I could hate him right now. I feel like I've been on a damn roller coaster ever since Colin confronted me. This day with Skull has done nothing to settle all the fear and upheaval inside of me. Now, after putting me through the wringer, he just stands there and tells me to strip.

I should tell him to go fuck himself. The problem is, he'd probably just find someone to replace me. This isn't about love. There'd be no love with Skull even if Colin wasn't in the picture. I'm not going to get love.

The image of Colin comes to mind. I bite down the panic and, instead, center my gaze on Skull as I fumble with my pants. I eventually get them off, but it's definitely not sexy and alluring like in the movies. I nearly fall as I kick them off. I feel stupid. I stand up straight and take a deep breath. Skull stands there not saying a thing. It's like he's daring me to go further, like he doesn't think I will do this. He probably has a good reason to think I won't. My nerve is about to fizzle out. The only thing that keeps me going is the memory of Skull's kiss and his fingers on my skin. That gives me the courage to pull the shirt over my head. Now I'm standing here in my underwear, watching him.

"Bra first, *querida.*"

I take another deep breath; it shudders through my body and comes out ragged. "You're kind of being an ass," I tell him, reaching behind me to undo the clasp.

"I like watching you, sweet Beth. I like giving you orders and having you carry them out."

"I'm not a servant..."

"In here only, Beth. I want you to take my direction. Do what I ask of you. Give me this and I'll reward you. It's my job to show you your limits and push them. My job to give your body exactly what it needs... and what it will come to yearn for."

His words cover me softly like another form of seduction. They make my knees weak and my body respond, but at the same time they make me sad. I won't get time with Skull, and I think I already yearn for what he can give me. Will it get worse after I actually sleep with him?

My hand covers my breast as I let my bra slip off one shoulder, then work up the courage to remove it completely. That's when I see his body tighten, his eyes glued to me. This strong, larger-than-life man covered in tattoos and scars is totally wrapped up in me right now. He's watching my every move. I have his complete attention and he's filled with need... *for me.* Something about that strikes me deeply. I might be the one following his orders, but I feel powerful right now. I drop the bra and try to be brave enough not to dive down onto the floor and find it.

"*Bella,*" he whispers. I need to learn Spanish. Colin and Matthew made me take French in school because the family has homes and businesses there. Once I get away, I vow that I will memorize and learn every word so I can relive these moments. I am already sure that anything that comes after Skull will never touch me like he does.

"Skull..."

"You are beautiful, *mi cielo,*" he moans. "So fucking beautiful." He's walked up to me. His words dance across my skin as his lips gently meet my shoulder, his large hands taking hold of my hips. "You take my breath away."

It sounds like a line, and maybe it is, but it makes me feel *beautiful.*

"Lie back on the bed," he tells me.

I bite down on my bottom lip to keep from telling him I'm not ready. I lie down, letting my head fall half on the pillow and half on the mattress. The bed is unmade and the sheets are rumpled. I worry he's had other women here, but once I lie down, his scent and cologne surround me, comforting me.

I gasp as his hands circle my knees and he pulls me back down to him. I watch him closely. He grabs the waistband of my panties and looks at me. He winks. Then, just like that, he tears them.

"I don't have any other—"

"I don't want you covering my property up," he says. "You won't wear them anymore, Beth. I want you bare under your clothes and ready for me whenever I want."

I start to argue, but that's something I can give for the few days I have left with him, so I don't. He pushes my ruined underwear to the floor and positions himself between my legs. Heat zaps my body, and a mixture of desire and embarrassment flush through me, turning my skin deep pink. I can feel the heat burning in me.

"Skull, I think, I mean…" I stop talking. I don't think I could say another word if I wanted to. It doesn't matter because all of my words stop. They lodge in my throat, unable to move, when I feel his tongue flick against the inside of my thigh, his breath against me.

"Lie back and just enjoy, Beth," he says, and I do exactly that—without arguing this time. I can't argue. I feel like I might faint.

CHAPTER 14
SKULL

" I'd die a happy man
with her on my tongue for eternity. **"**

I feel like a drowning man, losing myself in her. The scent of her sweet pussy envelopes me and I breathe it in ... the sweetest nectar I've ever dreamed of, finally within my grasp. I bite the inside of her thigh, marking it. My dick jerks in reaction because the fucker knows he's finally going to get to claim her.

I pull away and hastily shed my clothes, hoping she's distracted enough that the sight of my cock doesn't bring her fear to the forefront again. My experience with virgins is nonexistent. I didn't need Beth to tell me she had never done this before. It would take a fool not to see it. The mere fact brings me joy.

"Skull?" her soft voice questions, a mixture of excitement and nervousness.

"I got you, *querida.* I'm going to make you feel real good in a minute," I tell her. Then, I use my thumbs to pull the lips of her pussy apart. Her hard little clit is throbbing, drawing my attention. I flatten my tongue, darting inside her entrance. Her taste blooms on my tongue and I groan. A man could become addicted to her taste. *I* could become addicted. I push my tongue inside again, gathering more cream on it and fucking her with it. Her moans are the only encouragement I need. My thumb slides over her clit and instantly more of her cream pours forth. I flick that hard little nub with my tongue over and over as I slide two fingers into her. I give her just a small taste, sliding my knuckles in. She clamps down, her whole body tensing.

"You have to relax, *querida* ... Relax your body."

A shudder rakes through her body, but slowly I feel the muscles in her pussy ease.

"Skull …?"

"Yes, *mi cielo?*" I answer, sliding my fingers all the way inside her tight channel this time. I go slow, stretching her because she's so fucking tight. I can't wait to sink home. I start fucking her with my fingers, carefully and methodically, stretching her for my cock and giving her pleasure at the same time. I use my thumb to caress her clit again, giving her the extra pleasure she needs to bring her close to orgasm.

"What… what are you doing?" she asks when my tongue goes back to teasing her clit and licking up the cream that flows around my fingers. Her hips move against my mouth and the muscles of her thigh tighten against me as she tries to ride.

"Finger fucking you," I hum against her clit, drawing the throbbing morsel into my mouth, capturing it between my teeth and lashing it with my tongue. Her hands come down to my head, her fingers threading through my hair. She's pulling me into her pussy. It's all the more erotic because she has no idea what she needs. It's pure instinct. *Mine.*

"But, you… I thought we were going to…"

"Thought what, sweetheart?" I ask, pulling back slightly so I can watch the way she sucks my fingers inside. I let my tongue dance along the outside of her lips, touching my fingers and gathering her cream.

"I thought you were going to… *take me!*" The last syllable is cried out as I stretch her open with my fingers and make the perfect entrance for my tongue. I fuck her with my tongue and collect all of her sweet juice that I can. I push my thumb against her hardened clit, loving the noises coming from her. When I look up, she's sitting up so she can watch everything I'm doing to her body.

"*Amante dulce.* I am going to take you. I'm going to take you in every way imaginable … starting with consuming you," I tell her, or maybe I'm warning her. I wrap my arms around her thighs, pulling her pussy into my face. Then, I eat her. My tongue pushes inside, fucking her and adding the pressure of my mouth and nose. I release only to lick up to her clit and suck it in my mouth. "Fuck my face, sweet Beth. Take your pleasure. Take it." I encourage her as she tries to ride. I bring one hand back and thrust my fingers back into her pussy while I torture her with my mouth, eating, licking, teasing, fucking, and devouring her.

"Skull!"

She screams above me, but I can already feel the way her muscles are fluttering and squeezing me. Just as the first flood of cream bathes my face, I pull away, rise quickly while she's in the throes of her orgasm. Then, I slam home inside of her, tearing through her virgin barrier and making her completely mine. The walls of her pussy collapse against my cock, squeezing the fuck out of it. She cries out and looks up at me with tears in her eyes. It takes everything I have to hold myself still as her muscles flutter and squeeze against my cock, demanding I move. I can't. Not yet. I owe her this much.

"It hurts," she moans through her tears, even while her body still shudders from her earlier pleasure.

"Only for a moment, *mi cielo*. Can you feel how you're already making room for my cock? Stretching to fit only my cock? Mine…"

I bring my fingers between our bodies, seeking her clit and rubbing it gently in my need to arouse her further. After just a little bit, I slide a little further inside. Beth gasps, her head lolling back in pleasure. I keep working her clit until her hungry snatch begins taking me even deeper. When I bottom out, balls deep inside of her, I maneuver her body carefully so that I'm lying over her. I kiss her tears, taking them on my tongue just as I did the sweet juice from her pussy. They belong to me, just as her body does. She's mine now. Her fate is sealed and no one will take her away from me, ever.

"Shouldn't you be moving?" she whispers, pushing up with her hips and moaning from the sensation. I smile, feeling a happiness I have never felt before. I slide back out and her fingers bite into my arm as she tries to stop me. The heels of her feet curl into my ass; she clings to me almost as tight as her pussy does to my shaft, refusing to give it up. I leave just the tip inside.

"Beth," I prompt, needing to see her face.

"Skull…?"

"You belong to me," I tell her.

Somewhere along the way, I forgot that this was only supposed to last until I grew bored. I have been captured by this little slip of a woman and I do not want to let go. She heals something deep inside of me. She calms the beast that always claws from within, needing to break free. She doesn't give me the words back, but she licks her lips and nods her head yes.

That's enough. *For now.*

I thrust hard into her, letting my balls slap against her. I grind myself into her and then pull back, only to thrust again. I worry I should be making sure she's okay, but when her hips thrust up into me, I stop worrying.

Then she whispers, "More."

That's all I need. I push into her harder the next time, and I don't stop. Every thrust is deeper, grittier. Each pull grows faster until the two of us are frantically fucking each other, her body trying to keep up and meet my every demand. Even as she finishes her orgasm, I don't let up. My hand pulls her hip up at an angle so I rake the sides of her walls. She cries out from the added stimulation. My dick sinks even farther in, scraping her cervix. That's when I let my fingers go to her clit and manipulate it until she's crying out my name again and I feel her second orgasm crash through her. I slam into her, knowing I'm ready to explode. As she clenches against my cock and sucks me inside her heaven, I let go. I feel my seed flooding her womb, painting her insides with… *me.*

Before I'm done, every inch inside and outside of her will be marked and owned by me. *Only me.*

CHAPTER 15
SKULL

" I thought she would be something I tired of.
Instead, I found a reason to breathe. "

We lie there for a while. Our bodies are still joined because I'm just not ready to leave her yet. I don't know much about virginity, that's true enough. But I know I want to take care of her. What she just gave me was special. I didn't think I would feel that way, not consciously. But knowing that I was the first to bring her pleasure ... The first to own her body ... I'm a possessive, greedy fuck, and I find that now that I've had her, I don't want to turn her loose for another asshole. All my previous plans with Beth have been thrown out the window.

These are the thoughts racing through my brain after the best climax I can remember having. I hope I'm just drunk on pussy, but I have a feeling I'm not. I force myself to push off of Beth. I'd collapsed over her, and even though I move to the side, I fear I'm still squashing her. I hiss as my dick drags out of her swollen pussy, not wanting to let me go. Even now, after the workout I just gave her, her greedy little cunt is trying to suck me back in, unwilling to give up one inch. Fucking perfection, right there. Beth moans, and even though she's half asleep, she tries to pull me back to her.

"Where are you going? Don't leave, Skull," she says, her tired voice hoarse from her cries and filled with desire. My dick should be tired as a motherfucker, but instead, he's already perking back to life.

I look down at him and see the telling signs of her blood on my shaft and between her thighs. That should bother me, but it doesn't. I want to beat on my damned chest like fucking Tarzan while screaming for my woman.

"I'll be back, *mi cielo*," I whisper to her. She mumbles, curling back into the covers.

I go the bathroom and run water. I search through the bathroom supplies and find the bath salts mi madre used to keep here before she passed. I couldn't bring myself to dispose of any of her things. These may be out of date, but they will be better than nothing. I pour them into the water, hoping they work. My mom used them to help ease her muscles after a hard day of working in the garden. It didn't matter how easy I tried to make her life, she always had to stay busy. I'm hoping that the salts will help heal Beth, because fuck did I give her a hard workout.

As I look down at my semi-erect cock covered in a mixture of our combined release and her virgin's blood, I know I'm planning on working her out even more.

I return to the bedroom to pick her up in my arms. She's boneless, but curls in to me and kisses me on my chest. That Tarzan feeling does nothing but intensify.

"Where are we going?" she whispers, her beautiful eyes slowly opening.

"I need to take care of you," I tell her, heading to the bathroom.

"I thought you just did that. Like … a couple of times," she says with a ghost of a smile.

I laugh and, for the first time in years, I feel free. You would think she'd be embarrassed or shy after what just happened. After all, it had been pretty intense for a virgin. Not Beth, though. Maybe that's why we mesh so well. I slowly stand her up, holding her close to my body and not wanting to let her go.

"The lady has jokes," I whisper against her mouth before claiming it in a sweet, soft kiss, my tongue dancing with hers. She holds onto me, her tongue playing with mine, and we break away slowly.

"I'm taking a bath?" she asks, looking over at the water

running in the bathtub and then back at me.

"We are." I help her climb in. "Scoot up," I tell her when she's settled, then get in behind her.

"And to think I've always been a shower person," she says, reclining back into me. My arms slip around her while the water continues to fill.

"I'll show you how wonderful showers can be too, *mi cielo* … Don't worry."

She kisses my shoulder. I stretch to turn the water off, quickly wash my now-raging cock, then take the soap and begin lathering my hands.

"Tell me about your life, Beth. I want to know more."

"Not much more to tell," she says, but from the way her body tenses up, I know she's lying.

I decide not to push her—not *yet*. My hands go around to cup her breasts, massaging the soap in and just enjoying the feel of them. For such a small woman, her breasts are large. The nipples are a pale pink and about the size of a dime. I love the way they feel in my mouth, the way my tongue can torture them, my teeth imprison them. I nearly groan as my dick hardens into full launch mode.

The fucker can just calm down; there's no way she's going to be ready to go again. Soon, though. I'm not going to be able to wait long.

I pull on her nipples and her head goes back against my chest, her hips thrust up, sloshing the water around us. "Skull," she moans.

"You have beautiful breasts. So large and juicy… made to pleasure and bring a man to his knees," I whisper, still torturing her nipples. "And your nipples… They taste so sweet, so inviting…"

A picture slams into my mind, a picture of Beth nursing my child. My son or daughter's lips latching on and drinking from her body while her stomach is swollen with another child. You would think that would make my dick deflate. Instead, I feel pre-cum leak off the head and my balls tighten. It felt so fucking good coming inside of her, filling her full of my seed while my shaft was pressed as deep into her womb as humanly possible. It wasn't a conscious decision, but it was on purpose. I want to fill her with my babies. Lock her to me for eternity.

"Skull, sweetheart… Oh, God, that feels so good," she moans, her hands biting into my legs on either side of her, and she pushes her ass against me, further torturing my cock.

"You could be pregnant even now, *mi cielo*. We used nothing. My babe could be growing inside of you."

I didn't mean to say that, but fuck, now that I've had the vision, I want it. I fucking want it, and *now*. I wish I had kept that shit to myself, though, when her body goes rock solid against me and she pulls away.

"That can't happen," she whispers, standing up.

Jesus, is the thought of having a child with me so terrifying? But then, I've told her I will tire of her. She doesn't understand that having her and taking her virginity have been game-changers.

I capture her hand and she twists to the side to look at me.

"Sit back down here, *mi cielo*. Face me this time. I want to take care of you. I didn't realize the thought of my child was so repelling to you."

Something flashes in her eyes. I think she's about to call me on my earlier comments about growing tired of her. Instead, she turns and sits back down, this time facing me. I loop her legs on each side of me, pulling her as close to me as I can. I busy myself with cleaning the blood from the inside of her thighs.

"It's not that, Skull… though that would be insane. I'm not exactly in the shape to raise a child alone."

"You wouldn't be alone, Beth," I tell her, and for now, I will leave it like that. When I see in her eyes that she doesn't take me seriously, I vow to tell her the truth soon. I'm not letting her go.

"It doesn't matter, Skull. I can't get pregnant," she says while I'm rinsing off her sweet pussy.

The words are said so matter-of-factly and deadpan that I look up to watch her face. "What do you mean?" Inside I'm screaming *no*. It doesn't change my plans. She's mine and I'd rather have her and no children than anyone else. I'm grieving the loss of seeing her nurse our baby.

"You knew I was sick." She shrugs like it's nothing, but I can see moisture in her eyes.

"*Si.*"

"I had cancer. It's gone now and my latest tests last month confirmed it's still gone. The treatments, though, were rough. The doctor told me the aggressive chemo and radiation would make it impossible for me to have a child."

Fear. Have I known stark fear that is running as deep as this before? I don't think so. The thought of the world losing Beth to this disease... The thought that something inside of her could take her from me and there wouldn't be a damn thing I could do about it causes my heart to slam against my chest hard. I grab her by the neck and pull her lips to me, acting on instinct and instinct alone.

"You will not get sick, Beth. You will not leave me," I growl. I don't give her time to answer. Instead, my tongue invades her mouth and I pour all the anger and fear I have into it. I suck on her tongue, my fingers tightening into her hair as she pulls herself up on my lap, getting even closer. I plunder every part of her warm depths that I can. Our teeth clash, but I don't care. I just keep hearing her say she had cancer. I keep replaying what that could have meant: I could have never had the chance to touch her, to lie with her, to listen to her laugh or see her smile. Those are things I vow from this moment on that I will not take for granted.

When I break away, we are both breathing hard.

"Wow," she says, trying to smile.

My fingers search out her clit. I know I can't get back inside of her this soon, but I need to bring her pleasure. I want to chase away the sadness in her eyes and have it replaced with desire that

I put there.

"Skull," she moans, pushing her sweet little cunt towards me, eager for more.

"Shh... I will give you what you need, *mi cielo.*"

I pet her pretty clit. My mouth goes to her breast and I suck as much of it as I can into my mouth. My tongue works around the hardened nipple as I suck, then seize it with my teeth, biting it—*marking it as mine.*

"I want you inside of me," she cries, wrapping her legs around my body and pulling herself closer to me. My hands go to her ass to stop her.

"We can't, *querida.* It's too soon. You'll hurt yourself more," I groan, trying to be fucking noble. "I will make you come. Just relax," I tell her, letting my tongue go back to torturing her nipple.

I'm distracted by the taste of her sweet flesh, but she completely grabs my attention when her small hand wraps around my cock and guides him inside her body. She moves and impales herself on my rod. Sweet Jesus, he slipped in so easily and her greedy little snatch latches onto my cock, demanding more.

"Fuck," I moan. The hold on her ass changes now to push her farther down on my dick.

"God, you feel so good inside of me, Skull."

"We shouldn't do this, Beth. You're sore. It will hurt."

"It feels amazing," she whispers into my ear, biting on the lobe and sucking it into her mouth. "Fuck me, Skull. I want to feel you inside of me months from now and remember tonight."

What man can deny his woman when she says something that he wants even more than she does? Still, I can't hurt her, so I still refuse, doing the only thing I can at this point because there's no way in fucking hell I'm not going to give her my cock.

"Then ride your man, *mi cielo.* Take your pleasure, and show me how much you want my dick."

She freezes for a minute, looking into my eyes. Hers are

filled with need. Slowly, she begins to rotate her hips, sliding up and down on my cock. When she squeezes her pussy tight against my shaft, I moan.

"Yes, *querida*... Just like that. Ride me. Take us both over the edge."

My words seem to be all she needs, because she picks up her speed, and I can do nothing but get lost in the pleasure and how beautiful my woman is at this moment. When my fingers hone in on her clit and I pinch it between my fingers and twist before rubbing it over and over, she completely comes apart in my arms. She's riding harder and faster, her breasts bouncing and her hips twisting to get more. The inner muscles of her pussy clench and flutter all around my cock, sucking me in until my balls are pushed against her sweet snatch. I feel my climax coming and just as she screams out my name, I unload inside of her.

Those fucking doctors think she can't have a child? They haven't met me. I won't stop until her stomach is round with my baby. I wrap my fingers in her hair and bring her lips down to mine.

I vow that I won't stop until she's surrounded by my babies. That's a vow I plan on keeping.

CHAPTER 16
BETH

" *He's destroyed me.* "

My mind is a mess. This is the second straight night I've had with Skull. I'd ignored common sense and did not go back to the school. I couldn't bring myself to leave Skull. It might be just sex for him—and maybe it's because he is my first—but it feels real. *It feels like love.* I don't want to leave him, but I *have* to leave him and Georgia behind completely. Those thoughts keep intruding upon every minute I have with him, even now when I'm holding onto Skull while riding on the back of his bike. I'm full of need and emotion that's all centered on this man, but there is a part inside of me screaming about life's unfairness.

Skull pulls up against the sidewalk a block away and cuts off his engine. I don't make a move to get off. Instead, I hug him tighter, laying my head against his shoulder. He seems to know that's what I need because he doesn't move for a few minutes. His hand covers mine at his stomach and he squeezes it.

"Are you okay, *mi cielo?*"

"They could be looking for me," I mumble against his shoulder, knowing I need to leave and not wanting to.

"You mentioned that before. I doubt very seriously you have a reason to fear nuns, Beth. I will protect you if need be, though," he jokes.

I want to smile, but I can't. It's just a reminder of the bigger secret I'm keeping from him. I ignore the tinge of guilt I feel at not telling him the truth, then slide off his bike.

"What time is it?" I ask, holding my arms tight around myself

79

to ward off the chill. Skull puts a jacket over me, but the night air is cold. He wanted to drive me out to his favorite spot and I wanted to be anywhere he was.

"Are you really worried about missing curfew?" he asks.

"If they report it to my guardians, then yes. They'll take me out of school and have me finish in private tutoring or ship me off to France."

Again, I only tell him half-truths. None of what I just told him matters since I'm running away. He looks at me strangely as I try to remember exactly what I said. Did I give too much away? I only have one more night with him, really. I don't want to mess that up.

He parks his bike, grabs a rolled up blanket from his saddle bags, then joins me. He takes my hand and walks me down the grassy pasture-like area we're in. I can't tell anything about the area because it's dark. There's a large moon above us that gives light, but since I have no idea where I'm at, it doesn't help me. Skull, on the other hand, seems to know exactly where we are. His footsteps never falter.

In a few minutes, he comes to a stop and I look up. In front of us is a small dock that overlooks a calm lake. Even in the dark, or maybe because of it, it is beautiful.

"Amazing," I murmur, turning back to him with a smile. It's secluded and romantic. It's what you envision a lover taking the time to show you. *It makes me feel special.* Between this and the way he's treated me since our first night, I feel like I matter to him. Still, I know I'm probably just fooling myself.

He brings his hand up and holds the side of my face. I lean into it, loving the connection with him. His thumb brushes my lips gently, almost reverently. I capture the tip of it with my teeth and hold it between my lips, letting my tongue tease it gently before letting go.

"One day, sweet Beth, I will learn all of your secrets."

"Why?" I ask, confused.

"Because it's needed," he says cryptically.

I want to question him further, but I don't. I follow him to the dock. He spreads out the blanket he brought with us, then sits down and reaches a hand toward me. I join him and lean into his body as we watch the water and the way the light of the moon reflects off of it, making the beams dance.

"What happened to your parents?" he asks, and I can't help the way my body tenses up.

"They split up when I was young. My father took my sister Katie, and mom took me."

"*Pendejos*," he growls, squeezing me tighter. I look up in question. "Assholes," he translates.

I nod. "Pretty much, yeah. They just never saw life beyond what or how it affected *them*. Anyway, I haven't seen my father since. Not even for Katie's funeral. Mom remarried and my stepfather wasn't exactly a warm man. I don't guess I've ever been close to anyone in my life. I do miss my mom, though. Her and my stepfather passed away in an accident. My stepbrothers were left as my guardians."

"*Lo siento, amor,*" he whispers against my hair.

"Someday soon, I'm going to learn Spanish so that when I'm alone, I can think of our time together and understand all you've said to me," I tell him without thinking. Every time he uses Spanish, I mourn that I don't fully understand what he is saying.

He turns my face to look at him and, even with the darkness, his eyes draw me in.

"Tengo miedo han sido capturados. Nunca dejar ir," he says, the lyrical words rolling off his tongue.

"What'd you just say?" I ask, my heart beating faster.

He smiles and kisses my forehead before lying back on the dock, lifting me under my arms as he does and bringing me atop him. Our lips are just a breath away from each other. Our eyes, locked on one another. My legs slide along his body so that I'm astride him and I find myself wishing we didn't have clothes on.

"Come on, Skull. It's not fair. Tell me what you just said."

"I said that I fear your body has me captured. I need to fuck you again. Are you very sore?"

My face reddens at his frank words. But the instant he says them, I feel excitement pool between my legs. I *am* sore. Very sore, because Skull is not a small man. I don't have anything to really judge him by, but I can't imagine there are many—*if any*—larger.

But I know I won't get to keep experiencing the pleasure he gives me. I greedily want all of it I can have.

"I'm good. I want you again too, Skull."

"My sweet, sweet Beth," he moans, his hand brushing the side of my face and his lips finding mine.

It's a different type of kiss than the others we've shared. This one feels tender. Somehow, that moves me more than anything he's ever given me. I lose myself in his taste and the warm, wet texture of his mouth. My tongue curves around his, sucking it in further, needing the silky feel and the way it heats my body on the inside. His hands move up my back and then back down where he cups my ass and grinds my body into his. I can feel the hard ridge of his cock against me and moan in response.

"Are you sure?" his raspy voice asks as his kisses trail down the side of my neck. He hones in on the juncture where my neck and shoulder meet and bites on the tight tendon there. I cry out softly in response, trying to buck restlessly against him. His strong hands keep me in place.

"Teach me… in your language."

His tongue teases my skin, tracing my neck and under my chin, before looking up at me. "Beth…?"

"Teach me how to ask you to fuck me in Spanish," I demand. I don't know where the need comes from, I just know it's there.

"Soy todo tuyo," he tells me, and his eyes never leave mine as I say the words. It doesn't ring true to me. Rosa taught us all a bunch of Spanish curse words, and none of the words Skull just gave me match what she said was Spanish for fuck. It doesn't even match the words he said earlier. So, I commit these to memory—for two reasons. One, I want to know what he had me say. Two? I love the effect they have on him.

"Soy todo tuyo, Skull. Soy todo tuyo."

Skull growls, flipping me over while already tearing my shirt from my body.

Oh, yes. I definitely want to know what I've just said to him. *Definitely.* And once he has us both naked and his hard cock drives into my body, I say it again just for good measure. I say it over and over. Skull wraps his hand in my hair and holds my body exactly how he wants it as he pounds me relentlessly, pushing us both over the edge.

My body shudders in the last aftershock of my orgasm and I feel our combined fluids leak between my thighs. I moan and tighten my muscles upon his cock, which is still semi-erect and deep inside of me. I want to scream that I love him, but I don't. *I can't.* But when he whispers, "I am yours too, *mi cielo,*" I smile. I am pretty sure those are the words he had me say in Spanish, and I'm okay with it. I'm more than okay because it doesn't matter that I have to leave in a very short time.

It doesn't matter at all, for it is true: *I am his.*

CHAPTER 17
SKULL

**" It's the calm before the storm ...
a fucking shit storm. "**

It's the best fucking day I can remember having. I left Beth sleeping in my bed after fucking her again. Jesus, I've gotten lost in her body so much the last two days that my dick should be completely withered away. Instead, the fucker is still half hard.

Finally, I'm getting a meeting with the Donahues. I thought they were going to continue ignoring me and I couldn't let that pass. Word had come this morning. They planned a meeting at Paradise Ridge near Lookout Mountain, which is actually in Tennessee. I hated leaving Beth, but with any luck, I'll get this shit done and be back home to her before she wakes up. I left her worn out. The thought of the orgasms I'd wrung from her body over and over makes me smile. Her innocence calls to me. I'm a hard fucking man; there's an animal underneath the calm demeanor I show the world. Very few have seen it, and even less have survived to tell about it. I let shit go until I hit my limit. Beth somehow tempts the animal in me. It's almost as if he can smell her blood and is primed for the hunt, but then her touch soothes us both. She's the first woman who I could ever see myself with and not grow bored. If I feel this strongly after two days, what the fuck will it be like when I'm with her longer?

I left Beast in charge of Beth's protection. I know she'll be okay, but I can't deny I will not be resting easy until I'm with her again. Her protection is mine to keep. *She* is mine. It was no coincidence though that I left the one patched-in member of the club who has a steady old lady to watch over her. I look over at

84

the cocky look on Torch's face as we pull up in the parking lot and, yeah, I know it's fucked up, but I'm not about to let the fucker anywhere near my girl.

We all park our bikes and wait. I had a couple members go ahead to make sure we weren't walking into a trap. I also called in a marker, and I see him coming now.

Diesel walks toward me, his long lanky legs eating up the pavement. I tried like hell not to like the son of a bitch, but I can't. He's the president of a club in Tennessee called the Savage Brothers. They have a chapter in Kentucky, Florida, Ohio, and several other states. I've not had any dealings with any of them besides Diesel. There's been rumors that the president of the Kentucky branch is a fucking hothead. I hear he goes by the name Dragon. Hopefully calling my marker in with Diesel won't require me dealing with any of the others. I'd like to keep this as contained as possible.

Diesel and I shake hands. He claps my shoulder and I do the same.

"How are you, you sorry son of a bitch?" he asks. In some ways he reminds me of Torch, but life has been hard on Diesel. There's a story in his eyes. Then again, none of us became leaders without having it hard. It's what tests us to see if we can survive the fire.

"Diesel. I see you haven't changed, hombre. You ever going to cut that shit on your head?" I ask, motioning to the pile of hair messily trapped on top of his head. It's an old joke between us.

He flips me off in response, then asks, "You ready for this shit?"

"Ready as I will ever be. Are they here?"

This was a big marker. Diesel and his crew are a neutral host. They make sure I'm not walking into a trap, and I get my meeting. Hopefully we all get out of here without bloodshed.

"That they are, *ese*. I don't know what you did to piss Colin off, but I'd tread carefully."

"I wish to fuck I knew, too. That's what today is about. Let's get this shit done. I got a woman waiting for me."

"You always have a woman waiting for you," Diesel responds.

"Not like this one. This one's special."

"Don't tell me you're getting all bent out of shape over a woman," he says, shaking his head.

"I tell you, she's special."

"She got a golden snatch or something?"

I laugh at his words, but in a way he's not wrong. *Tengo miedo han sido capturados. Nunca dejar ir.* That's what I told Beth, and I was serious. Roughly translated, it means: *I am afraid I have been captured. Never let go.* I don't want her to. I like knowing that she has had no other man before me, that I stretched her to fit only my cock, that the blood of her innocence was on me, that I *claimed* it. It's *mine.* Fuck, I don't care if it's only been a matter of weeks or that she's only been in my bed two days. I'm claiming her and by God I'm keeping her.

"Skull?" Diesel prompts me. We're walking through the door of the local lodge's restaurant. It's shut down thanks to Diesel and his crew. Inside, I see Colin Donahue sitting at a table with two of his main henchmen. I guess he didn't feel the need to have big brother with him today. That's not fucking good. I hate dealing with the Donahues in general, but Colin is the most miserable fucker ever born. He's worse than his fucking father Edmund ever was—and that is saying something.

I motion to Torch and Sabre to stay at my six and remain standing, then I sit down at the table with the Devil himself.

Time to get this party started.

CHAPTER 18
BETH

" The pain is so huge, I can't catch my breath. "

"Skull, you in here?" I hear Torch in the distance. I mumble and dig further under the covers. My body is sore from the workout that Skull gave me last night, and I'm worn out because it was so late when we returned from the lake.

Tonight will be my last night with Skull. I'm praying the memories we've made will be enough to help me survive life without him.

Skull squeezes me and I smile without opening my eyes or acknowledging him. Since I've been seeing him, he's always touching or hugging me. He does it even more since I've been here. He kisses the top of my head, then I feel the bed shift as he gets up.

"Quiet, asshole, Beth's sleeping."

"Sorry, Boss. We got word this morning. Colin wants to meet at the Ridge."

"Did you tell Diesel?"

"Yeah, he set it up, just like you wanted. We need to head out now."

"Okay. Get our best men together. Beast stays to watch over Beth. I want him making sure she's safe and doesn't leave, got it?"

"I'll tell him now."

My body freezes as I hear the conversation. All signs of sleep are gone. I'm wide awake now and halfway into a panic attack. It takes all I have to keep my breathing even. I can't let Skull know that I heard them. Inside, I'm filled with panic and despair. I won't get one more night with Skull. The pain hits me so hard it robs me of breath. I keep my eyes closed tight and try to tune out the sounds of Skull getting dressed. I try to still the heavy beating of my heart as he leans on the bed behind me to kiss the top of my head.

"*Mi cielo...* I will return soon to you. I miss you too much to stay away too long," he whispers, and I block out the pain the words cause. The last two days and nights with Skull have been so wonderful that I've tried to convince myself there was a way for this to work out. After hearing this conversation, all my hopes die.

I manage to keep it bottled up until Skull closes the door. I sit up in bed the minute he's gone. I count to twenty in silence as the tears run down my face. When I think I'm in the clear, I allow my sobs to take over. My cries echo in the room as I accept that this is the end. I don't know how long I cry, but I make myself stop. I need to figure a way to get out of here.

Skull left Beast in charge of me, which means I need to figure out a way to distract him. Sadly, for Beast at least, I think I know how to do just that. I get up and try to use makeup to cover up the damage the tears caused. Then, I head to the kitchen, praying luck is on my side.

When I make it to the kitchen, Jan's there with one of the club girls that I heard Torch call Carla. They look at me with that barely disguised hate that I'm coming to expect from them.

They should be glad to help me leave.

"I figured Skull would have grown tired of your pussy by now," says Carla with a sneer. "He doesn't usually do repeats."

"Actually, I need to leave," I respond, keeping the pain out of my voice; I can't afford to show any weakness.

"Oh, poor thing. Did Skull kick your ass out?" Jan speaks up. Not for the first time, I think of what a bitch she is. From everything I've seen of Beast, he's a great guy. I don't understand how he got saddled with *her*.

"I just need to go home, but I need help."

"What the fuck for?" Carla asks.

"I need someone to distract, Beast. Skull has him watching me. I need him occupied so I can get away. I thought you might be able to help with that," I tell Jan, waiting for her response.

"What's in it for me?" she asks, her greed evident in her words and the way she watches me.

"Fifty dollars?"

I wait for her answer. I've only been here a couple of days and Skull's been keeping me busy, but even I have heard of Jan's problem. She's addicted to coke. It's not my place to worry, but I feel bad for Beast.

"It's going to cost more than a fifty to do what you're asking. Fucker won't ignore an order given to him by Skull. I'll have to suck his dick to even stand a chance."

"I'll suck his cock for a fifty," says Carla.

"Damn fucker won't let you. He hasn't been with another woman since he put a fucking ring on my finger. Shit, I leave just to get a break from giving him pussy. Drives me fucking crazy. He's the most boring fuck around."

I wince, feeling bad for Beast. I wish he could see what a bitch he's hooked up with. I may not know him that well, but no man deserves to put up with this kind of stuff.

"So, how much?" I ask, anxious to end this conversation.

"A hundred."

Guilt hits me as I hand her the money. I know it will go for drugs. Still, I try and justify it by admitting that if I don't get away, no one will survive. Colin won't quit until he makes sure of that.

"I'll be going in there in ten minutes. You better do what you have to do because I'm not about to make sure you're gone to finish him off."

She's just so freaking sweet, I think to myself. I listen as she gives me directions on how to get out of here and exactly what she will arrange, then hurry towards Skull's room, desperate to get away from her.

"Everything okay, Beth?" asks Beast, and I come to a stop right before I can make my escape.

"Sure," I say, trying to avoid eye contact. "Why do you ask?"

"Just checking. Skull and the boys will be back late this evening."

"Yeah, he told me. Hey, Beast?"

"What's up?"

"You're a nice guy, you know. I mean… I don't know you that well, but I can tell." I feel my cheeks flushing.

"Uh… thanks, Beth."

"Sure. Anytime. I… better go and take a bath. You can't be too clean, you know."

He grins. It's a stiff grin, but a grin nonetheless. I'm being an idiot. It's a wonder he's not laughing and making fun of me.

"Bye, Beth."

"Yeah. Bye, Beast. I really enjoyed talking with you and meeting you. You know. Just… everything."

He does laugh a little this time, and why wouldn't he? I sound loony. I just feel guilty that Jan's been talking about him the way she has and that I'm using it to my advantage. I wish I could tell him all about Jan, but I can't.

"Talk to you at dinner, Beth."

"Yeah, sure, okay," I tell him, opening the door to Skull's room and needing to get away before I break down and tell him everything I'm planning.

I grab my backpack and sit on the bed, trying to calm my nerves. I only had two days with Skull as his, but they were the best two days I've ever had in my life. The weeks I spent meeting Skull at the coffee shop and then here at his club are memories I shall take with me to survive the rest of my life.

I get off the bed and crack Skull's door and wait. When I hear Beast's moans of pleasures, I sneak into the large hall bathroom. Jan said she'd have Marker, one of the new prospects who was in charge of monitoring the back of the building, wait for me and get me out of here. I wonder if Skull knows how shitty some of the people he keeps in his compound are.

It takes some prying and a lot of cursing, but I manage to get the bathroom window open and shimmy out of it. My plan was to hold onto the ledge and then jump down, but my hands slip and I fall to the ground with a hard thump. It jars me and knocks the breath out of my lungs. I have to sit on the ground for a couple of minutes before I can continue. I stand up and find my legs weak, though I think it has more to do with nerves than from falling. I look up and there's a large man wearing a black leather cut just like Skull's. The only exception is there's no name or designation on it. It's blank.

"You Skull's whore?"

I wince. I want to argue, but I bite my tongue. Is it so far from the truth, really? Do I even care? Truth is, I would give myself to Skull over and over if I had the chance. It wouldn't even be a question.

"I'm Beth," I tell him.

"Whatever, follow me. I'm getting your ass out of here before one of the other men can catch me. You get caught, you never saw me. Got it?"

"Got it."

I take a breath and follow him. It takes all I have not to look back or run back to Skull's room and wait for him.

CHAPTER 19
SKULL

I didnt see that one coming.

"Colin," I acknowledge, sitting across from him.

He doesn't say anything. His cold steel eyes look me over. Everything about this motherfucker sets off alarm bells in my head.

"You have five minutes," he says, and my hands shake from the need to end the motherfucker.

"I need to know why you and Matthew called an end to our truce."

"We had no truce. You were merely inconsequential," he says, leaning back in his chair.

"Fuck that. Matthew and I brokered a truce and it's been pretty fucking effective the last few years. Then you and the Saints decide to come into my territory and make a fucking declaration of war. I demand to know why," I tell him, my voice hard. I'm not toying with the asshole. I don't care who he is.

"Matthew's not in charge anymore, *chico*," he says, the slur rolling off his tongue... a tongue I make a vow to cut off someday soon. *Very soon.*

"Does Matthew know he's not in charge?"

"My brother does not concern you. You're running out of time."

"And you did not answer my question satisfactorily. If you want war, believe me asshole, I can give it to you. I would rather not see the shedding of blood if it is not necessary."

"Are you afraid?" the cocky bastard asks, taking a drink from his glass. There's an empty glass in front of me and an aged bottle of scotch, but I don't trust the motherfucker not to have it drugged, so I ignore it.

"Not in the least. Enough of the song and dance, Colin. We both know you wouldn't strike without a reason, however fucked up it is. So tell me, what the fuck does this come down to? Or, we can both get the fuck out of here and war can begin. I got warm pussy waiting for me at home. I much prefer that to looking at you."

His lips curl in distaste. My fist clenches under the table so no one can see it. I keep my face impassive.

"Beth."

He says my woman's name and my insides freeze. My brain doesn't comprehend it at first. How does he know her name? Why is he bringing her up? *What the fuck is going on?*

"Excuse me?" I ask, feeling my way in the fucking dark and vowing to have a word with Beth when I get back. I planned on learning her secrets... but fuck me sideways, not like this.

"You think you can touch my property? You bought yourself a world of trouble, and the only blood that will be spilled... is *yours*. And that is a promise. This meeting is done."

"*Your* property?" I ask, my voice laced in ice.

"Mine," he states, and it takes all I have not to tear him apart with my bare hands.

"Does she know that? Because I don't remember her saying your name when she was begging for my cock."

Shock comes over Colin's face, then jealousy. I see it clearly before he locks it down.

"You're lying."

"She's got the sweetest pussy I've ever been inside of. Drains a man dry and begs for more. Too bad you didn't get a taste when you could, Colin, because she's *mine* now, and unlike you, motherfucker, I protect my property." I stand up. "*Now* this meeting's finished."

"Return her back to me and I might let you live, Skull."

"I'll see you in hell first," I tell him, not bothering to turn around. "Let's go boys," I call to Torch and Sabre. My mouth got away from me. I know there will be blood flowing in this fucking war, but I can't stop it. The son of a bitch is never getting his hands on my woman. She is mine, even if I'm going to fucking make sure she can't sit down for a week.

"Jesus, when you get serious over a woman, you make sure it's not simple, *ese*," Diesel says, following us out. I don't answer him. There's nothing I can say because he's absolutely fucking right.

CHAPTER 20
BETH

" My mistake was in thinking men could behave rationally. Clearly, that's impossible. "

I'm so tired that I stumble with my every step. I've been walking nonstop since Marker got me out of there. I kept expecting Beast to find me or one of the others out hunting for me, but so far I've been home free. I'm probably overestimating my value. I mean, just because I'm more than halfway in love with Skull doesn't mean he has the same emotions. He's told me several times that he'll grow tired of me. He'll probably get back and decide I'm not worth the trouble. Up ahead, I can see the bus station.

I find the sight of it brings me both relief and sadness.

I make it through the doors and go straight to the bathroom. It's been so dry in Georgia that I can feel the dust all over my skin. I freshen up and splash water on my face. Once I make it back to the main lobby, I stare at the big map of the states pinned on the bulletin board. I don't have a plan about where to go. If I go back to Montana, Colin and Matthew will find me and I don't want that. Colorado? Texas? Do I pick a small town, or would it be easier to get lost in a big city? There's so many decisions and I'm scared to death to make the wrong one. I send up a small prayer and hope I'm doing it right.

In the end, I decide to go with the bus that's leaving the quickest. In fact, this one's loading right now. I buy my ticket and head to the door. I'm putting my change in my purse and look up just in time to hear that voice hit me.

"Beth. Where do you think you're going?"

My blood runs cold.

"How did you find me?"

"A better question would be, why did you disobey me?"

I take three steps backwards until I'm pressed up against the side of the building.

"You had a meeting today…"

"And it's over. Imagine my surprise when I get a call that you're walking along the side of a road. Let's get in the car. We'll discuss the trouble you've caused me then."

"Colin, I don't want to go back. I don't want to be here. Let me go. We're not family, not really."

His cold face, which has always been scary to me, turns even colder.

"You are my property, Beth. You can't leave. You do as I say, when I say it. Get in the car. Don't make this worse on yourself," Colin warns.

I bite my lip and the coppery taste of blood releases into my mouth. I knew escaping was going to be a longshot, but I thought I would get further than I did.

I'm about to take a step towards Colin when another voice, this one from my opposite side, stops me.

"Beth, if you take one more step, I will tan your ass more than it was already going to get."

My heart turns over and then slams quickly in my chest, beating so fast I'm sure people can see it shaking my body. *Skull.*

"Skull…"

"Get over here, woman, and let's get back home."

"If she goes with you," says Colin, "I'll wipe you and your whole club out. That's my family you're messing with. It will not happen."

"You shouldn't be sporting a fucking hard-on for your sister anyway, Colin. Talk about disgusting," Skull taunts.

My legs quake. I wonder, if I took off running, how far I would get? When Beast blocks the door back into the bus station, I figure any hope of that is gone.

"She's not my sister, but she is mine."

"Beth. Now," Skull orders, ignoring Colin.

"You do, and you will live to regret it," Colin says to me, his eyes filled with hate and every bit of it is directed at Skull.

"She'll be fine. If I were you, Colin, I'd worry about myself, because I'm going to fucking *end* you. I told you, Beth was mine. I really didn't expect this of you. Who knew you'd be so eager to get my sloppy seconds?"

"Skull!" I gasp. I know he's just taunting Colin, but surely he knows how stupid this is. "Colin, he didn't mean—"

"I sure as fuck did. Told you before, Colin. I've had her, and I'm not letting go. That young pussy, *cabrón?* Fucking delicious. I broke in that tight little snatch and formed her to fit only my cock. I'm not giving that shit up, so you're out of luck."

"Beth…" they warn me together.

"Will you both hush!" I growl, stomping my foot. "I'm not *property!* I'm a real person! I want to leave. I'm not going back with any of you!"

"Beast."

"Got it, Boss," Beast growls and, before I know what to expect, he grabs me and throws me over his shoulder. He moves us behind Skull and the other men. Over my yelling, I can hear Skull in the background.

"You're giving me a license to wipe you off the map, biker. I don't think you want to do that."

"It's not going to be that easy. You want war, you got it, but I warn you now, Colin, I will fucking make it my mission to cut your head off and mount it for your brother."

Panic fills me. I have to stop this. Doesn't Skull realize how much he has to lose? Doesn't he know the kind of power that Colin and Matthew wield? Beast will not let me down and, in desperation, I plant my teeth into his shoulder, hoping the pain makes him drop me.

"Ow! Fuck, Skull! Your woman bit me!" Beast growls, trying to pull me away. I give up when it's clear he's not going to drop me.

"This isn't over," Colin says, motioning to the men around him. That's when I see Colin's men holding guns. Skull's men have guns pointed directly at them. How did I miss that? At Colin's signal, they back away but keep their guns aimed. "It looks like you got your war," he says and my stomach rolls with the implications of that.

"So be it. I'm not giving her up," Skull says.

My tears fall at that declaration. The thing I was trying to prevent just happened. How many deaths will be my fault? *Will Skull's?*

CHAPTER 21
SKULL

" A man's not a man
        if he can't protect what is his. "

Beth rides on the back of my bike all the way to the compound. I'm so pissed at her, I'm afraid of what I'd say right now. I need to calm down, but I don't see that happening. We pull into the garage at the compound. The boys are as silent as I am. This fucking shit is going to be bad. There's not a fucking thing I can do to stop it. I'm not giving up Beth. Hell, even if I delivered her back to Colin at this point, there'd still be war. Anything less would make me a weak motherfucker and I'm sure Colin feels the same.

Beth climbs off first and I follow. She's wringing her hands, betraying her nerves. I can't feel sorry for her. She should have fucking told me this shit from the get-go. I'm not sure it would have changed anything, but she knew what kind of fucking secret she was hiding. She might be young and inexperienced, but she's not stupid.

No. Instead, she made me the fucking last to know.

"Torch, increase all the security around the compound. Then, you call Church. If they wear a motherfucking Blaze cut, they are there. No exceptions. I also want Pistol's brother on the phone. It's time to batten down the hatches, motherfuckers. Nothing in or out unless I clear it."

"Got it, Boss."

I grab Beth by the arm and look at her. "Who's the motherfucker that helped you get out of here?"

"Skull…"

"Names, Beth," I warn her, at the end of my rope.

"I promised I wouldn't—"

"I think you've kept enough fucking secrets from me. Give me the names. *Now.*"

"Marker."

"Torch, chain his ass up," I order over my shoulder. "Who else?"

"Skull, I think this is something we should discuss in private," she pleads, her face pale.

"The time to discuss shit with me privately would have been before everything went to hell. Now you just fucking tell me. One more time, Beth. Who the fuck helped get you out of here?"

"The bathroom window was unlocked, really. I mean, I could have just got out on my own."

She looks down at her hands as she answers. She looks nervously over at Beast. It clicks into place.

"Beast?" I ask. Beth looks up, stricken with fear.

"No, Skull! It wasn't Beast! He even stopped me in the hall to make sure I was alright! I lied to him, I swear! He'd never betray you."

"Beast?" I prompt again, ignoring Beth. My hand is so tight on her upper arm that I know it will cause a bruise. That's good. She needs to remember the fucking stunt she pulled today. She needs to remember what happens when she keeps secrets from me.

"Yeah, Boss?"

"Your old lady. Was she around when Beth escaped?"

"Jan?" Beast asks and then I see it hit him in the face. His old lady is a bitch and, I'm pretty sure, a fucking cokehead. I'm tired of seeing my man keep blinders on his eyes.

"Fuck, Boss…"

"Beast," Beth tries to interject. Beast gives her a fucking look that most men would shrink from, then turns away from her.

"You lock your old lady down. Got me, Beast?"

"I'll get it taken care of, Boss."

"Get moving, boys. I know the Donahues aren't going to wait until we're ready to attack."

Everyone moves out, leaving me and Beth alone.

"Skull, please, just let me explain," she begs.

I ignore her, throw her over my shoulder, then walk her through the club and back to my room without stopping to acknowledge anyone else.

I throw her on the bed. "Skull," she says as she bounces on the mattress.

"What the fuck were you thinking, Beth? How could you not tell me that Colin and Matthew were your fucking family? Or that Colin wants to stick his fucking dick in you? Don't you think that's something I need to know?"

"No. I mean, you said you'd grow tired of me. I thought I'd be long gone before—"

"Were you always planning on fucking leaving?"

She flushes guiltily and betrayal dropkicks me. *Fuck.*

"Skull, it wasn't because of you. I just knew I couldn't stay here because of Colin. I had to leave."

"So you were planning on leaving me today regardless? You weren't even going to fucking tell me?"

"You're the one who said you'd grow tired of me! Remember? What are you getting so upset about?"

"When were you leaving me, Beth? *When?*"

"Tomorrow. I couldn't stay knowing Colin might take it out on you."

"And you weren't going to tell me. Right, Beth? Be fucking honest for once, since it appears you haven't been from the beginning. You weren't going to tell me a fucking thing. You were just going to disappear."

"Yes."

"You're locked in this fucking room. You manage to get some other bitch to help you, I'll make you sorry and I'll kill the motherfucker who helped you. Do not test me, Beth."

"Skull, if you just let me go—"

"I'm not fucking letting you go. Don't you get it yet, Beth? You're mine. I've claimed your lying ass and I'm keeping it. You're never getting away."

"You can't just keep me here like a prisoner!"

"The fuck I can't. Just watch me, *querida*. Just fucking watch me," I growl and slam the door.

I stomp back out to the club. It's been deserted by all except Latch. Before he can make it to the room where we have Church, I stop him.

"Latch, you're on duty with Beth. You go in that fucking room. You do not let her so much as take one step off the bed. She doesn't go to the fucking bathroom, she doesn't fucking do anything but breathe. You got me?"

"Got it."

"Good. I'll be back after Church. Sabre can catch you up."

He acknowledges the command and heads back to my room. I take a deep breath. When that doesn't calm me down, I plant my fist through the fucking wall. The sheetrock caves with the force of my hit and the pain hurts like a son of a bitch. I don't feel one bit better either. She was going to fucking leave me and I never would have known. Colin would have gotten his hands on her and destroyed her. I slam my fist into the wall again, ignoring my bruised and bloodied knuckles. I feel like I could pound the fucking wall for days and I'd still be pissed off.

I can't, though. I have to figure out how I can keep my men from dying, all while keeping Beth safe. This is war. Once I get that settled, then I'll deal with Beth. I just don't know what the fuck to do with her.

CHAPTER 22
BETH

" *I'm screwed.* "

I watch the door slam behind Skull. I just sit there. I don't know what else to do. I'm in shock. The last thing I expected was having Skull and Colin show up at the bus stop. Sometimes, being in small towns really sucks. I let out a large breath and try to sort through everything. I can't let Colin destroy Skull. I know Skull thinks he can handle this, but I've seen the way Matthew and Colin operate. Nothing good can come from this. Yet, I've got a feeling that getting away from here won't be that easy.

I tense up as the door opens. Surely Skull isn't back so quickly. It's stupid, but I'm more than a little disappointed when it's not Skull that comes through the door.

"Who are you?" I ask the stranger. I've seen him before, so I know he's a member, but he's one of the ones I haven't talked to.

"Latch."

Does no one in this club have a regular name?

"What are you doing here?"

"I'm your babysitter until Skull gets done and can come back to watch you."

"I don't need a babysitter."

"Apparently, you do."

"So I'm a prisoner?"

"Let's see. I'm not supposed to let you go to the bathroom alone, so I'm going to go with *yes*."

"This is ridiculous." I huff, looking away from Latch. I don't want him to read the fear in my eyes. I really need to get away before it's too late—*if it's not already.*

"Yeah, it is."

"Then why don't you go back out and do whatever you need to do? I'll just—"

"Run away again?" he finishes for me. "Ignore the wishes of the man who's putting his life and the lives of his brothers in jeopardy for you? Betray him? What *will* you do?"

His questions hit me with the force of a blow, and I'm stunned. "Just wait a minute here. It's not like that!"

"You didn't leave the compound when Skull made it clear you needed to stay here?"

"I needed to leave! I was trying to avoid putting Skull in danger! I don't want to put anyone in danger!"

"Kind of late for that," the asshole says, stretching back against the chair he's sitting in and looking bored.

"I know, that's why I—"

"The time to worry about that was *before* you spread your legs for him. Tell me, cupcake, did you even think about the fact that you were signing Skull's death warrant when you climbed in his bed? Don't you think you should've warned him?"

"No one was supposed to find out! That's why I was leaving!"

"Well, I guess we've seen how great that plan worked."

"You're an asshole."

"Been told that before. I don't see it myself."

"So what are we going to do in here until Skull gets back?" I ask when it becomes clear he's not going to leave.

"Play strip poker?" he asks, holding up cards.

"I don't think Skull would like that," I tell him, laughing despite my stress.

"Only if you lose," he says.

"How about just regular cards?"

"Boring as hell, but whatever," he says, kicking out the chair across from him. He moves the end table between the chairs and starts dealing.

I glance at the door before joining him.

"No one's saving you. I don't have a bitch that leads me around by the dick like Beast, so you're shit out of luck," he says, not looking up from dealing. I feel myself flush because I do feel guilty about that.

"Beast deserves better," I grumble, sorting through the cards.

"No argument here. So does Skull, though."

"I didn't sell him out," I argue.

"No. You just don't have any faith in him. He can handle the Donahues."

"You don't know them like I do. They are dangerous."

"You don't have any idea what Skull and our club are like when our hands are forced. If he's worth giving your pussy to, try having a little faith in him for the other shit, cupcake."

"I really hate that nickname."

"I hate playing regular poker. Sometimes you have to deal."

"Does Beast know she's hooked on drugs?"

"He does now."

"I'm sorry," I say lamely.

"That's the one thing you shouldn't be sorry about."

"You really think Skull can handle what Colin and Matthew will try?"

"I think if he can't, no one can."

"That's not totally reassuring, Latch."

"It's just the truth, cupcake."

"Skull doesn't have to do this. Maybe if I left, I could stop Colin from—"

"I didn't see anyone twisting Skull's arm back at the bus stop."

"Well, no. But—"

"Then I'd say he chose it. Your job is to have faith in your man."

"My man? He said he would grow bored with me," I whisper. The words still have the power to hurt me.

"I don't see anyone growing bored with you. Now go, will

you?"

I swallow at his words. *I'm scared.* I'm scared to stay and I'm scared to go. I decide to concentrate on the cards since I don't have any other choices right now. The only thing I'm sure of is, I can't let Skull get hurt because of me.

CHAPTER 23
SKULL

**War is where you find out
what kind of man you really are.**

"Meeting in order," I growl as I sit down. I don't bother with the fucking gavel. I'm not sure I wouldn't break the son of a bitch right now.

"We're at war with the Donahues?" Briar asks, getting straight to the point. He was one of the few main patched-in members I didn't take with me. It was on purpose. He and Pistol are close. I haven't talked with him much about all the shit, but I don't have time to deal with fuckers who aren't behind me.

"Yes." I sit back and watch everyone's faces, judging and monitoring their reactions.

"That's a lot to fucking swallow," Clutch adds.

It's a full table tonight. Normally, I only have Church with the officers. However, this will involve everyone. So the patched-in members, with the exception of Latch, are all here.

"Are you with me or against me?" I ask the one question that matters the most.

"You pick a fucked up time to start not one, but possibly two wars," Briar says. "Have you even spoken to Cade?"

Cade is Pistol's brother and my biggest worry about the situation. I need Cade's support right now. I sure as hell don't need him pissed off and coming at me.

"I'm going to, right after we're done here." I divert my attention away from Briar and back to the group as a whole. "Now's the time to speak up motherfuckers if you have a problem with the way I'm running things. Let me hear it."

"The situation with Pistol needs dealing with. We can't leave the fucker on ice, and he is a part of this club, a patched-in member," Briar says again.

"He disrespected me. Ain't no motherfucker gonna do that."

"Then fight it out or kill him, but do something."

"You're cool with that?" I ask Briar, because of all the men, he's the one friend Pistol has.

"It should've been dealt with a long time ago. I'm more than cool with it," he says, surprising the fuck out of me.

"I second that," Torch pipes up, and all the men nod in agreement.

There it is. I have all the brothers' support—even the one member I wasn't expecting it from. Contentment settles inside of me. This is why I chose to be president. This is why the Devil's Blaze MC is my home.

"Okay, then anyone want to weigh in about the Donahues?"

"Kind of late to worry about it. We back down now, we're a bunch of fucking pussies. They want war. We give it to them. But I say we better make a motherfucking statement," Beast speaks up.

"Is she worth the war?" Sabre asks.

"She's mine. I'm claiming her. That makes her one of us," I tell him, but I direct the words to everyone.

"She's awful young, Boss," K-Rex says.

"Fuck, you're claiming her? I was hoping to have a go at her. It'd be nice to get some strange around here, even if it's your sloppy seconds," Torch cracks, looking at me with that damned grin on his face.

"Stay away from her, you horny fuck. You already nail everything with a snatch in a ten mile radius."

"Hey, a man has needs."

"You're going to break your fucking dick before you hit thirty and be a sad-ass fuck popping pills to get a boner," I tell him.

"No danger in that. Torch is my name, and heating up juicy

little cunts is my game."

"Whatever, just stay away from Beth."

"Boss, you wound me," he responds and I want to lay into him, but I need to direct this meeting in the right direction. We have shit to do and I need my motherfucking bases covered.

"All joking aside, we're in for a fucking battle. I want phone conferences with the charters tomorrow."

"Are we asking for help from outside clubs, like Diesel's?" Sabre asks.

"We're going to need it eventually. I want that path cleared, but I won't ask them to join in until our hands are forced."

"What about our families and shit? I know my old lady fucked up, Boss, but I need to think about Annabelle," Beast says. I look at the big guy and feel bad for him. Jan is a miserable bitch. Beast deserves better, but he knocked her up and he's a loyal fucker. He's not going to turn away from Jan; he's going to take her shit until he can't no more, just to keep his daughter close. I'm not sure I can blame him. His daughter Annabelle is only three, and she's a beautiful little thing who luckily looks just like her dad and nothing like Jan.

"We're on lockdown. We increase the fucking security here and no one goes in or out. That means *no one*, Beast," I warn him, because he knows as well as I do that Jan will be pushing that—especially when she runs out of her stash.

"Got it." I can see from the look in his eyes that he does, so I let it go.

"Okay. We'll have another meeting tonight to check on the status of shit. Everyone here, no exceptions," I order, banging my hand on the table and making it vibrate with the force of the hit. Then, I walk out before anyone else. I have some fucking calls to make and I need to deal with Pistol. Maybe then I can go back to Beth without wanting to strangle her.

CHAPTER 24
SKULL

I fight. Every day, I fight. But she's like no opponent I've ever known.

It's dark outside by the time I get free enough to go to my room to talk to Beth. I sent word by Torch to have one of the men send her and Latch dinner, but I know she's probably pissed as hell at being confined to her room. I can't help it. She brought this on herself. She's lucky I don't have her chained to the bed. My dick moves and pushes against my pants to let me know he's still alive as I picture Beth chained to my bed. The damn thing can just die back down. I'm not fucking Beth again until I make her see what a fucked up thing she's done. I will not put up with her keeping secrets and lying to me. That's a deal breaker. I'm not going to be like Beast, being led around by my dick and being made a fool of. *No way.*

When I make it to my door, there's laughing going on inside and I instantly want to rip the door off the hinges and use it to beat one certain biker to fucking death. Instead, I open the door and stand there ready to snap his neck like a twig.

"What the fuck are you doing in here?"

Torch looks up grinning. I'm really getting fucking tired of that grin.

"Hey, Boss. I decided to bring Beth some dinner myself."

"Dinner was two hours ago, fucker," I growl, and my eyes dart to Beth, who is blushing but trying not to look at me. *She shouldn't.* The slightest thing will make me cross the edge right now.

"Wow, really?" Torch asks, fake-glancing at his watch. "Eh,

Boss, you know how it is when you have good company. Time gets away," he tells me, this time turning his attention back to Beth.

I'm going to have to kill the motherfucker. That'll make him behave.

"Yes, really, *Cabrón*," which is Spanish for *dumbass*, which is being nice. There's so much more I'd rather say to him. I don't bother, though. With Torch, it wouldn't matter, and I want to talk with Beth. When I look over at her on the bed and see the way her blonde hair falls over her face and her full lips making a half smile, I admit that I mostly want to fuck her. Between the Church meeting, talking with Diesel, and then with Pistol's brother, I am about talked out.

"I guess I got carried away talking to the lovely Beth. It's hard to concentrate on the time when you have such beauty in front of you."

"Why would she want to talk with a man who tries to flirt with all the ladies, but since his dick is only two inches long, gets nowhere?"

"Fuck you. My cock is legendary," he returns, then winks at Beth, adding, "In size and in experience, in case you were wondering."

"If you don't get the fuck away from her, you won't *have* a cock," I warn him, and I'm not exactly joking. Torch ignores me, but doesn't press his damn luck. He says his goodbye to Beth, gives me a motherfucking salute, then closes the door behind him. That leaves me staring at Beth wondering where in the fuck we go from here.

"He's interesting."

"You're taken."

"I wasn't looking. It was merely an observation."

"So you admit you're mine?" I ask, pissed off with myself because that's not the conversation we need to be having, but it's the only thing that keeps coming to mind right now.

"Skull, you need to let me go. You heard Colin. He won't

stop until he destroys you. I can't let that happen."

"I'm not letting you go, Beth. You're mine. I've claimed you in front of everyone. They all know it. The only person not seeming to get it would be you."

"Skull..."

"Strip."

"Isn't that how we started this mess to begin with?"

"It's not a mess, and if something works, then you stick with it. Now strip."

"I thought you were mad at me."

"That's why they invented angry sex."

"Shouldn't we talk first?" she asks, but she stands and raises her shirt over her head and throws it on the floor.

"We will be talking with our bodies. If you're lucky, you'll wear me out enough that I won't have the energy to punish you."

Beth steps out of her pants and kicks them off to the side.

"I should've ran the other way when I met you," she mumbles.

"But you didn't, and now it's much too late."

"You said you'd grow tired of me!" she complains, standing in her underwear.

"I lied."

"Skull," she begins, but I stop her.

"Lose the underwear, Beth. Then come stand in front of me," I tell her, sitting down in a chair, already naked.

"This doesn't sound much different from regular sex," she huffs, but she takes off her bra and panties.

"The angry part will come when I'm feeding you my cock. Now get over here," I tell her, stroking my cock and squeezing it tight because fuck me, I already want to come.

She looks at me, then down at my cock. Pre-cum drizzles from the head of my dick onto my hand as I continue stroking. Then, she walks towards me, her eyes glued to my cock, and that sweet little tongue of hers licks the bottom of her lip, which only makes my dick leak more.

Fuck, this isn't going to last long. "On your hands and knees, Beth."

She slides down to her knees on the floor. Her gray eyes sparkle with need as she looks up at me. If there's a more beautiful sight, I can't place it. This is nowhere near angry sex, but telling her I need her to submit to me—to touch her, to own her for no other reason than to reassure myself that she's not leaving—gives her too much fucking power. Beth has no idea how gone I am for her. She's young. Maybe she thinks a woman is something a man puts his life, his club, and the lives of his brothers in danger for so easily. It's not. I know what I'm asking of my club. I was completely prepared to override my brothers tonight. The fact that they all agreed with me, even Briar, leaves me humbled. It cements my reason for taking over for my *tío*. Being president of the Devil's Blaze is where I belong.

"Give me your hand," I tell her. She reaches for me and I clasp it in mine. Soft, smooth skin, pale white compared to mine. Our difference could be summed up there. Completely opposite of each other, but then there's so much about us that connects. She's young, but life has made her older than her years—at least in most of the ways that count. "So beautiful. How many times have I reached for this hand in the middle of the night? You planned on taking that away from me, Beth," I tell her, kissing her palm.

"Skull," she begins, but I don't let her talk.

"Quiet, *querida*. Your chance to talk has passed." I bring her hand to my sack. She holds my balls carefully. It's almost as if she's afraid. It's that innocence that makes me smile, even when my mind is a fucking mess. "Roll them, Beth. Tease them," I instruct, my hand going back to my dick. Her eyes follow my movements as I stroke myself slowly. I doubt she even realizes her head is tilting towards my cock. I decide to give her what she's silently asking for. I take the head of my cock and brush her lips with it, painting them in my pre-cum. Her tongue comes out to play and she licks the head, delving into the crease in the tip. "Do you want my cock, Beth?" I ask, my words coming out more like a moan. The sight of her tongue dancing across my head and her lips greedily taking my cum into her mouth will be one that I will remember when I'm a hundred fucking years old.

"Yes."

My fingers push into her hair, gentle for now. I let the texture float across my fingers, taking in the different colors in the strands. Golden sunshine, just like the light that having her beside me brings to my life. I never stood a chance. She knocked me on my ass from that first glimpse of her, and she may very well be my death.

All of that, and I still wouldn't change a motherfucking thing. "Take it, *mi cielo*. Show me how much you want it," I tell her, still letting her hair sift through my fingers.

I watch as her hand moves up to the base of my cock. Her fingers can't reach all the way around, but she squeezes it, and it feels so damn good. Her lips kiss my balls, sucking one into her mouth, then releasing it before nuzzling her face against them and planting more soft kisses. Her tongue flattens and slides along the underside of my cock in a long, soft glide until it reappears at the head and my pre-cum is all over her tongue. I can see it and feel the heat of need zap along my spine. I need to come, but I hold back. I want her to play. I want her to learn my body because it's the only fucking body she'll *ever* have. *Mine.*

I'm so intent on watching her discover my cock with her tongue that I'm not prepared when, on her third sweet lick upwards, her mouth goes down on my staff. I watch as I disappear into that wet, heated paradise. "That's it, baby. Suck it down," I encourage her. Her eyes go to my face and she slides further on my cock. I feel her tongue dance along my shaft. Her cheeks hollow out as she loves on my dick. Sucking him in so fucking tight, I can already feel my cum building. She goes down until her lips meet her hand and then goes back up. I watch her bob up and down on my cock and it's beautiful, but it's too fucking slow for what I need now. My patience is gone. My fingers tangle in her hair now, pulling tight. She looks up at me and I see the question in her face. She's afraid she's done something wrong. "Brace your hands on my knees, *querida*. I'm the one in charge now. I'll feed you my cock and you'll take every fucking inch."

My voice is hoarse from need. Her fingers bite into my legs and she hums around my cock. I feel the fucking vibration in that, all through my dick. I use the hold on her hair to push her further down on my cock, moaning as inch after inch disappears. I reach the back of her throat. She gags and I bring her back up.

"You can take it further, breathe through your nose," I tell her before pushing her back down. She gags again and I back off, leaving her to lick the head while I reach with my other hand and palm her breast. I tease the nipple, and her mouth goes back down on me, even though I'm holding her hair to keep her from going very far. She growls this time against my dick and I can't stop the smile. "You want it that bad, *querida*, you need to be prepared because I'll give it to you."

That's the only warning she gets before both of my hands tangle into her hair and I push her down on my cock, forcing her to swallow me down. This time, when I reach the back of her throat, I don't let her pull away.

"Work your throat and breathe through your nose, Beth. You can do it, sweetheart." I pull her back up and then push her mouth down again and this time, when I reach her throat, she works it like I've told her and she deep throats me like a fucking pro. "Oh fuck. Yeah, that's it, *querida*. That's it. Yeah, take that dick."

I work her hard on my cock and I can feel it. I'm about to explode. I could make her swallow it down. I want that— eventually. Not right now, though. Now, I need something else entirely.

I pull her off of me and she cries out in frustration. "No," she moans. "I want you to come."

"I'm going to," I tell her. "*Inside* of you. Climb up here on my lap, woman. You better be ready because this is gonna be a quick ride."

"In the chair? How?"

I hold my shaft steady. "Fuck yourself with it, Beth. Guide me inside."

She reaches down and takes control of my cock, holding it to her sweet pussy and pushing down on me.

"Oh, God," she moans, not stopping until I'm completely seated inside.

"You're soaked, *mi cielo*. Did you like sucking my dick that much?"

I take over her mouth before she can respond, tasting myself on her tongue. She pulls away, gasping, moving up and down on my cock and riding me like she's been doing it all of her life. My baby learns quick.

"Skull, I need more," she gasps, her voice sounding desperate. "Please, baby. I need—" She breaks off because I've found her clit with my fingers. She's so fucking wet, I glide easy over the hard little button. It's pulsing so hard I can feel it throb. "Oh, fuck. Baby! I'm going to come. I'm going to come!" she cries.

I can feel her shattering. I feel her sweet cream all over my cock and running down in streams. I grab her hips, slamming her down on my cock and grinding her against me over and over until I join her. When it's over, she lays her head on my shoulder and I hold her, taking in the scent of our lovemaking while our hearts and breathing slowly return back to normal.

"It gets better each time," she whispers. "I'm sorry, Skull. I should have told you."

"You should have."

"Do you really think you can defeat Colin?"

It annoys me that I can hear the fear in her voice, but she has a good reason to be worried. A fool wouldn't.

"It's not going to be easy, Beth. But I have something to fight for that Colin can't comprehend."

"What's that?"

"The mother of my children."

"Skull, I told you…"

"You'll see, *mi cielo.*"

Eventually, she will. There's not a doubt in my fucking mind.

CHAPTER 25
BETH

" *I love him, but I know in my heart I can't have him.* "

"I don't think I can move," I sigh, curled into Skull sometime later. I've lost track of time. All I know is, we've moved to the bed and now our room is dark. Neither one of us has made a move to turn on the light. I don't really want to. It's calm now, and it's like we're in our own world.

"Good. Maybe I can trust you enough to stay put so we can get some sleep," Skull grumbles.

"I was only trying to—"

"Leave," he interrupts.

"I didn't want to, Skull. I was trying to protect you."

"I'm a man, *querida*. If the time ever comes that I need to hide behind a woman to survive, I'd rather you just put a fucking bullet between my eyes."

"Will you please not say that?"

"Why? It's the truth. I did not get to be president of this club by being soft, Beth. I can take care of myself."

"They'll leave you alone if I go."

"Not now. I've called Colin out. He'd look weak. The time to worry about this shit would have been when we first met. You should have told me then who you were."

"I asked if you knew who I was. I didn't plan on hiding it from you."

"And when I told you no?"

"I kept saying, one more meeting, one more… and then I just didn't want to give you up," I tell him honestly, guilt laced in my

118

words.

Skull tightens his hold on me. One of his large hands still palms my ass. He squeezes it and pulls my center in closer to him. I don't know how, but his cock is already semi-erect. You'd think after everything we just did he would need recovery time. I pull my leg tighter over his hip. I love being close to him, and when I feel his cock brush against me, an answering wetness gathers between my legs. I'm addicted to him.

"It wouldn't have mattered, Beth," he tells me, looking into my eyes. He has a finger moving softly over my bottom lip. The rough texture of it teases me.

"What?" I ask so quietly I'm not sure he can hear me. My eyes are glued to the silver hoop in his lip and the way his tongue moves when he talks.

"I would have claimed you anyway, even knowing who you are. I may have played it differently, *mi cielo*, but I still would have claimed you."

"Why do you call me that?" I ask, my eyes almost closing as the heat of his body lures me to sleep.

"*Mi cielo?*"

"Yes."

"My sky," he says, pulling me so that I'm lying on his body.

Just like that I'm awake because I feel his cock rub against my pussy and slide in between the folds. I let my knees fall to the side of him and I push against him just once, testing. I nearly moan from the feeling. I could come like this, just using his cock to tease myself with. It doesn't even have to be inside of me.

"Your sky?" I gasp, doing it again, this time harder and sliding against him while tightening my pussy to get that delicious pressure right where I need it. *Oh, fuck yeah.*

Skull wraps his hand in my hair and tugs my head up so I can look at him. I pull against his hold because I'm dying to wrap my tongue around his hard nipple and suck the small bar he has there. When he moans, I feel like a queen. In response, he pulls on my hair harder, the pain making me look at him.

"*My* motherfucking sky. You are light, *mi cielo*... a fucking light I didn't know I needed. I want you shining on me all the time. I don't want you to leave, Beth. You're not fucking getting away because I won't let you. Your body, your mind, your fucking breath is mine. I'm not letting it go. I'm not letting *you* go, *ever.*"

His words are big, so big my breath stalls. They are like foreplay all by themselves. Skull is such a force. He seems larger than life itself, and yet somehow I shine for him. I shine for him so much that he wants to keep me. He *needs* me. That fact settles inside of me and I force my head down, ignoring the pain. My tongue plays around the nub, licking the hard, silver barbell and sucking it completely in my mouth. Skull's hands move from my hair down to my ass. He fingers bite into my cheeks as he shifts me so his cock rakes against my clit. I moan from the pleasure. As I release his nipple, I capture the piercing between my teeth, then tug. He growls, his hips thrusting up and driving his cock harder into the wet valley my pussy has created. I use my hand to torture his other barbell in much the same way.

I look and discover he's watching everything I do, his dark eyes setting me on fire.

"On your knees, Beth. Get on your knees, now."

His order and the hoarse growl in his voice sends vibrations of need through my body, and I instantly obey. I get up on my knees as he half-sits underneath me, then leans back to rest against the pillows. I brace myself on the headboard and wait for his next move. It doesn't take long. He takes his large cock in his hand, stroking it slowly. There's something so breathtakingly beautiful about his large, inked, rough hand stroking his hard slick cock. I bite into my lip, watching him stroke it from root to tip.

"Jesus, *mi mujer*, my cum is running out of your pussy even now."

I look down and see he's right. I didn't bother cleaning up after we made love, and this is our third round after all. Besides, I like having him inside of me. As I watch his cum slide from my pussy, my muscles quiver, wanting to claim it and draw it back inside. Skull must have the same thought because he gathers it on the head of his cock then guides it into my entrance. He braces one hand on my hip, then holds his cock still as he pushes it inside of me inch by glorious inch. He stops when I have half of him inside of me. I thrust into him, trying to take more. His fingers bite into my hip, refusing to let me.

"Skull…" I whine, my pussy clamping down hard on his shaft.

"What is it, *mi cielo?* Does that greedy cunt need more of me?" he asks, feeding me a little more.

Then, all at once, he shifts his position. He grabs my hips, pulling me back down on his lap, and thrusts hard. His cock is completely inside and I can feel his balls press against me. We're sitting now staring at each other. We did this before, but it's different this time—the emotions have changed. He maneuvers me again and helps get my legs around him. The heels of my feet dig into his back, my pussy already quivering around his dick as he rakes the inside of my walls and tunnels in and out of me.

It's a slow pace at first, our eyes locked together and just enjoying the feel of being a part of one another. I can't stop myself from holding the side of his face. My fingers skate over his nose, then pet the soft skin of his eyelids. I want to memorize every inch of him. I don't know how long I will have him, so I want to memorize everything. I run the pad of my thumb over his eyebrows.

Slowly, his eyes open again, his body still gently rocking in and out of me. I'm working with him now, our rhythm in sync. I'm going to come. I can feel the climax raking through my body, but I'm glued to the heat in his face.

"Beth?" he whispers.

Perhaps he sees it in my look or senses it through my touch. Maybe it's even by the way my body is clinging to his, wanting to be as close as physically possible… I don't know. But I'm sure he sees it before I even say it. I see the flair of recognition. So, I give him the words, the words which have been true since our first meeting.

"I love you, Skull. I love you."

He growls. Then, using his hold on my hips, he angles my body to the side, picking up his speed. His body slams into mine repeatedly, and he grinds himself against my pussy with each inward thrust. I tighten my muscles around him.

"Come for me, *mi cielo*. I want to see you fall apart in my arms while my cock's buried inside of you. Feel your pussy squeeze the fuck out of me so you take me with you," he commands as his hand moves down between us. He pinches my clit, twisting it.

I disintegrate into a million pieces. Skull follows me just a few seconds later. His cock jerks inside of me, the heat of his cum bathing and coating my insides. I squeeze him tighter, greedily wanting every drop.

When we're finished, he keeps me lying on top of him, his cock still inside. He brushes my hair and kisses my shoulder.

"*Te amo*, sweet Beth... *Te amo*."

I may not speak Spanish, but even I know what that means. Skull loves me. My eyes flutter shut, but I smile.

He loves me.

CHAPTER 26
SKULL

Five fucking days and not a word has come from Colin. The fucker's going to strike, I know it... I just don't know where or how. I feel it in my bones.

"You got a minute?"

I look up at Pistol standing at the door. His eye's black still, his arm is in a sling, and his ribs are taped. His brother asked me to give him one more chance, even knowing what a fuck-up he was. My gut instinct was to say no before Cade sweetened the deal: I get the support of his club and his charters in my war. He's even sending up a crew of a hundred as backing. This is why that motherfucker Pistol is still breathing enough to be standing. I beat him down. I took out every fucking frustration I had on his ass. He got a few hits in, but not very many.

I lean back in my chair and look at him. Why the fuck not? I've just been spending the day twiddling my damn thumbs. Why not just cap off my piece of shit day?

"What's up?"

"We need to settle this between us, especially if we're in a war."

"I thought we settled it on the court... when I kicked your ass."

The court is a ring out back in our common area where we fight. We either beat each other to vent frustrations or to prove a point. It was the latter between me and Pistol. If he had one thought in him that he was strong enough to overtake me, I beat that shit out of him.

"I was being a dick, I get that. But fuck, what do you expect? I'm second here. It's my club, too. I have a right to be worried about your choices."

"Maybe, but you don't have a fucking right to talk shit to me. You bring your concerns up in Church, motherfucker. You call for a vote. You challenge me to a fight. I don't give a damn which you choose, but what you do *not* do is talk shit and mouth off to me in front of my men. This is my club. *Mine.* I will not be disrespected or undermined."

"Point made. We don't have to be enemies. Not during this. No matter how we feel about each other, we both care about the club. Can we work together to protect it?"

"You can work with me, but I warn you, motherfucker, one wrong step and your brother won't save you this time."

His face closes off, but he gets points for the way he pushes down the hate and continues looking me in the eye.

"What are you thinking?" I ask.

"The Donahues use the Saints to do a lot of their fucking dirty work," he tells me. "Shit they think is beneath them. I'm pretty sure they think you are beneath them."

"You think they will have the Saints attack?"

"I think they will use them," he answers, and the idea is not without merit. He may be onto something. I can't deny having the same thoughts.

"What do you suggest?"

"We plant someone in the Saints."

I sigh. "I doubt we could get anyone in there they will talk freely with. Especially if they are helping the Donahues."

"Maybe, but I know someone in their clubhouse who hears a lot of shit."

"Who?" I ask, alarm bells going off. I don't trust Pistol. This sounds too easy.

"Claire."

"A muffler bunny?" I shake my head, discounting his

suggestion. "No way they'd be stupid enough to talk in front of a woman."

"We wouldn't. The Saints aren't that disciplined. I'm telling you, this could work."

"You trust this Claire?"

"Fuck no, but I trust her to jump on money if it was offered."

"Without setting us up?"

"That won't be on the table. All we need is for her to give us a heads-up if she hears them planning."

"You deal with it. If you think it will pan out, we'll try it."

"Got it. Are we good?"

"I don't have to like you. We're good as long as you don't pull that fucking shit again."

"Fair enough. I'll let you know if I hear anything further from Claire."

"Sounds good."

I stare at the door after it closes. I'm not sure how I feel about what just happened. I have warning bells going off in my head, but that may have more to do with the fact that Pistol's involved. I rub the tension at the back of my neck, studying the file in front of me. Colin's ugly face stares back at me.

"What are you planning, you son of a bitch?" I ask the ugly face. "And just when the fuck are you going to strike?"

I don't do well waiting. I don't like not taking the first strike. I thought about going on the offensive, but I know in my heart that this battle is going to be bloody. I'm not ready to put lives on the line until I have to.

I pick up my Bowie knife off the table and stab it into Colin's picture—right between his eyes. *I fucking hate waiting.*

CHAPTER 27
SKULL

There might be worse things than waiting..

"Still no word from Colin?" Beth asks when I come through the front door. The club's been on lockdown for the last week and the motherfucker still hasn't made a move. It's a game to him, I know. My only problem is, I'm not sure if it would pay for me to strike first. I do know I fucking hate being on the defensive end.

"Not a fucking word."

"What about your contact, Pistol? Anything?" Torch asks, and all eyes turn there.

"They've been keeping it nailed down. Word is, they've been dealing with a higher up who is unhappy with Colin's choices."

"Who's higher up than Colin?" asks Beth. "I thought he and Matthew were in charge since Edmund and mom passed."

"There's always someone higher up, *querida*," I answer. "Speaking of Matthew, where *is* that fuck? He's not made one move good or bad in this and that's the fucker we had the truce with."

"No one seems to know. Maybe your girlfriend knows," Pistol says.

I let that shit pass. Until I get through this crap with Colin, I don't give a fuck what Pistol says; that motherfucker's out of chances.

"Matthew went on vacation in France to the villa there. He hadn't come back, the last I knew," says Beth, staring at Pistol. I squeeze her hand and she turns to give me a smile, though her

126

face looks a little lost.

All this shit is driving her crazy. She's blaming herself for all of it. Nothing I say is making it better. I'd like to take her away from this shit for a couple of weeks, but that's not possible. When we get this crap behind us, I'm taking her away and spoiling her rotten. That, and fucking her raw. I adjust my cock; fucker's had her pussy a hundred ways—two to three times a day—and he's still not worn out. I got a feeling he never will be around her. Shit, I'll be ninety and still trying to nail her.

"Torch, you find out who this higher-up is who's unhappy with Colin. That can only be a handful of people. Maybe we can get this fucker from the inside."

"On it, Boss."

"What about the list of businesses and shit that Beth gave us?" I ask, squeezing her hand again. "Were there any surprises in there?"

"Nah, not really. We had all of their holdings down except one, and I'm not really sure why they own it. It's a freaking fruit market and gas station in Jelico, Tennessee."

"A fruit market?"

"Yeah, and near as I can tell, boss, that shit is a legitimate business."

"Do they use it for money laundering?"

"If they do, they're hiding that shit really good. I'm gonna dig deeper, but I can't even tell if they have anything to do with it, other than the fact that the licensing comes back to Beth's mom."

"My mother? She never owned a business," says Beth, confused. "Well, not that I know of. She was always too busy getting her hair done and partying. I swear, if I thought she had anything to do with the business, I would have told you, Skull."

"She would have, too. She's real good at ratting out people who are trying to help her," says Jan from across the room.

I pick Beth up in my arms, sit down in her seat, then settle her in my lap. We're having an informal meeting and I probably should have took it to my office, but the only ones allowed in this main part of the club while on lockdown are patched-in members and old ladies, which explains why Jan is running free. However, I'm not about to put up with her shit. In my book, the woman never looks good, but today she's looking even more haggard than usual. You can tell lockdown is wearing on her. I wonder how long it's been since her stash has emptied because you can tell just from looking at her that she's going without drugs, cold turkey.

"Beast," I growl, letting him contain his old lady. Only reason the bitch is still here is because he said he'd make sure she was under control.

"Got it, Boss," he responds, rising to go to his woman. "Come on, Jan. I told you it's not safe up here. Let's get back below," Beast tells her, taking her hand. "Annabelle will be wondering where we're at."

There's a storm shelter below. It's a basement of sorts, but more like a bomb shelter. I've had it all tricked out with special ventilation, steel-enforced blocked walls, and lighting that mimics the sun. It's a huge area complete with fifteen bedrooms and adjoining bathrooms, a huge kitchen and dining area that can easily handle up to two hundred people if need be, a bowling alley, poker and pool area, club and open bar, and another large playroom for kids. It's one of the main things I did when we chose this place for our compound. We don't go on lockdown often, but when we do, I want to make sure I can take care of my men and their families.

"Fuck that shit. *She's* up here," Jan slurs, pointing at Beth. It's obvious she's been hitting the bottle. I can see my man cringe. He's embarrassed of this shit and should be. This bitch is a piece of work.

"We're going over the information she gave Torch so we can try to end this lockdown and war before it hits," Beast explains.

"Yeah, that little bitch is good at being a narc."

"I didn't—" Beth tries to defend, but I squeeze her to get her to hush. She owes this cow jack-shit.

"Tell that to Marker, you bitch! Did you know they kicked him out of the club? They beat the fuck out of him because of you. He had to be carried back to his apartment! All because of your prissy ass!"

Beth tenses up in my arms. I've had enough.

"He was beat down for betraying his club," I growl. "He got the same fucking thing you deserved, but Beast saved your ass. Why he keeps doing that, I don't fucking know. But you better listen well, Jan: you so much as look at Beth or breathe near her, not even his ass will save you from here on out. You get me, bitch?"

This time, it's Beth who calms me. Her hand cups the side of my neck and her thumb grazes over the vein and pulse point.

"Let's go, Jan," Beast says when she doesn't respond with anything but looks of hate. She jerks away from him, pulling away so hard she nearly falls. She staggers and finally steadies herself.

"Fuck that. I don't want you around me. If I have to look at your fucking face again, I'm going to scream. I was only getting you off because you were giving me money and shit. I can't stand to look at you. You're always touching me, wanting to fuck. It makes me sick. You make me sick. You're a weak-ass little boy. I couldn't even stand the smell of your breath if it wasn't for the money you give me!"

"Jan, let's go back downstairs. Annabelle—"

"Annabelle isn't even yours! You didn't even know! You're so stupid you didn't even realize I was fucking your brother every time your dumb ass wasn't around!"

"Jan!"

"Sometimes he fucked me when you were there. Didn't know that, did you? You'd be in there watching your football games and your brother would be in the bathroom fucking me against the wall and getting me off in ways you can never fucking manage! He's Annabelle's dad! Not you! You should have been the one to die in that fucking prison riot. You. Not him! Terry was more of a man than you'll ever be!"

Beast lets off a guttural scream that sounds like it's torn from his very soul—and it probably is. Beth hides her face into my neck and I can't blame her. I wish I wasn't here to witness my brother's misery. Someone needs to pinch that bitch's neck. Beast slams his fist into the wall mere centimeters from Jan's head. I think that might have sobered the woman up because she suddenly seems to be smart enough to look scared. She should be. Beast is one of the most controlled people that I've ever met. My brother is fucking raw right now, and after the news he just got, who knows how in the fuck he will react.

"Get this fucking bitch out of my sight before I kill her!" Beast screams. I motion over to Sabre, who grabs Jan and drags her off, though she's obviously not fighting that hard. I think it's finally hit her what the fuck she just did. Beast yells again and slams his fist right back into the wall.

"Brother," Torch says. Beast turns around to look at him, and the look in my man's eyes nearly guts me.

"Annabelle is mine," he growls. "She's *mine*. I'd know if she wasn't." But he's not looking at Torch; he's looking at me.

"I know she is," I respond. "Anyone who's seen that little girl knows she's yours, Beast." I'm not talking about biologically because, knowing that lying cunt, this was the one time she was telling the truth. Regardless, Beast is her dad in all the ways that count. He's been both mom and dad to that little girl.

"She's mine, Boss. I don't give a fuck what that bitch said. She's mine. She was just drunk."

"I know."

"I got to get out for a while. I can't be here. I can't be around her right now," Beast growls slamming his fist back into the wall. The good news about that is, instead of three separate holes, there's just one big one.

"Torch, you and K-Rex go with him. Stay with him. Watch his back and your own."

They get up and follow Beast out the door. The room stays silent for a few minutes.

"I hate her," Beth whispers.

"We all do," Pistol grunts, and for the first time in forever I'm in perfect agreement with the bastard.

CHAPTER 28
BEAST

> Some pain slices you open and you think it will kill you, but that would be too easy.

My life has been fucked up for over four years. I got between that bitch's legs one night without using a condom, and I've been paying for it ever since. The men bitched at me all the time. They thought I was being pussy-whipped, but that wasn't it. I wasn't like them; talking to women didn't come easy for me.

Shit. Talking to people in general fucked me up.

I doubt I would've ever been a member if I hadn't grown up with Skull. He's a brother, the closest I've ever had to one. The only constant in my life was Skull's madre, Maria. None of the others know that. That secret is mine and Skull's and, as far as I'm concerned, not one fucker will ever know it. My old man was loaded. He had more money than God. What he didn't have was time for me or my mother. Then again, my mother was a miserable drunk who only had time for her tennis instructor—and she didn't know how to play tennis, not even a little bit.

Skull's mother Maria lived in the adjoining coach house with Skull and, though she cooked and cleaned in our home, it was that small coach house I remember as the only home I've ever had. When my father died of an unexpected heart attack, I didn't grieve for him. My mother and her lover ran off together leaving me with Maria, and I fucking rejoiced. When I turned twenty-one, the only contact I had with my mother was when I got my trust. She had burned through her money and wanted mine. I had no use for the money. She dropped my half-brother Terry in my lap saying she had to have a way to support him. I took Terry in, but I spat on her and walked away. I never liked Terry, but I tried. He was a miserable son of a bitch, and if what Jan said was true, I should have given up on him way before I did.

The only smart thing I've apparently done in my life was give my money to Maria and Skull. We used it to fight the cancer and make sure Maria was comfortable. When Skull's uncle came into the picture and Skull decided to become a prospect to Devil's Blaze, I followed him. It wasn't because I wanted to be part of the club so much; rather, I couldn't imagine not having Skull beside me. He was all I had left. Maybe it's my fucked-up past, but if you don't get close to people, they can't fucking hurt you. They don't get the chance to. Women were too much effort. So besides the occasional fuck, I didn't bother with them.

Fucking Jan without a condom trapped me. I got drunk off my ass one night and woke up in bed with her the next morning, damage done. I panicked the whole fucking time, terrified she'd be knocked up. I prayed even. Not that I knew much about praying, but it seemed like the thing to do. When she turned out that way, I stepped up. Made her my old lady, even though Skull did his damnedest to talk me out of it. I didn't listen. I didn't want to put much effort into having a woman. This made that easier. The only fucking time I had to talk much to Jan was when she wanted something and that got me sex. It was easy and it protected my child. I may not have wanted Jan pregnant, but I did want Annabelle.

It's four in the morning and I've drunk so much that I've come full circle—I'm practically sober again. My head is foggy and it hurts to breathe, but I don't think that has shit to do with the hangover. Torch and a couple of the boys grabbed a cage and insisted I ride with them to the Boot. The Boot is an old honkytonk. It doesn't get much business, and that's what I wanted. I didn't want to be bothered; I wanted to sit at a bar and drink my ass off, and that's exactly what I got. The men know me, so they didn't talk to me either. They just watched my back. Still, I didn't want them around me. They saw that fucking shit with Jan and I didn't want anyone to realize what a sad fuck I was or how stupid I'd been.

I make my way down into the shelter part of the club. I should have stayed topside in my room up there as far away from Jan as I could. I need to see Annabelle just once. Her and Jan's room is separate from mine, and Jan stays in there sometimes. I doubt it's out of any motherly feelings; she's a piss-poor mom. It's probably to get away from me, and I'm okay with that.

Luckily, the bitch isn't here tonight.

I clean the loose money out of my pockets. I'm not sure how much is there, four or five hundred dollars. Hell, I think I tipped the bartender two hundred. I lay it down, as well as the keys to the Durango that Torch threw me when we parked up. They drove me home, but it was my cage. I guess he trusted me not to take off again tonight. Softly, I lie down on the bed beside Annabelle. She's truly beautiful: dark-brown hair that glistened, a cute little button nose, and the longest eyelashes I've ever seen. You can't see them right now because her eyes are closed, but when they're open, her irises are a mixture of browns, golds, and greens, and they sparkle. I have blue eyes. My baby's eyes are totally different and always makes me smile.

I find myself thinking how Terry's were the same color.

The knowledge is burning a hole in my gut. It's tearing me up inside and mostly because I think Jan's words might be the truest thing she's ever said. Terry is probably Annabelle's dad, not me. The one thing I've ever done in life that I was proud of, and…

My hand comes up to hold my daughter's. It's so small and delicate, so pale and white compared to the sunbaked, inked-up dark complexion of my own. We're so different, especially in ways that a father and daughter ought to be at least a little similar.

That hole in my gut burns brighter, harder.

"Daddy loves you, Belle," I tell her, letting the tears run free. They're silent, but they're torn from me because I'm broken. It won't matter. Terry's rotting in the ground and that fucking bitch

Jan is one line away from snorting her last. She'll overdose without me watching over her and I don't fucking care anymore. Nothing matters but my daughter. And she is mine. I may not have fathered her with my seed, but I've been there. I held her when she had high fevers and Jan was out partying. I read her bedtime stories, rub her stomach when it hurts, chase off the monsters that she insists hide under her bed… I've done all of that and I'll continue to do it. She's mine. "Daddy loves you, Belle," I whisper again, dried tears on my face as my eyes close and I finally let alcohol and sleep claim me. *"Daddy, loves you…"*

CHAPTER 29
JAN

" I'll get what's mine. He won't hold me back anymore. "

I really fucked up tonight.

Spending an hour sucking some damn prospect's dick didn't help shit. The asshole told me he could get me a key to one of the vehicles outside. After I got him off, he told me Skull and Torch had taken all the keys during lockdown. Bastard could've told me that shit *before* I swallowed his pencil dick.

I need to lay low until I can find a way out. There's no way I can face Beast until I have a plan. He's an idiot, but I doubt he'll even buy that I was lying about it all. Now that I've ripped the blinders off, he has to know that Terry is Annabelle's dad. Shit, I never even fucked Beast that night. I knew I was knocked up, and Terry and I drugged his ass so that when he woke up, he'd think he could be the father when I told him.

Terry was the love of my life, but he didn't have a dime to his name. Beast was loaded, and Terry was already facing ten to fifteen in jail for attempted manslaughter. We needed Beast, so we used him, plain and simple.

And I still can't believe I fucked it all up last night.

I freeze when I get to Annabelle's room and find the bastard lying on her bed. He's huge, way over seven-foot and he looks like the side of a house, he's so fucking big. His dark hair is long and he constantly wears a beard—entirely too much hair. He can't even carry on a conversation unless you count grunting. I hate him. He could've kept Terry out of jail.

I look at him lying beside my daughter and figure there's a

way I can make him pay. Finding the money and keys on the nightstand just makes it that much easier. I quickly pack the whelp's overnight bag. She annoys me almost as much as Beast, but she's the last piece of Terry I have. I grab the money and the keys and stuff them in my pockets. Beast is snoring loudly. Fucker always did—another reason to hate him.

I pick up Annabelle. "Mommy?" she asks sleepily.

"Quiet, Belle. You'll wake your daddy," I tell her, choking on the words. "We're going to run out and get a surprise for daddy."

"We are?" she whispers excitedly. "What are we gonna get? A puppy? Daddy likes puppies!"

"That's it. Exactly. But we have to be quiet so no one sees or hears us. We have to sneak out so it will be a real surprise," I tell her, and I could nearly laugh out loud when she does as I tell her. She's going to have to toughen up in this world. She can't be as stupid and clueless as a man. Women have to make their own way. I've depended on Beast, and he just kept fucking me over and holding me back. This will be a new start.

Annabelle's car seat isn't in the vehicle. Fuckers must have taken it out when they went to drink. I just buckle her in the seat without it. That's good enough. I get in the car, start it, then drive through the lot. The tricky part is, there's a gate up ahead. I slow down. That fucker I sucked off is manning the gates—him and another prospect.

"Where do you think you're going?" he asks through my window. "Skull said no one in or out."

"Beast gave me his keys. I have to take my daughter to the doctor. She has a fever."

"They didn't tell me. I think Beast would've said something, or else be with you. I'm going to have to clear it with them before I can let you go."

Son of a bitch.

"What? Why? I just sucked you off! You owe me, you miserable fucker!"

"Please, you weren't even that good," he says, walking away

and grabbing the phone inside the small guard shack.

He's going to ruin it all. I can't let that happen. I look over at Annabelle. "Hold on. Mommy's going to drive through the gates so we can get out of here."

"But mommy... daddy can go with us to get the puppy! We don't have to—"

Her voice drones on, but I ignore it, jerking the car into reverse, then pushing the accelerator to the floor. It lurches backwards, then I brake hard. That stupid idiot jumps in front of the Durango like he can stop it. I jerk the lever back to drive, floor it again, then bounce him off the hood. Annabelle screams and even that makes me smile.

Yeah, I'll toughen her up. She'll learn what the real world is about.

We slam through the gates and they break away with the sound of crashing metal. Once we make it through them to the main road, I don't slow down. I'm laughing louder than Annabelle's crying. *I'm free! I'm finally fucking free!* I don't let off the accelerator. It climbs to fifty, fifty-five, sixty, and then something strange happens. At sixty-five, there's a loud click. I can hear it over everything else, even Annabelle's screaming. The car loses power. There's a loud boom from the back of the vehicle, startling me out of my laughter. Heat swallows us from all directions.

"Daddy! Daddy! I want my daddy! Take me to my daddy!" Annabelle cries, her tears and sobs racking her little body. Fear blooms through me. I look in the rearview mirror just in time to witness the explosion. Fire consumes everything—*including us.*

CHAPTER 30
SKULL

" I wont take prisoners. I dont want
one fucker breathing when this war ends. "

It's a fucking mess. Beast's kid and that bitch Jan are gone. There's nothing left of that vehicle. We finally got the fire out, but there's... nothing. Beast won't even have true ashes to bury.

He went crazy. It took four men, myself included, to pull him away from the fire. We finally had the club doc tranquilize him. He gave him a double dose and still the fucker fought it. His hands suffered horrible burns, his face and chest too. Another member had to beat the flames out while the four of us held him down. They took him to the hospital while we stayed here and tried to regroup.

We haven't told anyone but the patched-in members. I don't want Beth to know. She's already feeling like this is her fault. If she finds out about Beast's kid, she'll completely lose it. Me? Fuck, I'm dealing with my own guilt. I made my choices and I didn't even think how it would affect my brothers. I guess I didn't realize this type of blood. All of us know that death can come at the drop of a hat. We know it and embrace it; it's part of why we live wild. We take our freedom and we make our own rules because that freedom was built with our brothers' blood.

But nothing can prepare you for the death of a child.

I caused Annabelle's death. I did this. I should have just taken Beth and left my brothers out of it. This is *my* war. Instead, I went full steam ahead. If I could go back, I would have done things differently. It's just too fucking late now.

I look over at Pistol. "Call your brother. We need the men

now. We attack at nightfall and we attack hard."

"Plan A?" Torch asks, and for once, the motherfucker isn't cocky. No, he's something else entirely: he's *furious.* That's good. We all need to be.

"Plan fucking A. Saddle up, boys. Before dawn breaks tomorrow, I want every piece of property and every business the Donahues own hit and in flames." My words are met with a huge battle cry. My men scatter, except for Briar. I grab him by the arm. "I need you to stay with Beth. I want her away from the others. Tell her there's been a breach in security and I'm doing all I can to make sure she's safe until I'm back. Do whatever you have to do. I don't want her to know about Beast or his family until I can be the one to tell her. I can't take the chance she won't go off half-cocked."

Briar doesn't look happy, but I didn't expect him to. He's like the rest of us: he wants to get revenge.

"Boss," he starts, but I stop him.

"I can't trust this to a prospect, Briar. Torch and Sabre are in charge of the explosives. Besides him and Beast, you're the only one I trust my woman with. I know you want your ounce of blood, but I need you here. I promise you'll get your shot before this is over."

"Okay. I'll do it, but she's not going to be happy."

"I know. I'll deal with it. I just need to not worry about her right now."

"Okay. Go make the motherfuckers pay."

I slap him on the back. "That, I can promise."

I walk off. I want to go check on Beast before we ride out. It will take Cade's men a couple hours to get here. They've been held up at the state line to avoid detection from the Donahues. I pull Beth's cellphone out of my pocket, staring at it. I go through her contacts and hit dial when I find Colin's number.

"Beth. It's about time."

Figures the sorry fucker would give her his private number. I'm going to hang him up by his balls.

"Wrong, motherfucker. And you just made a big mistake."

"I see you found our present," the smug bastard answers. "Sad that we didn't take you out, but you had three of your finest in that car, right? Irresponsible, really, to leave your vehicle unwatched when you're at war. Then again, I don't expect much better from you. You're outclassed here, spic. Time for you to pack up and get the fuck out."

His slur rolls off of me. I could give a fuck what he says.

"No, you fuck. You killed a woman and a child. A three-year-old girl who did nothing to anyone. All you managed to do to me and my brothers was piss us the fuck off. We're coming for you, asshole. We're coming."

I click the phone off, slam it on the ground, then stomp it under my boot. My whole body vibrates with anger. If the fun we have planned for tonight doesn't kill him, then I will kill him myself, slowly, and enjoy the fuck out of it.

I walk to my bike, surprised to find Pistol there.

"You going to see Beast?" he asks.

"Yeah."

"I'll ride along."

"You need to spend your time making sure your brother's men are on their way and things are in place."

"Already done. I may not agree with some of the shit you choose, Skull, but Beast is my brother too, and you're still my president. I'm watching your back. The Donahues may be monitoring the hospitals."

I shrug, not about to waste more time arguing with him. There's too much shit to accomplish today. Besides, he's right. I peel out of the compound, avoiding looking at the burned Durango we've hauled back inside. The men are busy repairing the gates. I've ordered a stronger gate, military grade. Wish to fuck I'd done it sooner. Apparently I've got a little to learn about being in a war, too.

Hopefully Colin won't see the hits we have planned coming.

CHAPTER 31
BETH

" I'm starting to feel like I'm home.
It's settling somewhere inside of me. "

This is ridiculous. Skull's had me locked in my room all day. I thought things were good between us. Now, I have no idea what's going on.

Briar—seriously, if that's not a road name, I feel sorry for him—has been with me all day and refuses to let me leave. He had our breakfast and lunch brought in. The only thing he told me was that there were some new developments and Skull wanted to make sure I was protected. He refuses to tell me what these developments are and, trust me, I've asked him a hundred times.

It's been boring as hell, so I did the only thing I could think of to make Briar sorry that he's stuck in this small room with me. We're on our third movie of the day. We started with *Bridget Jones Diary*, moved on to *Pretty Woman*, and now…

"What the ever loving fuck?" exclaimed Briar. "You mean she's not even going to move her fat ass over and let him float on that damn piece of wood? Jesus, two of him could fit on that shit."

"You're missing the point. He loves her. He's going to *die* for her."

"Big fucking deal. If she wasn't a selfish bitch, she'd scoot her ass over and they'd both survive."

Now, it should be said that I totally agree with him. However, I find I enjoy arguing with Briar. Well, that and I'm bored out of my mind. "She lives a full life because Jack loved her."

"She's a selfish cow. Why can't she die? I mean, this story would be a fuck of a lot better if Jack survived and lived high on the fucking hog with that damn diamond."

Okay, actually that sounds like a more interesting movie if you think about it, but I ignore him. "Hush, Briar! There's a happy ending, wait and see. You'll love it!"

"Yeah, I'm sure," he says sarcastically. It's all I can do not to laugh.

"You know, if you told me what happened last night to have Skull worried about me, I might consider turning this off and letting you watch football."

"Nice try, but no cigar, babe."

"I guess we could watch ballet. There's one on channel—"

"You turn on that fucking shit and I promise you I will put a bullet in the television. I'm drawing the line at this movie and that's only because the redhead has some decent knockers."

Okay, I snort at that comment. It'd take a better woman than I not to laugh. We're silent through the rest of the movie until the end. Then, I thought poor Briar was going to blow a gasket. He literally turned red in the face.

"You've got to be kidding me! What the fuck?"

"What? They got their happy-ever-after!"

"They're dead!"

"Well yeah, but they're together."

"Fuck, that's just messed up. Is this really the kind of shit you chicks get off on?"

"It's a great movie. Very romantic."

"No fucking wonder," he says.

"What are you talking about?"

"If this is the kind of shit you like to watch, it's no wonder you bitches give us men such a hard time. Relationships would be a lot easier if women would just watch porn."

"Is that a fact?"

"Fuck, yeah. Porn is straight-up, man. No bullshit. Instead of Ol' Jack dying, he'd be helping her fiancé feed her dick."

"Oh my God!"

"It's the truth. I actually watched the porn version of *Titanic*. It was grade A. I think it even won an award."

"There's a porn version of *Titanic?*"

"Woman, there's a porn version of every movie."

"You're kidding me."

"Nope. Name one and I'll give you the porn title."

"And if you can't, you have to let me out of this room."

"That can't happen, but since I know all the titles, hit me with your best shot."

"Okay. Umm… *When Harry Met Sally!*"

"How old are you again? Were you even alive when that movie came out?"

"It's a good movie!"

"*When Harry Ate Sally*," he says calmly.

"Oh my God." He winks at me. I sigh, digging deeper into my vault of favorite movies inside my brain. I'm a movie buff. Heck, before Skull, movies were my excitement. "*The Terminator!*" I exclaim suddenly.

"You really are making this too easy. *The Sperminator*."

"Holy shit."

Briar laughs. "Ready to call it quits yet?"

"Okay, I got it. *Gone in Sixty Seconds!*"

"*Blown in Sixty Seconds*. Sadly, not a favorite."

"I bet. Okay I've got nothing. I cave."

"But we were just getting started! There's *Robocock, Saturday Night Beaver…*" he continues.

"You're making this shit up!"

"And every woman should watch *King Dong*."

"Get out of town! There's a movie called *King Dong?*"

"It's a very touching movie. It's about a little boy who's picked on because his dick is three times as big as everyone else's. He was bullied mercilessly."

"I'm sure," I say sarcastically.

"He was. It's very touching, really. All the football jocks

hated him."

"Probably because all the cheerleaders were letting him under their skirts."

"Well, yeah, that too. Still, it's a touching movie."

"As in, there was a lot of *touching* of King Dong's... dong?"

"You're a smart one."

"How big was King Dong's *aong* anyway?"

"Is there a reason you're talking about dicks with my woman?" Skull asks from the door.

The two of us turn toward him, startled by his sudden appearance. He looks super tired, and I'm more than a little pissed at him, but I'm ecstatic to see that he's safe and back home.

"Oh, hey boss. Sorry, we were just discussing—"

"The size of King Dong's dong," I finish, looking up at Skull and smiling.

"And... who is King Dong?"

"The guy in the porno that Briar is trying to get me to watch with him," I explain, doing my best to look innocent.

"What the fuck?"

"I was not, Boss. We were just discussing porn titles," Briar clarifies, shooting me an *I'm-going-to-kili-you* look. I stick my tongue out at him, not bothering to hide my amusement.

"Why were you even talking about porn with my woman?"

Briar shuts up and gives me that look again. I smirk.

"I'm out of here. Everything go okay today?" Briar asks as he walks by Skull.

"Hopefully. We'll know in about an hour when Torch and Sabre start detonating. We'll be watching in the office on the screen."

"Got it. I'll meet you there."

I look at Skull once Briar leaves. My heart is beating hard against my chest because it didn't escape my notice what they were talking about.

"Detonating?" I finally ask, trying to keep the fear out of my voice—*and failing.*

Skull nodded somberly. "Colin and Matthew's calling card is bombs, *querida.* So I decided to show them how it felt to be on the receiving end of one of their surprises."

"How many are you detonating?" I ask, the fear in me beginning to run bone-deep.

"A lot."

Shit. This isn't good.

"What did Colin do to make you do so much, Skull? And don't lie to me. I know something has happened or else you wouldn't have kept me locked away all day."

I wait for Skull's reply. I can already tell by his face I'm not going to like the answer.

CHAPTER 32
SKULL

" Guilt can crush you and make you stupid. "

I can't remember ever feeling this fucking tired and old. I'm lying in bed with Beth and she just now fell asleep after crying for over an hour. She demanded I take her to see Beast and I put her off until tonight. I want to go check on my brother too, but I'm going to be in the office watching as I blow Colin's fucking empire to smithereens. I'm hoping to get the holdings in France too. I have some connections working on that.

I hate seeing my woman hurt, and I know it's my fault. I should have handled this shit differently. I'm dealing with a lot of fucking guilt for the hell I've asked my brothers to step into. I'm dealing with even more of it when I think about what I cost Beast. He's going to undergo quite a few skin grafts. There will be some horrible scarring on his body and his face, and it's not even certain that he'll be okay. A body can die when the burns they suffer are too bad and extensive. The main problem is, when he comes out, I'm pretty fucking sure he's going to want to die. Fuck, when I think of that beautiful little girl of his, I can't say I'd blame him.

I kiss Beth's forehead and my finger catches a stray teardrop she either shed while sleeping or had trapped in the corner of her eye and just now escaped. I ease off the bed and pull the covers over her, putting a pillow where I was laying. Beth doesn't move. She's exhausted from the tears, I'm sure. Hell, I can't even suppress a yawn that escapes when I stand up, stretching the kinks out of my back. I'd love nothing more than to crawl in bed with my woman. Was it just a day ago we were fucking happy and I was mapping out our future?

It seems like a lifetime ago.

I make my way topside to the office. I don't bother shutting the door; the only ones stirring around outside of the shelter are patched-in members and we all know what's happening tonight. We're just hoping it's successful. The mood is a mixture of sadness, stress, and nervous hope. The result is that there's tension in the air so thick you could cut that crap with a knife.

"Hey, boss. Beth okay?" Briar asks.

I slap him on the back of the head. "Motherfucker, talking about dicks with my woman. Much more of that shit and you won't have a dick, and all you'll be able to do is talk about them."

Fucker just laughs and I flip him off.

I take my usual seat. Above our table, there are a total of six flat screens hanging on the wall. The screens are about twenty-seven inches, big enough to see clearly. Each screen has a different piece of property. There's the casino, the gym where the underground cage-fighting takes place, a bar, a couple strip joints, and finally the estate where Colin and Matthew live. Tonight, it's these six. Tomorrow night, a different six have been staked out. I expect security will increase after tonight, so they'll be harder to do, but not impossible. Nothing's impossible if you have a reason to do it—and we do, a fucking big reason and a thirst for revenge.

"How long 'til show time?" I ask Torch.

He looks down at that damn watch he's always wearing. "In about two minutes, Boss man."

I nod. And we all sit and just stare. We're quiet, all of us. Even Pistol has cut down his sarcasm. Sabre is sitting at a laptop and Torch gives him a signal. You can hear the tapping of the keys, the room is that quiet. Then, the screen in the bottom starts as the bar explodes. Wood and other debris go everywhere as flames swallow the screen.

My men don't celebrate; real lives were just taken. Collateral damage sucks and it makes it hard for me to continue, but fuck, you have to do what you have to do. The Donahues called war on me, and I can't exactly tell everyone to leave the bar if they want to live.

Up next are the strip joints. A similar scene to the first one unfolds on the second television followed by the one beside it. The gym makes me smile. That one's not collateral damage; every fucker in that joint was dirty and owned by the Donahues. There's a pause before the next one hits. It's huge. The casino starts with one explosion in the back of the building. I hear Sabre typing on the computer again, and another explosion goes off in the same building, closer up, then another, and another. In total, a series of six bombs combine to bring that fucker down. I watch as people run from that building; I hope the innocent ones got out, but again, it's out of my control.

I release a breath of air that I didn't even know I was holding. The next hit is the most important. Hell, I'm even praying that we take out Colin with this one, even if I do know it's a longshot. Torch already warned me there will be a five minute delay between it and the other bombs. I look around at my men. Each one is a good man, a man who for one reason or another pledged themselves to my club and my leadership, and I do feel like I've let them down.

"Men," I say, addressing them. "I should have thought more about how my actions would affect each of you. I don't normally back down from a fucking fight—and Beth is my old lady, that made her one of us—but doing that cost Beast something so precious I can't begin to imagine how he will live with that. That's on me. This is my fucking fault. I shouldn't have claimed Beth and went full steam ahead."

"Boss," they all start. Well, not all; Pistol's shooting me I-told-you-so's from across the room, even if he isn't giving them voice.

"No, let me finish," I insist. "I made a mistake, and for that

I'm sorry."

The room is silent.

"You would have let her go and backed away to keep from going into war?" This comes from Briar and I can hear the disgust in his voice.

"Fuck, no. I would have claimed her anyway. I just would've thought twice about making it my club's problem. Beth's my woman. I'm not giving her up for anyone."

"Then fuck you. We're a club because we have each other's backs. That includes Beth. Besides, I like her."

"Same here," Torch speaks up, but he doesn't look away from the monitor he and Sabre are working on. In fact, every member here, even Pistol, seem to agree. I still feel the guilt in my stomach, but that tight knot inside me loosens at their support.

Then the fireworks start. Colin and Matthew's house blasts apart before our eyes. Honestly, we put twice the charge in that fucker. We had to. We knew we wouldn't get a second chance, and it was harder than hell to get through the gates, even disguised as groundskeepers and security guards. Still, it's done, and every fucker in the room cheers.

In a few days, their private yacht and some of their favorite things will be toast. They wanted war and the motherfuckers are getting it, one delicious slice at a time.

CHAPTER 33
BETH

> *" Never get comfortable. There's no place for me here. That's crystal clear now. "*

When I woke up and found Skull gone, my heart hurt. I still can't believe this mess went so horribly wrong that it took Beast's beautiful little daughter's life. I'm consumed by guilt. If I had just given Skull up when Colin demanded it, none of this would have happened. What makes that thought even worse is that, despite everything, I don't know if I could go back and give him up. I don't know what kind of horrible person that makes me, but I know it's disgusting.

I slide out of bed and decide to go and find him. I want to hold onto him. I hope tonight delivers the message that Skull wants to get across. I'm praying it ends the war before it can escalate further. I just don't think it will. I look around the hall of the shelter, but luckily everything looks pretty deserted, probably because it's so late. Skull said he'd hoped to be back by nightfall, but they had some problems infiltrating the house that Colin and Matthew owned even with me giving them security codes. I can't figure out why they hadn't changed the codes, but I figure it's arrogance. I honestly don't think Colin thought I would betray him. Then again, he thinks I'm eventually going to cave and accept that I will be his one day. I'd rather die.

Once I'm at the main structure, I make my way to Skull's office. The door is open, but I'm frozen in my tracks as I watch the explosions on the television screen. My hand comes to my mouth as I try and stop sound. I recognize each of the places, of course, and one after one I watch as they are destroyed. As I watch each of the businesses go up in smoke, I feel hope bloom in my chest. Maybe Skull was right and Colin didn't know who he was messing with. I should have had more faith. I start to go into the room to be there with Skull. I want us to be side by side as we watch Colin's house go up in flames. Maybe a little of Skull's attitude is rubbing off on me. I smile at the thought, but before I can take one step, I freeze.

"... Beth is my old lady, that made her one of us—but doing that cost Beast something so precious I can't begin to imagine how he will live with that. That's on me. This is my fucking fault. I shouldn't have claimed Beth and went full steam ahead."

His words strike me and each feels as if someone is driving a nail through my heart. The final blow is the one that wounds me in ways that I will never heal from: *I shouldn't have claimed, Beth.* I knew Skull would regret it. All along I did, but he kept insisting he wouldn't. He got upset with me when I tried to leave and now he's just as good as telling his men I shouldn't be here, that being with me was wrong... *is* wrong.

I feel the tears fall again. I need to get away before Skull sees me. If he does, he's liable to lie to me again because he doesn't want to hurt me. It's better I found out his true feelings now. I can't even be mad at him. I felt the same way before he convinced me I was wrong.

I back away slowly and, only when I'm at the end of the hallway, far away from Skull's office, do I take off running. I make it back to my room, slam the door, then lay on the bed and let the tears fall. There's a chance that Skull is successful tonight, and if he is, maybe it won't matter anymore.

In truth, me being here has already cost Beast everything. Will he be able to survive everyday with me here as a reminder of what I cost him?

I need to see Beast. I dry up my eyes. I'll go to the hospital with Skull. I'll stay by Beast's side and nurse him through, then make my decision. If Beast hates me, I need to leave. If Skull is wrong and this strike doesn't take Colin down, then I still need to

leave. Skull says he loves me and I know I love him. I can't turn
my back on that if there's any other way around it.

I'm going to hold out for a miracle.

"*Mi cielo?* Are you okay?"

I look up to see Skull standing there. I ignore his question. He
knows the answer to it, even if he doesn't know that I heard him
upstairs. "Were you successful?" I ask him instead.

"I think so, *sí.* We'll find out more in the light of day. We'll
begin phase two then, too."

I give him a tight smile. "Are you ready to go see Beast?"

"Are you sure you're up to it, *querida?*"

"I want to see him. Do you think he will care if I'm there,
though?" I ask him, worried.

"They have him drugged right now because of the pain and
other things. I doubt he'll know you're there, sweetheart. We can
go tomorrow if you'd rather."

"Can we do both?"

He looks at me for a few minutes. I'm afraid he can read my
thoughts.

"You do know this is not your fault, right? No one's to blame
for what happened to Beast's daughter—except *Colin. He* did
this, *not* you."

"He did it because of me."

"Bullshit. If anything, he did it because of me and my mouth.
You hold no blame in this, sweetheart."

His words hurt me because I just keep replaying what he told
his men. I swallow down the pain and try to give him a smile. I
don't exactly succeed, but I try. "Let's go," I urge him, walking
over to him.

Skull takes both of his hands and places them on each side of
my face. He pulls me closer to him and I breathe in the scent of
oil, leather, and man that I've come to associate with Skull. He
kisses my forehead gently and holds me like that for a few
minutes. Then he pulls away, takes my hand, and leads me out of
the room.

CHAPTER 34
SKULL

" She's planning something. I just can't figure out what the fuck it is. "

This is the third day straight that Beth insists on staying at the hospital. I would say absolutely not, but she's probably safer there than at my club right now. I'm having Briar and K-Rex stay with her, and we have no less than ten men from Cade's crew monitoring every exit of the hospital.

The fight with Colin has gone quiet since our attacks. We have confirmation that we didn't manage to take out Colin, and that fucking sucks. There are rumblings though that our strikes have caught attention of the higher powers in the faction. We've been unable to get a name, but eventually I will. In the meantime, we're planning attacks on the personal holdings of the Donahues. We'll hit the apartment downtown, the country home that Matthew has claimed as his own, the private planes at the small airport they own, and finally the yacht. These strikes won't do so much about hitting their bank accounts, but it will hurt them personally, especially Colin, and that's my goal right now. I want the fucker to hurt, bleed, and go to hell. I'm making it my life's goal to achieve that.

I call Beast's room and stare off into space as it rings. Eventually Beth picks up, and when her sweet voice quietly whispers, "Hello," I feel the tension inside of me ease. She has that effect on me. She calms me like nothing ever has or ever will.

"Hey, *mi cielo*. How are things?"

"They've just taken Beast down for surgery."

They're going to check out his healing tissue as well as begin their first repair on his face. The surgeon warned us not to get excited, that it would take several surgeries, but in truth, not one of us gave a flying fuck. We just wanted our brother alert and talking to us again. We're all worried about how he's going to react when he comes back through and has to face the fact that Annabelle is gone. My men got some ashes in an urn for him. There's no way of telling if the ashes contain any of Annabelle, but we hoped that at least having something physical to grieve over would make it all easier.

"That's good. Any word on how long it's going to last?"

"No. The doctor said the surgery could last anywhere from an hour to several hours. It just depends on how he heals and what they find once they start exploring."

"You'll keep me updated?"

"Of course. Are you doing okay? Anything going on?"

"I'm fine, *querida*. I told you to stop worrying. Colin will need to regroup before he even thinks of striking back."

"I know, I'm just worried."

"I got this. Have some faith."

Beth grows quiet and I get the sense that once again she's planning something. I've had this suspicion for a few days now. The only problem is, I don't have any idea what it is. I've done the only thing I know to do: I'm having her watched and guarded heavily.

"I love you, Skull."

"I love you too, *mi cielo*. I'll show you tonight. I find I'm missing my woman," I tell her and I'm not joking. I've not been between those thighs in at least two nights. She was so upset since Annabelle's death, and I couldn't bring myself to do anything other than hold her and let her know I love her.

"Finally."

"Hey, if you didn't like it, you could've jumped my bones," I tell her, deadly serious.

"I'll make note of that."

"See that you do. You call me if you need me, and keep Briar and K-Rex with you all the time. I don't know Cade's men, but I trust Briar and K-Rex to make sure you're fine."

"Yes, sir."

"I think I like when you talk like that, Beth."

"Don't get used to it," she laughs.

"Talk to you this evening, *mi cielo.*"

"This evening," she agrees. "Love you, sweetheart."

"You too," I tell her with a smile, hanging up the phone.

I have a surprise for her this evening and I'm hoping she doesn't turn me down. When I pick her up, I'm going to run by an ex-member's house. The dude is crazy as fuck, but he has a license, and I'm marrying Beth.

I want her as my wife as well as my old lady. Part of it is because if Colin manages to get his hands on her, I don't want him to be able to claim her. I know the fucker will try. This way, he'll have to get rid of a husband before he can. Our surveillance has shown that he's been meeting with a wedding planner about his wedding with Beth. Fuck that shit.

I haven't told Beth; she's got enough on her plate. Besides, it's not all about that. I know she said she couldn't have kids, but I was serious with her. I'm not going to rest until it happens. I have a vision of her nursing my child and I want that so fucking much. I won't stop until it happens, and when it does, we will be married. No child of mine will be born out of wedlock. I might make up my own rules, but my madre would come back from the dead and scalp me if I didn't follow the rules she held dear.

Tonight, Beth will be mine in all ways that matter. Colin can suck it.

CHAPTER 35
BETH

" How strange it is to have your biggest desire and fear answered all in the same day. "

I'm alone in Beast's room. I can't remember that ever happening. K-Rex is right outside the door and Briar just left to go talk with Cade's men. Still, for the first time I can remember in forever, I'm actually alone. I'm above ground... and alone. I would almost celebrate, but instead I feel vulnerable and scared, and I *hate* that.

I'm using the laptop Skull bought me to finish my studies. I'll be taking my GED in a few days. There's no way I could finish high school the old-fashioned way, but Skull knew how important it was to me, so he's helping me work around that and achieve it in a different way. I wish I'd met him under different circumstances.

The phone rings again. It's only been an hour since Skull checked on me. Surely he knows I'll call him the minute I know anything about Beast.

"Skull, sweetheart, I told you I'd call you the minute I knew anything about Beast," I say, answering the phone.

"Elizabeth."

My heart freezes. Only one person ever calls me Elizabeth. And, if it had been ten minutes, ten hours, or ten hundred years, I would know that voice... I used to adore that voice.

"Dad."

"I've missed you, sunshine."

I say nothing. There's nothing to say. How can he miss someone he gave away?

There's silence for a few minutes, then I hear his heavy sigh. "I need to see you, sunshine."

"I can't right now. There are things going on. It's just not possible," I tell him. It's truthful, but what I leave out is that even if nothing was going on, I never want to see him. I don't even want to look at him. How could he think I would? He took my sister away from me. He chose her over me. There's a list of offenses he's committed and I'm not about to forgive any of them.

"Elizabeth—" he starts.

I don't let him finish. "I'm sorry. I have to go. I don't know how you tracked me, but please pretend you never did," I say, and I'm pulling the phone away from my ear when I hear him say the one thing that would make me stop.

"Skull's life depends on this, Elizabeth. You need to talk to me."

I get this sick feeling in my stomach. How can Skull's life depend on it? Why would this war involve my father in any way? I try and breathe through my panic and pull the phone back to my ear.

"I'm listening."

"Not over the phone. It's not safe. You will need to come to me."

"There's no way to arrange that. Skull, unlike some men, makes sure the people he loves are safe. He has men with me all the time, especially when he can't be here himself."

My father sighs, and I know my verbal strike hit its target. Too bad I can't feel any joy from it.

"In fifteen minutes, Pistol will show up and take Briar's place."

Again my father manages to take my breath away. How does he know Skull's men? How does he know their names? Worse, how does he know what's about to happen?

"How do you—"

"That's not important right now. Listen closely. When Pistol gets there, he will escort you down to the cafeteria. You will follow him and *not* alert anyone to what is about to happen. When you get there, excuse yourself to the restroom. Once you're there, there's a small hall off to the right. Pistol will lead you to it. That goes to the kitchen. Someone will be waiting for you there. Don't mess this up, Elizabeth. I'm trying to save lives here, but if you don't cooperate, that won't be possible."

"Why should I trust you?"

"Because you don't have a choice, sunshine. I'll be waiting," he says, then hangs up.

My hand is shaking when I put the receiver back into the cradle. My heart is slamming against my chest. I've imagined seeing my father in a million different ways, and none of them included this one. The door opens and I look up to see Briar. My first instinct is to ask what's going on, but right behind him comes Pistol—*just like my father said.*

"Beth, are you okay?" Briar asks. I can't stop my eyes from going to Pistol. He looks at me impassively, but his hands are on the gun he keeps in a holster just beneath his leather cut. He makes sure I see it. The bastard knows exactly what he's doing. I take a deep breath, trying to steady my nerves and look back at Briar. I can't risk him getting hurt.

"I'm fine," I insist. "Just worried about Beast. The surgery seems to be taking a while."

"That's why I'm late. The doctor tracked me down at the nurse's desk. Beast pulled through and the surgeon was encouraged by the results."

"That's great," I tell him, genuinely relieved.

"Yeah, it is. I'm going back to report to Skull and do a few things. Pistol here will be taking over for me. K-Rex is going to stand guard over our vehicles because one of Cade's men got sick. If you need me, all you have to do is call."

"Sounds good. I'm actually getting a little hungry now that I know Beast is going to be okay. Could you take me down to the cafeteria, Pistol?"

He clears his throat and his disgusting voice has a tinge of joy in it. I want to hit him in the balls. "Sure thing. Getting a little hungry myself."

"Great. I'll ride down the elevator with you two, then," Briar adds.

We all go out and I'm doing my best to walk and keep my shaky legs from giving out on me. I manage to laugh or respond where it's needed as Briar talks. We part ways when the elevator stops on the first floor, then Pistol puts his hand to my back and leads me to the cafeteria. When we get there, right away I recognize one of Cade's men. Skull made sure he introduced me to every one of them so I'd know who they were if I needed help. Ironically, I think it's these men who may be helping to hurt me. Well, them and Pistol, obviously.

"I need to go to the restroom," I announce, loud enough so Cade's man can hear me. He starts to come forward, but Pistol waves him off.

"I got this. Come on Beth, I'll escort you."

Asshole.

I follow him. As soon as we're out of the other's vision, I jerk away from him. "Skull will have your head," I hiss.

"He won't ever know."

"You're disgusting. Skull thinks of you as his brother. Don't you have any ethics?"

"I'm not dying over some fucking whore of a woman. Now hurry up. Daddy waits," he says. I really seriously *hate* him. If I survive this, I need to make sure Skull knows he can't trust him.

We walk from the hall into the kitchen and there, surrounded by the silver counters and lunchroom equipment, is the one person I never thought I would see again in my life.

"Hello, sunshine."

My fucking father.

CHAPTER 36
ROGER

❝ Men like me should never have children.
They weaken you. ❞

I look at my daughter, and she's beautiful. I've missed both her and Katie. They might be twins, but they're as different as night and day. Beth was always the one who had the more innocent personality. That only grew stronger as they aged. I know she hates me. Why wouldn't she? I've done everything wrong with them from the beginning, including their mother. How I ever got ensnared by that bitch Isabel is beyond me. She cost me everything. I can't let emotion get involved here, though. I have to protect my daughter, even if she hates me. That's the only thing that's important. I lost my chance at being a father a long time ago.

"I'm here. What do you want?" she asks me, and I doubt she realizes how much like Katie she actually sounds in this moment.

"I know you're upset with me, sunshine, but I really am trying to save you here."

"I didn't ask for your help. The way I see it, you gave up all rights to even be involved in my life years ago. Now, I don't know how you got these men to help you, but I would suggest that you—"

"They work for me," I tell her, interrupting before she can continue. The hate in her voice is slowly killing me. My words, at least, stop her.

"What? ... How?"

"There are things you don't know about me, Elizabeth."

"*Imagine that*," she says harshly.

"Are you going to listen or not? Our time is limited here and I thought you'd be interested in saving your boyfriend."

"Why would you save Skull?"

She's suspicious of me, and she has a right to be. Hell, I don't give two shits about that damned biker. However, thanks to the moves that Colin has made, I'm left with little choice.

"My name isn't Roger Bailey."

Beth tenses up with my announcement. I hate to tell her like this, but I have no choice.

"What's your name?" she whispers, her face pale.

"Redmond Donahue."

"Donahue?" she asks, even paler than before.

"I'm the leader of the family, Elizabeth." I tell her. Shock comes over her entire face, her body swaying, and I know she's going to faint. I see it coming. I lean over and catch my daughter right before she hits the floor.

CHAPTER 37
BETH

> **" *Was I cursed at birth? All signs point to yes.* "**

I come to slowly. I don't think I've been out long because I'm lying in Roger's... Redmond's... *whoever-he-is 's* lap. We're still in the kitchen. His face is laced with concern and I try to block that out. He doesn't have a right to be concerned about me. Not now. Not ever again. He gave away that right. I jerk up fast and instantly regret it because the world swims.

"Easy, sunshine," he says.

"*Stop calling me that!*" I scream, and I don't care if it does sound like a temper tantrum. He left me! He gave me away and now I find out he's not even the man I thought he was all this time! I jerk out of his arms and stand up without his help. I back away to put distance between us. His face briefly twists with pain. He doesn't deserve that either. He should try being a little girl and finding out her father, the only person she thought ever really loved her, gave her away. Then he'd understand pain.

"Elizabeth, time is running out."

"If you're a Donahue, why can't you make Colin pull back? Why do you need me here?"

"Because your boyfriend declared war on Colin, but I'm the one who runs the family. To step back after all of the attacks he's made will make me look weak. You can't be weak in this line of work sun—Elizabeth. That would only sign my death warrant."

"What are you doing?" I ask him, worried about what he's doing to retaliate. I may have to give Skull away, but I couldn't handle it if he dies. I just, couldn't.

163

"It will be a small strike. Nowhere near what I'm capable of. But, I will pull my punches, if you work with me."

"Work with you? Why would I do that?"

"Because I'm trying to protect you. The family is already viewing me as weak. I have to watch my steps before that bastard Colin succeeds in overthrowing me."

"Why did I never know you were part of the Donahues? How are you kin to Edmund? Did mom know?" I ask my questions. I have so many of them now and I'm trying to hold them back, but I find I just can't.

"I tried to retire. It's something hardly ever done in the family. Isabel had just found out she was pregnant with twins. I wanted to take her and my babies away from all of it, to try and be... a real dad."

Disgust rolls in my stomach because I know just how miserably he failed at it. "They wouldn't let you?"

"For a while, but Isabel started talking to my brother. She told him the name I was using and where we were. She hated not being part of the family. She wanted the power and the prestige that came with being one of the Donahues. By the time I realized Edmund had found out where I was, it was too late."

"Edmund was your brother? Why did it matter if he knew where you were?" I ask. It doesn't surprise me about my mom. She's cold, always was. She also loved everything about money.

"He was younger than I was and because of that, I inherited the throne, as it were. Edmund always resented that. Even when I stepped down and he took over, he wasn't satisfied. The only way he would ever be happy is if I was dead and my heirs contained."

"Contained?"

"In Katie's case, it was a hit on her life. In yours, it was to groom you to be Colin's bride."

That's always disgusted me, but now... "He'd be my cousin! *My first cousin!* That's not just gross, I'm pretty sure that's illegal!"

"That doesn't matter to Colin. He's trying to forge ahead with his Dad's plans and that means claiming you to gain his position in the family. As long as you and I are alive, Colin's chance to rule will never happen."

This family is even more fucked up than I thought, and that's saying something. "Let's cut the bullshit, *aaa*. What do you want me for?"

"Believe it or not, all I want is to save your life, Elizabeth. Help me to do that. I can't strike out at Colin right now. He has too many on his side and I'm weak. I have targets through which they can strike out and hurt me. Help me to save your life so I can gain complete control of my empire once more… and I'll let your boyfriend live."

My heart stutters to a stop before pounding erratically in my chest. I don't know why, but somehow I know his plan will destroy me. The problem is, I love Skull. I'll do anything to save him.

"What do you want me to do?"

"Leave Skull and pretend to die."

He says it so simply, so matter-of-factly… the words seem so benign, so easy and unassuming. They aren't, though. Just the thought of those words rips my heart out. I keep hearing Latch tell me I need to have faith in my man. I'm already shaking my head no and backing away from this monster who wants to call himself my father. Unfortunately, I back straight into Pistol. He grabs my arms, refusing to let me leave.

"Listen to him," whispers Pistol in my ear. "If you stay with Skull, you're both going to die. There's nothing to stop it."

"Elizabeth. It's the only way. I can save your man," my father joins in, and my stomach is turning so much that I want to throw up.

"Why?" I whisper. "Why would I trust you, let alone *help* you, in this crazy scheme?"

"Because I have something you want, and proof that I can protect you and this Skull."

"What's that?"

"Your sister, Katie."

"What?"

"Katie is alive, Elizabeth. Alive and happy."

If I had it in me, I'd faint again. If I had the courage that Latch says I have, I'd run straight to Skull. Instead, I stand there as *Redmond* hands me pictures of a blonde who looks so much like me that we could be twins—because we are. It's Katie. There are at least twenty pictures of her. Pictures of her growing up, pictures of her laughing, pictures of her singing, pictures of her blowing out birthday candles—all pictures of Katie. *My twin.* The woman I thought was lost to me forever. My best friend. My... *sister.*

I'm crying my eyes out, sinking slowly to the floor. I hold the pictures to my chest like you would something precious... *because they are.*

My sister is alive.

CHAPTER 38
SKULL

> **"** *Im learning to bend. She's making me bend.*
> *I hope she doesnt break me.* **"**

"What are we doing here?" Beth asks, looking at the small white house I've parked in front of. She's been different ever since I picked her up from the hospital. I asked her what's wrong, but she only said she was tired. I can't help but feel like it's something else. Still, I'm not pressing her on it because there are more important things to deal with.

"This is the local circuit judge of the county."

"Judge? Is something wrong?" she asks, looking at the house like it's haunted.

"No," I tell her, grabbing her hand. "Beth, I think we should get married."

I don't know what I expected, but it wasn't for her to look at me as if I'm trying to kill her. Suddenly what I thought was a great plan doesn't quite seem that way.

"*Mi cielo?* You said you loved me. Don't all women want marriage?"

"Skull, I can't marry you!"

"Why the fuck not?"

"Because! We're in the middle of a war with my family!"

"The Donahues are not your family. Your mother might have been stupid enough to connect you to that clan, but you *querida* are not a Donahue. You don't have that slime running through your veins. Do not even put yourself down suggesting you do."

Her face goes whiter. I hate that we're going through this. I need to fucking kill Colin, and soon.

"I can't marry you right now. We don't even know what tomorrow will bring."

"My baby could be in your belly. I want my name on you, too."

"Then let the war pass, and if we're still standing, we'll get married!"

"What the fuck do you mean 'if we're still standing'…?"

"I'm just saying we don't know what tomorrow will bring. Look at what happened with Beast's family," she whispers, and the tears are in her eyes. I catch a couple on my finger and pull her close so our lips are barely a breath away from each other. The only thing between our bodies is the console of the SUV we're in.

"That is not us, Beth. We are meant to be together."

"Skull, I want to believe that, I do," she whispers tearfully, and the sob that escapes from her sounds like someone is ripping her heart from her body. "There's just so much. I don't want to marry you with all of this hanging between us."

"Beth…"

"Please…?" she begs, and I doubt she even knows the pain she's causing me with these words. Before I can respond, Torch is banging on the window. I give Beth one last pained look, then hit the button to roll the window down.

"You okay, boss? It's not safe to stay out in the open like this too long," Torch says, and he's right. As it is, I'm in a cage and have five men following me on their bikes. I feel like a sad fucker, but I can't take any chances with Beth. "Boss?" he prompts when I don't respond.

I don't look at him. I don't take my eyes off of Beth. "Change of plans for now. We're going back to the compound."

"But, boss…"

"I said we're going home. Load them up."

"I'm sorry," Beth says, still crying. I wish I knew what the fuck to say to her. I turn back around and start up my vehicle.

"So am I," I mutter. "So am I." Then, I pull out onto the road.

It's a quiet ride back to the compound. I chance a look over at Beth every now and then and she's just staring out the window while silent tears fall down her face. If she's so torn up over this shit, then why wouldn't she say yes? I don't get it. How the fuck did I get here? I should have just carted her ass in the house and told her didn't have a choice, but hell. I want her to say yes because she *wants* to be my wife. Jesus. Listen to me. I sound like some sad *Dear Abby* fuck. I never wanted to get married in my life and here I am, bending for a woman. Fuck that, I'm bending over backwards.

We get out and I know I have to let off some steam or I'm going to say something I regret. "Torch?"

"Yeah, boss?"

"Make sure Beth is safe and gets back to our room below."

"Hey wait, Kemosabe! Where are you going?" Briar asks me.

"To pound something," I growl back.

"Skull—" Beth cries.

"Later, Beth. Just... *later*," I tell her because I'm just about done for the night. I need to go pound the gym bag, something to vent. I don't want to hurt her. I know she's dealing with a lot too, but *son of a bitch,* that shit... hurts. Jesus, I do sound like *Dear Abby.*

"Can I join you, boss?" Sabre asks.

"Only if you don't mind me pounding your ugly face," I tell him, still walking and not turning around.

"Same goes, boss. Same goes."

"Skull!" I hear Beth call my name. Maybe I'm a fucking bastard, but I still don't turn around.

CHAPTER 39
BETH

" I'm hurting him and soon I'll probably destroy him.
What if I'm making the wrong choice? "

I watch Skull walk away and I want to run after him. What can I say? Do I tell him about my father? How will he feel when he knows I do have Donahue blood? I can't barely understand or believe all of the things I've learned today. When Skull told me he wanted to marry me, I panicked. I wanted to scream, jump, and shout *yes!*

But how can I marry him if I know that I'm going to end up leaving? Am I going to leave? Can I stay and risk Skull's life?

I'm supposed to meet with Redmond tomorrow. Jesus, it sounds so weird even calling him that. I want to scream at him and ask where he was when I was diagnosed with cancer. If he's so concerned about saving me, where was he when I truly needed him back in my corner? How could he stand to let my mother just leave with me? I have so many questions. So, regardless of what my final decision is, I know that I'm going to see Redmond again and hear him out. I can't stop myself.

I go through the motions on autopilot getting ready for bed. Brush my hair, teeth, clean off my makeup, slip on one of Skull's t-shirts, and the pink boy-cut panties he likes so much.

By the time I'm done, he's still not back. This is bad for me because it gives me way too much time to think. I need to talk to Skull. If I tell him about Pistol, what will the fallout be? Will I end up getting Skull killed? What if I tell him about my dad? What can I tell him that won't make everything a hundred times worse? I close my eyes and try to still my brain. Immediately, a picture of Skull comes to mind.

I don't want to leave him. I think the best thing to do is wait. My father won't like me putting him off, but I need to think. Skull could be right. He could win this war. My father admitted he had taken some serious hits. Latch's words keep coming back to me. I need to have faith in my man. That's what he said and he's right. I love Skull. I want to spend the rest of my life with him and I need to have faith that he can handle this.

Just as I come to that decision, I hear Skull's voice from the meeting the other day admitting to his men he made a mistake. What would Latch say now, knowing that even Skull realizes he underestimated everything? Again I find myself full circle, torn between what I want and what is probably best for Skull and his family. When the door opens, I snap my eyes to it hoping it's Skull, and perversely at the same time hoping it's not. It would be easier to leave if he pushed me away.

"Hi," I tell him nervously, hoping he's going to talk to me. I think he grunts back. There are definitely no words. That's when I notice his face. How long had I been worrying? It had to be a while because Skull's got a bruise under his eye, his jaw is swollen, and his knuckles are all bloody and scraped. There are several gashes open and still bleeding. I forget my nervousness and jump up, running to him. "What did you do?" I cry, holding his hand gently to inspect the damage.

He jerks it away from me. "Beat the fuck out of Sabre," he grumbles, walking around me to get to the restroom.

"Why would you do that?" I ask, following him.

"Because the fucker offered, and I needed someone to pound on. Since your stepbrother's nowhere near, it worked. Anymore stupid questions, Beth? Or, do you think I could be left alone so I can drag my sorry ass into the shower before the soreness sets in?"

In the time we've been together, Skull has been in several different moods, but not once, even when he was in his most irate, has he ever treated me like this. I know I've hurt him and I may even deserve him being hateful, but how much worse would he be if he knew the full extent of what I'm thinking? Can I live with myself if I hurt him? I've got to think. *God, I have to think... I have to breathe...*

"Skull, don't treat me like this, please."

I hate that when I talk to him, I can hear the desperation in my voice, the weakness, the fear. I am not a weak person. You don't live through cancer by being weak. I'm a survivor. But tonight, I feel weak. Tonight, I feel like my world is coming apart at the seams. I saw my father today for the first time in forever, the same father who didn't even bother to contact me when I thought I was going to die, the same father who took my sister and left me with a mother who didn't really care for me, the same father who didn't comfort me or hold me when my sister died. I found out the man also ran the family that I've come to hate. I found out I'm not just married into that family but a part of them. I found out that my sister is alive. I turned down a marriage proposal from the man I love and hurt him. I'm contemplating leaving him forever.

How much can a woman stand before she breaks? It doesn't matter how fucking strong she is; there has to be a point when she shatters. I'm so fucking close to the edge right now, I know I'm going to fall over it and break into so many pieces that there will be nothing left. *Nothing.*

Surely I can be forgiven for sounding weak.

"Treat you like what? Maybe I'm not remembering right, but I'm pretty sure I asked you to marry me. You're the one that turned me down."

"I didn't have a choice!"

"I guess not. I don't want to fight about this anymore, Beth. You made your decision, and it's done. I'm sore, I'm tired. I have to get started early tomorrow. So I'm going to shower and sleep."

He turns away from me to get undressed. I feel desperation cling to my insides. I want to scream.

"This isn't all about you, Skull! You don't get to just shut me out!" I yell. His back is to me and he's bent over adjusting the shower knob. He turns to me. Any other time, I'd be caught up in the brilliance that is Skull totally nude and standing before me. Now, I'm only hypnotized by the anger radiating in his eyes.

"It's starting to show," he whispers, his voice deadly.

Show? Show what?

"This is where it starts to show," he growls, grabbing a soap holder off the bathroom sink and slamming it against the wall. I duck, despite myself, then look up at him in shock.

"What are you talking about?" I ask, my heart beating hard.

"You're too motherfucking young. All about me, sweetheart? Fucking hell, *mujer!* You're the one it's revolving around. I took my men into war for you! I'm putting everything I care about on the line for you. It's not about me, it's all wrapped up in *you* and *you* can't even bring yourself to marry me! Fuck this shit!" he growls, then pushes his way around me and leaves the bathroom.

Like an idiot, I chase after him. "Where are you going??"

"I don't know, Beth. What do you care? I'm going to go find a drink, maybe a fucking bunch of them, then maybe find some pussy I can fuck and forget, because it's fucking clear I don't have what it takes to claim a woman."

"You aren't leaving this room!"

"Try and stop me, Sweetheart."

"You can't sleep with another woman! You said you loved me!"

"You said *you* loved *me*," he growls in return, standing there staring at me like I'm insane. Maybe I am. I'm so emotionally spent, I literally could be. I just know I will die if Skull goes and find one of the women who hang around the club. I couldn't handle it.

"I do!"

"Then marry me!"

"I don't want to rush off and get married just because we may not have tomorrow!" I cry. The tears break and I can't hold them back if I tried. They fall so hard and fast that I can't catch my breath. Sobs rake through me and I look at Skull with my heart torn apart. "I want to walk down an aisle and know that I get you forever. That I will never be without you, not even for a day." Skull stands there looking at me and I can do nothing but cry. "I want a fairytale," I whisper inanely, sinking to the floor and giving in to my misery.

CHAPTER 40
SKULL

I watch as she sinks to the floor. Her small body rocks with the force of her sorrow and I feel like a jackass a million times over, even as my anger still simmers. I rub the stress headache I feel banging against my forehead and close my eyes, wishing things were different. Then, I go to my woman and gather her up in my arms. I carry her to the bathroom and sit on the commode with her while I tug at her clothes, gently pulling them from her body.

"What... are... you doing?" she asks, shuddering between each word, the tears not bothering to slow down.

"We're going to take a shower."

"I thought... you were leaving... me."

Once I have her undressed, I carry her into the shower. Luckily, the water is still hot even though we've left it running all this time. I lower her, keeping a hold on her neck so her tear-filled eyes stay on mine.

"I was upset. I'm not leaving you, Beth. It was all talk. You're the only woman I want, the only woman I will ever want for the rest of my life." I bend down and take her lips. The salt of her tears mingles with the sweet of her mouth. I let my tongue soothe her, plunder her, and love her all in one kiss. She's mine. Regardless of what happens, I never want her to forget that fact. When we break apart, the sadness still in her eyes physically hurts me. I walk her backwards further into the water and help her tilt her head. Once I have her hair completely wet, I move her again, and this time my back is to the water while I pour shampoo into my palm and begin washing her hair. "Will you promise me something, *querida?*"

"What?" she asks, her head going back as I massage her hair with my fingers, lathering it.

"That once I prove to you that we will survive this and everything will be okay, you will marry me. I'll even give you the fucking fairytale if that's what you want."

She goes quiet, and I find myself wishing I could see her face.

"I promise," she whispers, her voice thick with emotion.

With her agreement, I feel a little better. I rinse and condition her hair. I love the feel of it, so silky smooth in my hands, and the weight of the water pins it to me. I've never washed a woman's hair before; never felt the need. Beth isn't like anyone else, though. I love her. I'm so busy thinking about all of the emotions I have tangled up in Beth that my body jerks in shock as I feel her hand on my stomach.

"What are you doing, *mi cielo?*"

"Bathing my husband," she whispers, a bar of soap in her hand as she moves it over my body.

"Your husband?" I ask, watching as she pulls back so she can rub the soap between her hands. Once she has enough lather, she puts the soap on the small shelf. Her small hands wash up my chest. She pulls on the rings I have looped in my nipples. The sting of pain goes straight to my dick and I growl.

"I, Beth, take you, Skull, as my lawfully-wedded husband," she says, still teasing my nipples but kissing down my stomach. My head goes back in pleasure and my eyes close as I drink in the sensations. "To have and to hold," she whispers at the same time her hand wraps around my cock, squeezing and holding it tightly. "I pledge to love you for the rest of my life, to put your welfare before my own, to ease your burden, to bring you comfort," she goes on. As she strokes my cock, her lips suck my nipple into her mouth and her tongue pulls hard on the ring.

"Oh fuck, Beth," I groan.

"I promise from this day forward I will belong to you and no one else for the rest of my life," she whispers against my chest before biting the nipple and kissing down my stomach, going to her knees.

"Beth," I moan as her hands cup my balls and rub them, her fingers petting them right before she takes them into her wet, warm mouth, sucking them and torturing them with her tongue. "Fuck, baby," I groan, unable to remember anything feeling so good. She hums against them and I swear I can feel that fucking vibration through my entire body. She releases them from her mouth slowly, sucking until the last minute and releasing each of my balls with a soft *plop* from her lips.

"I promise to worship your cock every chance I get," she whispers, looking like a fucking sex goddess with the water running down her naked body, sitting on her knees in front of me as her tongue slides up my hard shaft. She licks it like fucking ice cream. When she makes it to the head, her tongue dives into the hidden crease, seeking pre-cum and making my body tighten in need. My hands twist in her hair as I watch the show she's giving me. Blood thrums in my ears and my balls are already swollen with the need to unload.

"Now *that's* a fucking vow," I growl just as those big beautiful lips of hers begin a long, slow, teasing glide down my shaft. *Jesus, fuck.* Nothing better… there's just nothing better the world has to offer. I pet the side of her face as her cheeks hollow out and she sucks my cock tight in her mouth, her tongue sliding and pleasuring as I go deep into her throat. When I hit the back, I think she'll pull away, completely expecting it, but Beth keeps going. I break through the tight valley as she swallows around my head. Her throat encloses me, working my shaft. "Motherfucker, that feels good," I praise her, my fingers clenching wildly into her hair, not wanting her to stop, unable to keep from touching her. She pulls off of me, but just a little, before she goes back down. Her beautiful gray eyes watch mine the entire time. When her hand cups my balls, squeezing and kneading them right before she takes me into her throat again, I lose it. Heat slides down my spine as I watch my woman give me the greatest fucking blowjob in the history of blowjobs. Even as I think it, I know it's more: she's giving me a piece of her soul. I see it in her eyes, I hear it in her words, I feel it in the way she loves me. That's what it is: love. I may have no experience before Beth, but I feel it now. I feel every bit of it.

She pulls back off my cock, holding me in her hand, her lips just at the head and her eyes still on mine. "I vow to love you for the rest of my life and whatever comes after," she says, and I know she's sincere. I feel it.

Then, she takes me all the way back in again, but this time her movements are less slow and tantalizing and more desperate and needy. She bobs up and down on my cock, demanding my cum. I feel my pre-cum running out, my balls so fucking tight it feels like they might tear free from my body. Beth growls against my cock. The vibration rocks me.

"I'm going to come, Beth," I warn her, but even as I say it, my cum is barreling out. It jets out into her waiting throat. I yell out her name. I can't remember ever coming this hard. Beth growls in response, her fingernails biting into my thigh, her other hand tight on my cock as she sucks me harder and harder, draining every damn drop.

I lean against the back of the shower wall. My fucking legs are shaking from the orgasm I just had. I look down at my woman, thinking to praise her. Her sweet little tongue comes up to gather some cum that was left in the corner of her mouth. Water pours down the side of her body. Her eyes are full of emotion and she's making sure she drinks the last ounce of cum I've given her. Even with all that beauty that is Beth, I'm still surprised when she leans into my body, buries her head against my cock and bites into my thigh, marking me with her teeth.

I thought I was spent, but just like that, I know I'm going to have her again. My dick is already demanding it.

CHAPTER 41
BETH

" *I have to hold on.*
Please, God, give me something to hold on to. "

I'm lying against Skull, my head on his chest. His heart beats in my ear and the sound reassures me. My body is pleasantly numb while still humming from the workout he gave me.

After our shower, he dried me off and took me to bed. He bent me over the bed and took me hard and I loved every minute of it. I smile as I feel the way Skull's hand slides up and down my lower back. I love this. Almost more than the actual sex, the after time when he holds me close and I feel so connected to him. It feels as if it answers a need deep inside of me that I never knew I had. Until Skull, it felt like everyone I ever cared about left me. Skull is the first person who makes me feel like he would die before leaving me. *No.* That's not right. The truth is, he would die *for* me. He's already proven that. He loves me. As screwed up as my brain is right now, I'm sure of that.

"Your body is tense, *mi cielo*. What are you thinking? Do I need to work the stress out of you again?"

I smile and kiss his chest, pushing my body into him with a giggle.

"Is that what you just did?"

"I thought it was. Though, maybe I need to do it once more if you're already stressing out again."

"I was just worried about what's going to happen," I confess, carefully choosing my words. "I promise you, I never realized what would happen when we met. I would have tried to warn you—"

"Shh," he whispers, his hand moving up to brush my hair. "It is not important, *mi cielo*. I told you it wouldn't have mattered anyway. Besides, I did a partial background check on you. I could have pushed Torch to dig further, but I didn't. That's on me."

"Why would you have? Most women don't come attached with baggage that's pulled from the demons of hell."

Skull snorts, going back to brushing my hair. "*Querida*, you were mine the minute I saw you standing on the street. It wouldn't have mattered if you belonged to Lucifer himself. I still would have claimed you."

"What happens next, Skull?"

"We will wait another day or so, then attack again. I won't stop until I bury Colin."

"I wonder where Matthew is?"

"I'm not sure. We've been running checks and there's not been one word from Matthew. It appears Colin is spearheading this. Though, there is talk of Edmund's brother taking the reins again."

My heart slams against my chest. I turn to the side, hoping Skull can't feel it. I do my best to keep my body relaxed. I don't want to give myself away. "Is that good or bad?" I ask, trying to figure out how Skull feels about this situation. Would he be willing to work with my father? Could they join forces and be rid of Colin? If I could arrange that, maybe I wouldn't have to give him up. Maybe...

"None of it is good, *querida*. Besides, the strikes we made go farther than just the Donahues. They are just one faction inside a bigger one. Retribution will be sought. No, our only hope is to bury any of the Donahues we can. If we can cause enough problems and draw attention to them, the family will deal with them too."

"Won't the family lash out at you?" I ask, not quite grasping what he's hoping to accomplish.

"Probably," he says, and my stomach flutters.

"I was kind of hoping they'd back off after you struck back," I whisper stupidly.

"We just keep going, Beth. Eventually we'll find something to bring it to a head."

That one sentence makes my heart turn over in my chest. I can't stop the tremor of fear that moves through me, and I know Skull feels it too because he pulls me up his body so I am forced to sit up, straddling him.

"I know you don't think so right now, Beth, but I promise you it will be okay. *We* will be okay," he insists, his hands holding my hips loosely and his eyes boring into me, willing me to believe him. Again, Latch's words haunt me: *You need to have more faith in your man.*

"I'm scared, Skull," I whisper. It's the most truthful I've been with him in what feels like way too long. "I'm terrified."

He reaches over to the nightstand drawer and pulls out a gold chain. He holds it up, letting the gold wrap around his inked fingers. It gleams with the light of the lamp. At the end of the chain is a locket in the shape of a heart. It has two letters woven together—an S and a B. I recognize them before the tears flow heavier and it blurs everything. He holds each side of the chain apart, never turning away from me. I bend my head and he pulls it down so it rests against my neck. The heart lands perfectly between my breasts. The cold metal sends a chill through my bare skin. His hand comes to my cheek, holding it gently, and I lean into him.

"I take you, Beth, as my lawfully-wedded wife. To have and to hold from this day forward, for better or for worse, in sickness and in health," he whispers to me, his eyes never leaving mine, and I don't bother stopping the tears as his love wraps around me as surely as his words do. "From this day forward, we shall walk hand-in-hand in this world and into the next. I promise to love, honor, and protect you. Put no one or nothing before you. I vow to worship your body night and day and never let you forget who you belong to, and not stop until you come so hard in my arms every night that your fucking toes curl, your body is weightless, and you hear angels singing."

"Now *that's* a fucking vow," I whisper, returning the same words to him that he'd given me earlier.

"Just wait till I deliver on them, baby," he whispers, leaning up to take my mouth.

The last thought I'm able to hold onto is that Latch is right. I need to have more faith in my man. I'm going to hold on. I don't have a choice. With my decision made, I give myself to him and lose myself in his touch.

CHAPTER 42
BETH

" *I'm trying... I swear I am.* **"**

"Rise and shine, *querida*," Skull tells me. He's standing at the foot of the bed. Me? I'm curled in a ball under the covers. It's too early to be that cheerful.

"What? Why? What time is it?"

"It's six, sweetheart. We have to leave early to go to Beast if you're spending the day there. I have a meeting with Diesel and his crew today when they make it in from Tennessee."

"I don't want to go to the hospital today," I yawn, trying to ignore the sliver of fear that hits me. "I thought I'd stay here today and be close to you. That way, if you got some time, you could sneak off and make good on your promise."

"My promise?" he asks.

I smile up at him, my hand going to the locket he gave me. I slept in it because I can't bear to take it off. "Yeah. Remember? The whole worship-my-body thing? I think I heard mention of my toes curling and angels singing, too," I joke. I know every word he said. I'll never forget last night for as long as I live.

"Is that a fact?" he says. He's smiling and, for the first time in days, I see happiness in his eyes.

"*Sí*," I tell him saucily. "And it was my wedding night, so I'm hoping you weren't overestimating your abilities."

He throws his head back and laughs.

"That does it," he says, undressing.

"What are you doing?" I ask him, which is a stupid question, but I wasn't really expecting this reaction. He yanks me out of the bed, tugging on my hand. Then he takes my mouth in a hard kiss. When we break apart, I look up at him. "What are you doing?" I repeat like an idiot.

"Giving my wife good morning sex. Now turn around."

He kind of manhandles me so that my back is facing his front. I smile at his use of the word wife. My arms rest upon his, which are wrapped around my waist, and I take in the heat of his body for a minute. I love the way it feels when his skin presses against mine. It never fails to give me a feeling of contentment.

"Skull, sweetheart, I know I'm the new one at all of this, but I kind of think you have to turn me around to get to the goods."

"Oh, *querida*, I'm afraid I'm been neglecting your education." He hadn't, not really, but I decide to play along.

"I probably didn't marry well," I tell him with a playfully heavy sigh.

His hand comes up to my neck, holding me with force. Chills of excitement course through my body. I feel the graze of the stubble on his jawline rub against my neck. A second later, warm breath touches my ear.

"You may pay for that one, my darling wife," he whispers right before I feel a hand glide down my side. It moves against my ass, then lower. His fingers dive between my legs, pushing just beyond the lips of my pussy. I can't stop the moan that escapes as I push my ass against him. "*Querida,* you are soaking wet."

I gnaw on my bottom lip as his fingers slide up and drift over my clit. He's right; I'm so wet I can feel it from the sound of his fingers pushing through my cream. "I need my husband to fuck me," I moan. His hand stills and I tighten my legs against it, trying to push him further into me. When it doesn't work, I whimper with disappointment.

"Say that again, *mi cielo*," he growls.

"I need my husband to fuck me."

His hand comes back to my neck. When his words hit me this time, they're hoarse and full of need. "Bend over and hold onto the bed, *mi cielo*. This is going to go hard and fast." I do as he orders, my fingers digging into the rumpled covers on the bed. "Spread your legs and tilt your ass higher, Beth."

Anticipation runs through me. Once I get my feet planted, he massages my ass, his hands biting into the flesh, then he shakes my ass roughly, pulling the cheeks apart. I feel cool air hitting the wet needy skin of my pussy and I know I'm completely exposed to him.

"So fucking gorgeous," he groans, and the pleasure in his voice is so thick I can't find it in me to be embarrassed when I feel my cream slide down my thighs. I gasp when I feel his cock rub against my thigh and the cream found there. "Who does this pussy belong to, Beth?" he asks, his cock now teasing my opening, not going inside yet, but pushing just enough to let me know he's there.

"You," I gasp, when all at once the head slips and grates against my clit before he brings it back.

"Who am I, Beth? Say it," he demands.

"My husband," I tell him because I know that's what he wants.

"That's it, *querida*. That's it," he moans, and the sound mingles with my cry because he slams inside of my pussy without warning. I feel his balls bounce against me and I'm stretched fully as he stays right there, not moving. He folds down over top of me, his hand wrapping in my hair. He yanks back my head and his voice is almost deadly. "Put your fingers down there and rub your clit, Beth. Do it while I fuck you hard because I'm not going to last long and I want you with me. I want to feel that pussy coming apart all around my dick."

When I do as he tells me, his hands move to my hips, the fingers pushing into my skin, and then he fucks me. He rides me hard, slamming into me over and over, jarring my whole body. One hand begins kneading my ass while he crashes in and out of me, taking what he needs without worrying about anything else. I love it. I love that he's so desperate and lost in his desire that he demands I take care of myself. He didn't need to bother; I'm so excited that I'm sure I could have come just from what he's doing, but I slide my fingers over my clit, rubbing over it. My juice is thick, making the glide easy and reminding me of how it feels when Skull licks me. I twist and pinch my clit just as Skull slams into me again.

Then I hear him shout my name. I feel his cock jerk inside of me. I tighten my pussy as he slams into me again, and then I feel him release inside of me. The streams of cum are so forceful that they feel like thrusts themselves. My hands move faster and faster over my clit. I feel Skull pull out, then shift somehow and slam right back in, hitting a spot inside of me that makes me fly.

"I'm coming!" I yell, and I only go higher when Skull reaches around and pulls on my breasts. It seems like I come forever. I feel my arm give out as I fall upon the mattress, mini-shocks from my orgasm still running through me. I can feel Skull's weight on me and he kisses my back.

"*Te amo*, Beth. *Te amo.*"

He loves me.

CHAPTER 43
BETH

> " *Hope dies hard.* "

"Fuck, *querida*, you're going to kill me some day with that hungry little pussy of yours," Skull whispers in my ear, his fingers combing through my hair which sticks to my neck.

"Definitely going to have to shower, if I can ever feel my legs again."

Skull laughs and I realize I said that out loud. He rolls on his side and pulls me so I'm half-draped over him, our legs hanging off the end of the bed. I close my eyes as he holds me close, wishing we could stay like this and never leave this room.

"Does that mean quick and hard worked for you, *mi cielo?*"

"I'm not sure. I may need another example to be positive," I mumble. Skull's head goes back in laughter and happiness surrounds me. I wrap myself up in it, hugging him by clenching my body tight into him. I love that I make him laugh. I love that I can give him joy. It *is* joy too, because I hear it in the tone of his voice and see it in his face.

"You do realize, when all this has passed, I'm going to want a real marriage, Beth. I want you to belong to me in all ways. When I see you, there's this inner voice inside of me that screams *'Mine'!* I want the world to know it." He kisses the top of my head.

"You mean inner caveman. Are you going to have your name tattooed all over my body too?" I ask jokingly. Skull's body tenses up and I manage to finally open my eyes to look at him. His eyes are dark with need. "Okay, see, I love you, and in my

187

brain we're already married in all the ways that count, but once this is done, if that's what you want, sure."

"And—"

"I'm allergic to pain," I cut him off. "I'm small, not some big bad over-muscled biker who apparently loves needles. It's a good look for you. I totally approve. But I had enough of needles when I was sick. There'll be no tattoos on this body. No way, no how. No dice."

"I'll make you change your mind," he says, and from the gleam in his eyes, he's taking my declaration as a challenge.

"Yeah, good luck with that. People in Hell will be wearing snowshoes before it happens."

"We'll see."

Crap.

"I need to go, sweetheart. Thanks to you seducing my poor abused dick, I'm running late."

"When will I see you again?" I know that sounded needy, but I can't stop it. Things are easier and I'm stronger when Skull is beside me.

"I'll see if I can break away around dinner time to feed you."

"When you say feed me, do you mean food or dick?"

"Jesus, I've created a monster." He says, getting up and dressing. It makes me sad because a man like that should never have to put clothes on. He's more beautiful than any museum statue.

"What? I was merely asking for clarification," I grin, sitting up. I will admit I'm not covering up; I sit there naked with the cold air hitting my breasts, hoping he finds me irresistible enough to come shower with me. His fingers stop buttoning his jeans and I know a moment of victory—just before he dashes my hopes.

"Stop it, you little minx. I have to go to this meeting. Cover up those tits or I'll bend you over my knee and smack your ass for teasing me."

His words hit me and I feel a flutter deep inside. I don't know if it's from fear, or maybe want. I'll decipher that later.

I grab the cover and pull it over me. "Spoil sport."

Skull gives out a chuckle before pulling on his cut. "I'll give you what you need later, *mi cielo*, I promise. I have to go now. My men are waiting on me."

I stand up, letting the cover fall. I walk over to him and reach up, loosely wrapping my hands at the back of his neck and stretching against his body. His big hands rest on my ass and his head tilts down to look at me. There's a big smile on his lips.

"I'll let you go, but it should be noted that a husband should always shower with his wife in the mornings."

"I must have missed that rule," he says, bending down to kiss my eyelids, squeezing me tighter against him.

"It's in the new husband rulebook, page ten."

"Damn, I didn't know there was a rulebook. I've always been the kind of man who goes against the rules, forging my own path," he whispers, his voice dropping down as he kisses along the side of my neck. "I like to feel my way, you know? Explore, experiment, and conquer... That's always been my motto."

While he speaks, he nibbles on the skin of my neck, and his hands move inwards on my ass so that his fingers are skimming the valley between the cheeks. My pussy trembles and I have to wonder if he's going to make me come again, even without really touching me. He's *that* potent.

"Maybe we could throw away the rulebook," I moan, tilting my head as his lips capture my earlobe and sucks it into his mouth. He bites down on it and the sting of pain causes my pussy to spasm. Was it just a few minutes ago I was completely worn out?

"Good plan, *mi cielo*," he says, but his hand comes to my neck and he pulls away just a fraction to look into my eyes. "I have to go, *esposa*."

"I know. I'm just going to miss you."

"I feel the same. *Te amo*, sweet Beth."

"*Te amo*," I whisper before his mouth comes to mine. This

kiss isn't like one we've shared, at least in a long time. This one is sweet, gentle, and almost delicate. It makes me feel cherished.

When he pulls away, it physically hurts, and I do my best to beat down the panic that swamps me. It's not logical, but I honestly don't want to be away from him. I'm scared I'm going to lose him. I might be listening to Latch's advice, but that doesn't stop the fear. I think Skull sees it, or maybe he can sense it. I'm not sure. He looks like he's about to say something when there's a heavy banging on the door.

"Boss? You alive in there? We're late."

"Fuck," he mumbles. "I got to go, *querida*."

"Go. I'll be here waiting, but please be safe."

"Always. I have too much to lose now," he says, kissing my forehead, then he pulls out of my arms. He reaches behind him and gets the t-shirt he had on yesterday and pulls it over my head. He fishes my locket out and lets it fall on top of the shirt between my breasts. I raise my eyebrow at him. "When I open that fucking door, Torch will do his best to look in here and the fucker is not seeing any of what is mine."

"Yes sir, Captain Caveman." I smile, wrapping my arms around my waist and mentally trying to ignore the desperation inside of me that makes me want to beg him to stay and not leave me.

"Damn straight, woman," he agrees, turning away from me. A thought comes to me, and I can't let him go without trying to warn him.

"Is Pistol going with you?" I ask, and when I see the questions flare in his eyes, I bite my lip.

It's wrong, but I can't tell him about my father. Not right now. If he knows, will that be the thing that makes him push me away forever? Or will he attack Roger... *Redmona*... and get himself killed?

"*Si*. Why do you ask, *querida?*"

"I don't know. I just don't trust him. Will you be extra careful around him?" That's the best I can do to warn him without giving him the full truth. I feel like all I do is lie anymore.

He studies me for a moment. Finally, he says, "Always. We'll talk this evening, *mi cielo.*"

Did I give too much away? He turns and opens the door to leave. I stand there watching because I can't make myself look away.

"Fucking hell, boss. I thought you got lost."

"Screw you. I was giving my wife a proper goodbye."

"Your wife?" Torch says.

"*Sı. My wife.* Let's make sure you don't forget that, fucker," Skull grumbles before their voices completely disappear down the hall. My hand goes to the locket. I hold onto it. I just keep holding it.

That's exactly what I'm doing when my cellphone that Skull gave me rings. Thinking he's calling to tell me he misses me, I run to answer it like the crazy school girl I am and sometimes forget.

"Elizabeth, you are not here," my father's voice tells me at my giggled hello. And just like that, I'm no longer happy. I'm not even warm. I feel cold all the way through.

"How did you get this number?"

"That's a stupid question," he says, and it is. He could probably get it a million different ways, but I'm sure it was from Pistol.

"I'm hanging up now," I tell him. My hands and voice shake, and fear flows through my system where only moments before there was hope.

"You were supposed to meet with me today."

"I'm not coming. Skull and I were married last night. I'm going to have faith in my husband," I tell him defiantly.

"Funny, I was told you said no."

Acid churns in my stomach. My hand holds tight to the locket.

"Then your spies don't obviously know everything," I lie.

"I think they do. You turned Skull down because you know in

your heart that you are going to give him up. Your decision is already made. You're just having trouble coming to terms with it. Stop fighting it, sunshine. Let me save you. Let me save all of us."

I hate him. I fucking hate him.

"Goodbye, father."

"You'll regret this, Beth. What's about to happen is beyond my control. It could have been avoided if you had listened though. I'm sorry, sunshine. I really did try."

Something in his voice terrifies me. That isn't hard, considering how panicked I already am.

"Wait! What's about to—?"

The call drops. Silence is the only answer I get.

CHAPTER 44
SKULL

" Why do days that start so fucking good end in total shit? "

"You're late, *ese*."

"It happens," I tell Diesel. We're sitting across from each other in a little diner just at the Tennessee state line. Diesel picked the place. I don't really get it. Then again, I'm not much for truck-stop food.

"Any news?" he asks. Beside him is his second-in-command. He's an okay dude, nothing special, but he and Diesel seem to get along well. He's quiet. Too quiet for my tastes, but then again I'm used to Torch's constant fucking chatter.

"Not since the attacks. It's been nothing but radio silence," I tell him.

Beside me is Sabre. Torch is out with the others keeping watch on the perimeter. I gave the job to Pistol, but I don't trust that motherfucker, even with him swallowing his pride down and getting with the program.

Also, something about Beth's question today doesn't sit right with me. There has to be more to what she asked. I saw something flash in her eyes. I'm going to have to quiz my lovely *esposa*. My dick pushes against my pants at the thought. Who knew having a woman you want to put a ring on would make your dick so fucking hard? Then again, everything about Beth does that to me.

"We've been picking up more chatter about Redmond Donahue. Supposedly, he's been spotted just on the outskirts of your town," Diesel said. "Bell, give Skull the file," he says to his second-in-command.

I open the folder. There's a picture of a man standing by a limo in a perfect three-piece suit. He stands there looking straight at the camera that snapped the picture, like he knows they're there.

I study his face. He's Edmund's brother, but they look nothing alike. There's nothing similar about them, except maybe the coldness in their eyes. Something about Redmond hits me. Something about him seems familiar. His facial features, maybe... or the way he holds himself.

I shrug it off, closing the file to look at it more later. "Thanks. It doesn't matter, though. The plan stays the same," I tell Diesel. "I just need to know if you're in with me. I know it's a lot to ask."

"Fuck that shit. The day I back down from a fight, they can throw my ass in a hole six feet down and cover me up."

"It's not your fight, *hermano*."

"You mean you wouldn't have my back if the roles were reversed?" Diesel asks, looking away to acknowledge the waitress who comes to our table.

"What can I get you boys?" she asks.

She's pretty. Before Beth, I would have been tempted to talk to her. She has dark hair, the color of a raven. Her face is almost too sweet for the circles she carries under those deep brown eyes. She does nothing for me, but when I look over and see the way Diesel is drinking her in, I'm starting to understand why he picked this shithole to meet in. She does pack some serious dynamite for her small frame. In fact, the faded pink t-shirt she wears is stretched so tight over her chest, you figure her tits can burst out at any minute. I'd estimate Double-D's, easily. Diesel always was a breast man. I guess some things never change.

"Just coffee, *bonita*," I tell her.

"Same here," Bell and Sabre join in.

"And you?" she asks Diesel, looking bored and obviously ignoring his not-so-subtle looks.

"I'd rather have you than coffee," he says, and I want to roll my eyes. The motherfucker is usually so easy with the ladies, but that's one dumbass pick-up line.

"Coffee, it is," she says, not responding even a little to Diesel, then walks away.

The table erupts in laughter. Diesel just strains to look around the side as the waitress walks away.

"I don't think she's buying what you have to sell, amigo."

"She just hasn't seen me unleash the whole package yet, Skull, my brother. Just wait. She'll fall. They all do eventually."

"That's how you got your son, if I remember correctly."

His face loses that easygoing attitude. Apparently, there's more to that story than I thought.

"That was a mistake," mutters Diesel, "though I have Ryan. So I don't regret it. His mother, though? Pure bitch."

"Ever hear from her?"

"Only when she wants money. I don't think she's seen Ryan more than twice since he was born."

"Fuck," Sabre says, his voice full of disgust.

"It doesn't matter. Ryan is worth everything to me. You will see. You too, Skull. Don't tell me you aren't trying to knock up Beth every chance you get."

I flip him off with a grin, not bothering to deny it.

The waitress comes back and puts our coffees down, again ignoring Diesel. I can't help but laugh. Diesel looks at me and shrugs it off. "Fuck you, Skull."

We're just about to dive into the particulars when gunfire breaks out. Outside the window, I see my men with Diesel's pulling out their weapons and running for cover. The window shatters as a bullet drives through it and hits perilously close to our seats.

"Motherfucker!" Diesel yells out, and my grunt can't be heard, but it's right there with him.

We all move away from the booth and grab our weapons, but not before more bullets shower in. I feel a sting hit my shoulder and I know I've taken a hit. I glance down at it and notice it's a through-and-through, which is good. I've had a sawbones dig around inside of me for a fucking bullet before and that's not something I'd like to revisit.

I hear a loud grunt of pain, then clanging of the metal table. My attention jerks up to see Bell's taken a hit. He's not as lucky as I am. Blood blooms from his chest, the crimson color overtaking the pale gray t-shirt he's wearing.

I help Diesel drag him to the ground. Sabre is in position and fires back. The few occupants in the diner are screaming and crying, hiding under their tables. The waitress that Diesel has his eye on is huddled to the side of the bar looking panicked. We drag Bell over to her. Diesel grabs her apron roughly, ripping it from her body. She screams. He ignores it.

"Hold this to his chest to stop the bleeding," he commands. "Do you have a fucking cellphone?"

"W-What? Yes," she answers, instantly pressing the wadded fabric to Bell's chest.

"Call 9-1-1. Tell the dispatcher to tell a Detective Grady that Diesel said he's going to want to be here."

"What? Why wouldn't—"

"Just fucking do it!" Diesel yells as a bullet wizzes by his head and he pulls away from the woman and his buddy.

I'm shooting now too, but we're basically shooting blind because I can't tell where the fucking bullets are coming from. There are a few close up, but the ones hitting in here are snipers.

Sirens ring in the distance. I doubt it has anything to do with the waitress's call; there's not been enough time. I watch as I see two more of my men fall down. I scream. I can't tell who they are—there's just dust and chaos out there. I see their jackets as they fall. I'm going to kill the fucking Donahues. There's not a doubt in my mind that this is their doing. This is their strike back. Fuck. I should have had more men watching the mountains. This is on me. Why didn't I even think about snipers?

Fucking hell.

CHAPTER 45
SKULL

❝ Blood of your own stains your hands
in ways no one can see but you. **❞**

I rake my hand down the side of my face. *Carnage.* It's everywhere. There's no other word for it. Fifteen dead in total. Three of my own. Prospects with the exception of K-Rex. He was a good man. A man who had barely begun to live... and he's gone. Diesel lost his Vice President Bell and five other men. I feel the weight of their deaths, too. The rest of the casualties were civilians. Innocent bystanders who walked into the diner for lunch and will never leave. Their blood is on my hands, too.

"Boss?" Torch asks, worried. I pull my eyes away from the county coroners and paramedics who are covering bodies with sheets while the cops interview witnesses.

"Yeah?" I ask, my voice hoarse. I'm feeling fucking old.

"You going to let them look at your arm?"

I glance at my shoulder, the white cloth tied around it soaked in blood. I had forgotten it. It doesn't matter. It's nothing compared to what my men took, compared to the lives lost.

"Nah. I'll get our man to stitch it up when we get back home," I tell him, clearing my throat. My eyes can't stop going back to all of the chaos in front of me.

"We're coming with you," Diesel growls. I turn to look at him. I can see the fury in him. He's normally easygoing, reminding me more of Torch. Now he looks ready to kill everyone in his sight.

"I think this war has cost you enough, brother. I didn't mean for—"

"Fuck that shit. You know what it means when we go to war. We live this fucking life for a reason. We're the men our forefathers envisioned for this country. Not the watered-down bureaucrats who run it now."

"I should have thought about snipers. This is on me. The Donahue's calling card has always been 'go big'. I had our men monitoring for bombs and toxins. *Jesus.*"

"Colin's calling card is bombs, *ese.* This Redmond is different. All bets are off."

"We're going to need more intel on him, Torch," I order, feeling old and tired. I want blood as much as Diesel does. I'm fucking wondering how many are going to die before we're done here. "You sure about this, *hermano?*" I ask Diesel.

"We're at war and we band together. I'm going to need a couple of hours to see to my men and have their bodies sent home."

"Same here. You got a cage Pistol and Keys can use for transport?"

"Yeah. Got you covered. My connection with the state police and the sheriff's office are running interference, too. You should be good to go."

"I'm not sure it's going to be easy to get the bodies right now, Skull. No matter what Diesel says. Besides, he was the one who picked this damn place. Perimeters should have been more secure," Pistol says.

"Make it easy. Grease the wheels, use your charm if you have any, or fucking guns. I don't care, I just want my men home." My hand goes to Diesel to hold him back. He growls at Pistol, shooting him a look that could kill.

"Got it," says Pistol, looking at Diesel, but not adding fuel to the flame right now.

"Okay, we'll meet up at Pigeon River in two hours. Everyone have their shit together and be ready to move out. Torch, Sabre, and Briar, you're with me."

"Where're we going, boss?" Briar asks.

"We're gonna see if we can figure out where the snipers went. If we can capture one of them, that might be useful."

"We've been looking for the last hour, Skull," Pistol says. I'm really getting tired of the bastard. If I didn't need Cade's men right now…

"Then it won't hurt for us to look some more. Didn't I give you a job to do?" I ask over my shoulder, already walking off. I hear him grunt and take that as acceptance.

Diesel slaps me on the shoulder, which jars my fucking arm and hurts like hell, but I ignore it. "Your man needs to be taught who is in charge."

"I've taught him. He's just too fucking thick to remember."

"Cut off his testicles. That's not so easy for a man to forget."

My hand rubs my sack in reflex.

"I'll keep that in mind. For now he stands though, I need his brother's firepower. See you in a couple hours, *hermano*."

"See you then," he says, slapping my back again before walking in the opposite direction.

I hop on my bike and take off, my men following me. I need to get this shit done and get back to Beth. I've got to keep her safe. This attack was different from anything the Donahues have done before. I have to tighten the circle around her even more… *and soon.*

CHAPTER 46
BETH

**" I didn't know you could feel your world ending.
I felt it all the way to my soul. "**

Skull's late. Dinner was hours ago and it's dark outside now. I asked Latch if he had heard from them. He got this strange look on his face which worried me, but all he said was that they'd run into some trouble. He swore to me Skull was fine, but it feels like he's keeping something from me. My phone rang three other times today. It was my father each time, and each time I hit the button to decline the call. I can't talk to him. I have to keep holding on to hope.

It's all I have.

I spent all day cleaning the compound like a crazy person. The muffler bunnies were giving me the evil eye, and the men were all looking at me like I'd lost my mind. I have. Until I know if Skull can end this war and contain my father, I'm going to be certifiable.

"You're looking better these days, Beth," Latch says.

I'm organizing the back of the bar while Latch sits on a stool in front of me nursing a beer. I blow out a large puff of air because if Latch knew what a mess I was inside, he probably wouldn't say that.

"I'm trying to have faith," I tell him.

"Good to know," he says, taking a drink.

"Tell me about your sister." I need something to take my mind off of things.

"How do you know about Lucy?"

"I heard some of the girls mention that you help take care of your sister. They think that means you're sweet and caring."

"You know better?"

"I think you probably care about your sister, but the fact that you step up to the plate to help her doesn't make you sweet."

"Is that a fact?"

"Yep. I think it just means you use that to get into women's pants."

"Sweetheart, I don't need help to get into women's pants. They see me coming and that shit just magically falls off."

"I'm sure," I tell him, shaking my head. I'd argue with him, but after watching him and Sabre in action, I don't even try. My phone beeps and I pull it out of my back pocket.

"Well, look there. Looks like Skull and the boys are back," Latch says, using his drink to point to the security monitor that shows bikes and cars pulling into the parking lot outside. "You coming to say hi to your man?" he asks. I don't look up though. I have a text from my father. It's a file and I can't see what it is because it hasn't downloaded completely.

"What? Oh, go ahead. I'll follow you in a minute. I want to… freshen up."

"Women. Geez, you spend all day mooning over Skull and now you're putting off going to see him. I can tell you he won't care what the fuck you look like. He'd rather you meet him first, then freshen up."

"Go on, will you? I'll be there in a bit."

He says something else, but I don't hear it. My attention has turned to my phone. The file pops up; it's a video. The screen shows a silver and red building that says Edna's Truck Stop on the outside. My hand shakes as my thumb reaches up to hit the play button on the screen.

I watch as the scene unfolds, sending my body into shock. At first I can't see what's happening, but then it becomes all too clear. Men are diving to the ground and crawling behind bikes and cars as gunfire erupts everywhere. The camera zooms in, and from that angle I see a shattered window to the diner.

Then I see it. Skull is standing there and his arm is bleeding. The video shuts off, but another message arrived while I was watching. I hit play again—not wanting to know, but afraid not to. This time, Skull stands there looking out at a line of bodies. There are paramedics covering them in sheets and ambulances with their lights flashing. The video stops just in time for a text to appear on my screen:

I spared him this time. I won't the next, Beth. The choice is yours.

My fingers shaking, I text back: *Why are you doing this?*

One painstakingly long minute later, I get a response: *If I don't take him out or end this, Colin won't rest until he has you. I can't allow you to be used against me, Beth. You need to make a choice. Skull's life is in your hands.*

I hear voices coming through the doors. My heart pounds against my chest and a cold sweat covers my skin. It's time. After what I just saw, can I truly make any other decision? At one point in that video, a red dot had been on Skull's head. He could have killed the man I love; he had him in the gun-sight and Skull's death would have been my fault.

I take a breath. I close my eyes. My hand grips the locket around my neck. I don't think I have any hope or faith left. Now, all I have is the will to make sure that Skull doesn't die for loving me.

I make my fingers move: *I'll be at the hospital tomorrow morning.*

Once I text him back, I put my phone up and walk around just in time to catch Skull entering the room. I run and wrap him up in my arms, letting the tears fall.

"Shh. I'm okay, *querida*. It's just a small wound. Barely more than a scratch," Skull says, trying to calm me. He thinks I'm upset over the wound. I am, but that's not why the tears are flowing unchecked.

I'm going to have to give him up. I can't keep Skull. He's not mine. He never was. The truth of that nearly destroys me. I stand there in the middle of the room surrounded by his men and let him hold me while I cry out my pain—or at least a little of it.

CHAPTER 47
SKULL

**" War is hell on the home-front.
When I see Beth's face,
I finally understand what that means. "**

It's been a fucked-up day. I just got Diesel and his men settled. They're in sleeping bags in the main entrance to the bunker. Fucker refused my offer of bedrooms, told me I was getting soft. Hell, maybe I am. I'd take a warm bed over that fucking hard floor any day of the week.

A warm bed with Beth in it is even better.

I softly close the door to our room, hoping she's asleep. I should have known better. She's sitting up in bed doing something on her phone. She looks up when I come in and shuts her phone off, setting it on the bedside table.

"Everything okay?" she asks, her voice worn out and hoarse. She cried for an hour today after I got home. Even when I finally got her to calm down by showing her that the wound wasn't that bad, she still cried. This is taking a toll on her. I see the worry and the pain etched on her face and I fucking hate it. I need to end this fucking war; I just don't know how, short of cutting someone's head off. Trouble is, I can't tell whose head I should take. Colin's or Redmond's? And where the fuck has Matthew been all this time? I can't even find the son of a bitch in France where Beth thought he was. I keep thinking I'm missing the big picture here. It's driving me crazy.

"Yes, *querida*. Just had to make sure Diesel and his crew were settled for the night."

"You have his men here and Cade's. How many more do you think it will have to take? How many more lives will be on the

line because of me?" she asks, her voice weak and quiet. I almost
have to strain to hear the question.

I sigh deeply. I knew it would come to this. I hope I have the
right words to tackle her worries. There's nothing she can do
about it now; I'm never letting her go.

"*Querida*," I start, but she waves me off.

"You know I'm right, Skull. If not for me, none of this would
be happening."

I throw my clothes to the floor and join her in the bed.
Getting settled under the covers, I pull her body next to mine.

"We didn't start this, *mi cielo*. The only person to blame here
is Colin and Redmond." Her body tenses in my arms and I stroke
her arm tenderly.

"Redmond?" she asks.

"*Sí*. He's Edmund's brother. Word has it that he's the one
pulling the strings, not Colin. There's a pull for power going on
in the Donahues' camp, *querida*. I think we're just getting caught
in the crossfire."

"What will you do?"

"Keep attacking until the main target slips up. He will; they
always do."

She doesn't say anything else, so I just continue to stroke her
skin, letting my touch calm her.

"No matter what happens, Skull, I want you to know that the
day you walked into that small coffee shop and sat down at my
table was the best day of my life."

Something in her tone worries me. I pull back and lift her
face up to talk to me. "We're going to be okay, *querida*. This will
pass and things will get better. I need you to believe that. *I need
you to believe in me.*"

Her eyes seem to bore into mine, and I see a million
questions, but she asks me none of them. Instead, she buries her
head into my chest and places a kiss above my heart.

"I know you're extending the lockdown and tightening
security, but do you think you could let me go to the hospital to

spend the day with Beast? They're removing his bandages tomorrow and checking out the results from the first surgery."

"Is he talking to anyone yet?" I ask. They brought Beast out slowly, but he's not talking to anyone. The doctors are starting to worry his voice has been affected.

"No. He ignores everyone. I just don't want him to be alone. You have the place surrounded. I'd be okay."

"I don't know, *mi cielo*. I don't like the idea of you being away from the compound."

"I'll be fine. I promise to keep at least one of your men with me at all times."

I smile. She doesn't know it yet, but she won't have a choice. I don't feel right letting her go, but Latch spent the evening telling me how she cleaned the place from top to bottom. If I don't give her something to do, she's going to work herself to death.

"Okay, *mi cielo*. But you will come home early. Tomorrow, I will be busy early on setting up our next attack, but after that, I want you in my arms for the remainder of the day."

"I'm pretty sure that can be arranged," she says with a smile, but the smile doesn't touch her eyes. Gone is that playful front she had before I left. I know it's because I was shot. I just don't know how to fix it.

"It better be. I'm practically wasting away from lack of attention here," I tell her, trying to lighten up the somber mood.

"Is that so?"

"Complete truth," I sigh.

"I'll have to see if I can fix that then," she says, sliding under the covers. My baby does like sucking on my cock. When I feel her hand wrap around it, I groan.

"I like a woman who takes matters into her own... hands," I whisper, my fingers combing through her hair as she loves on my cock, my shaft disappearing into her mouth. I don't even mind the sting of pain that comes with using my arm.

It's more than worth it.

CHAPTER 48
BETH

" You don't sign in blood
when you make a deal with the devil. "

"You're looking beautiful, sunshine," my father tells me when I walk into the kitchen. Of course, Pistol is by my side. If Skull had any idea, the man would be dead—and he really needs to be. I thought about bringing a gun with me and doing the job myself. I didn't, though. One thing stopped me: he told me Katie was alive.

"Please cut the crap," I say tiredly. "I've cried all night and morning. You caused those tears and I look like hell. I'm here because I don't have a choice and we both know that. You didn't give me a choice."

"Elizabeth—"

"I want to know about Katie. You said she was alive. Where is she? Does she know what a bastard our father is? Why hasn't she ever reached out to me?"

"You need to watch yourself, Elizabeth."

"You have five minutes and then I'm walking out of here. All thoughts of a bargain is off the table."

"What makes you think I would let you walk away?"

When he asks that question, I finally see the mask he's been trying to wear slip. There's an evil, cold bastard lurking under his attempts to try and be my father. Suddenly, I worry about the life my sister endured. It never occurred to me that I might have gotten the better deal.

"If you don't let me go, your plan fails. Skull will know that you took me, and he will move both Heaven and Earth to get me back again, because that's what you do when you love and care for someone, *father*. You put them above anything—especially yourself."

"Is that what you think your boyfriend is doing?"

"I know it is. It's also the only reason I'm here. I love two people in this world, Skull and my sister, so stop pulling your punches. I want proof Katie is alive. Then, I want to know flat-out what you expect in exchange for leaving Skull and his men alone."

"It's a pity I didn't choose you, Elizabeth. I see myself in you. You could have ruled alongside me. Your sister never had a head for business. She keeps her thoughts consumed with animals and that damn farm she owns. I blame Isabel's genes for that failing."

My sister owns a farm?

"Your time's running out," I tell him. I'm trying to copy Skull; I've seen him when he's ordering his crew around. I do, however, sit down at a stool in the corner because my legs are weak and if they give out on me, there's no amount of acting in the world that will bluff me out of that. Then the Devil will know he has me. That's who he is to me now: the Devil. I apparently never had a father. I was just the spawn of Satan. The truth of that hurts me. Then again, my disappointment in my parents is something that's lasted a long time.

"Your boyfriend is getting ready to attack tomorrow. He will take out several things I hold dear. I'm letting that pass because of you—"

"Naturally," I interrupt him, unable to contain my sarcasm. It gets me another look from the Devil and another piece of his mask slipping. I don't know why I find joy in that, but I do.

"I know the time of the attacks and where they've planted the charges. I even have the codes and where the cameras and video feeds are. So, you see, I am truly the one in charge here."

"Let me guess how you would have gotten all that information." I look over at Pistol and he has the gall to look satisfied with himself. "I really hope I get to see Skull kill you someday," I tell him directly. "It couldn't happen to a nicer snake."

He makes a step towards me, but Satan calls him off. At least I wiped that look off of Pistol's face. Score one for me, even if it was a small one.

"So, you have all the info. What does that have to do with me?"

"We have the feed at the yacht spliced. I'm going to have it appear that when Skull blows up the yacht, he does so with you onboard."

The glee in his eyes chills me. He's such a cold and evil man. How can he be the same man who used to rock me to sleep and tell me bedtime stories? How did this happen?

"So you're killing me," I mutter in a monotone. I don't really have emotion about it. Without Skull, I already feel dead. How hard would life be to live without him? I can't do it.

"No, sunshine. I just need for your boyfriend and Colin to believe I have, then there's no more leverage against me, no weaknesses."

"I don't get it. Why not just kill me for real and eliminate these 'weaknesses' as you put it?"

He looks disappointed in me, not bothering to answer my question. Instead, he looks at me and asks the one thing I'm not ready to answer.

"Do we have a deal?"

"What about Katie? I want to see Katie."

"When it is safe, I will take you to see her."

"Safe? What does that mean?"

"I have plans for you, Elizabeth. Katie is my insurance plan. First, you need to walk the line."

With that, another piece of the Devil's mask slips. The thought of what plans he could possibly have for me scares the hell out of me. I swallow it down. One thing at a time.

"How do I know that if I agree to this you won't kill Skull

anyway?"

"Killing Skull won't accomplish anything. He's just a nuisance—inconsequential at best. It's the bigger picture I'm trying to secure, for you, for Katie, and for myself."

Call me crazy, but I don't want to know what the bigger picture is. I'm afraid of the bigger picture; it's all I can do to keep my thoughts on *this* one. I've still not decided. Skull asked me to believe in him, and I do.

I take a deep breath and prepare to turn the Devil down, telling him to go back to Hell where he belongs, when he surprises me.

"You're indecisive. I thought that would be the case. Truly, you are a lot like me, sunshine. Always weighing your options. It's very smart. Perhaps I have something that will make you decide."

A cold chill runs through me at his statement. "What's that?"

"Pistol. It's time."

I watch as Pistol walks away to a small supply closet. He reaches inside the closet and, when he turns back around, my stomach clenches, my body quakes with fear, and a cold sweat breaks out over me.

Pistol drags Katie toward me. She's changed since I saw her last, that's true. She's got the same hair as I do, the same eyes, and the same tears—because we're both crying. Her shirt is torn and smudged with dirt, her hair knotted up, her face bruised, and her pants torn.

I look back at the Devil like he's lost his mind. "How can you do this to your own daughter?" It's a stupid question. After all, what he's doing to me doesn't exactly nominate him for father of the year either.

"Someday, I will answer your questions, sunshine. For now, all I need is your answer. Yes or no?"

He reaches out his hand. I look at him, then back at my sister. Then, I do it. I strike a deal with the Devil. All I had to promise him was my soul.

CHAPTER 49
SKULL

" She's every fantasy I've had, come to life. "

"You okay, *mi cielo?*"

We're sitting in the main room of the bunker. There's music playing and the bar is open. By our standards, it's a quiet party. A few of the girls are dancing, but even Sabre and Latch have pulled it in tonight. Hard to celebrate when you've lost some good men.

Beth sits in my lap while I'm playing poker with Diesel, Sabre, and Briar. Beth tried to excuse herself and go back to our room, but I just couldn't talk myself into letting her go. I pulled her down on my lap and ignored her protests. Having her at the hospital today without me was one of the hardest things I've ever been through. I don't know how to tell her she can't do that again. She's already talking about going back in the morning. I love that she feels for my brother and wants to help Beast, but she's not responsible and I won't have her blaming herself forever.

"I'm okay. Just thinking," she says, giving me a small smile.

I wrap my arm around her and squeeze. Then, I whisper into her ear where only she can hear me. "*Mi cielo*, did I tell you how much I love that dress you're wearing?"

"It's the one I was wearing when we first met," she whispers.

I play my card on the table, then find her ear again. "It's driving me crazy. I'm dying to slide my hands up under it, rip off your panties, and fuck you right here, right now."

"I wouldn't say no."

My dick pushes so hard against the zipper of my jeans, the fucker probably has marks branded on it. Beth wiggles in my lap, letting me know our talk is getting to her too. "Makes my cock so fucking hard to feel your ass against it. Every time you move, I want to carry you into our room and fuck you so hard you can't walk tomorrow."

She drapes an arm around my neck and pulls my ear to her lips now.

"Skull. Please. I need you inside of me. I want you to fuck me so hard that I feel you inside of me for months," she whispers, a hint of desperation in her voice.

The fact that she needs me so much settles inside of me. I throw the cards on the table. "I fold," I tell them, standing up with Beth in my arms.

"Where you going, boss? We just started..." Sabre complains.

"I'm going to go fuck my woman," I growl back. Beth buries her head in my chest.

"Go get her, *ese!*" shouts Diesel as the others holler out lewd remarks.

I leave their shouting behind and walk down the hall to our room.

I'm barely in the room when I feel her teeth nibble up my neck, then her sweet little tongue following the same path. Her hands dive under my shirt as she drags her nails across my stomach.

"My woman needs her man tonight," I whisper through the moan she pulls out of me when she sucks on the small ring I have in my nipple.

"I'm dying for you. *Hurry*," she whimpers.

I slam the door with my foot before pushing her up against the wall.

"*Mi cielo*, you're driving me crazy," I mumble against her neck. "Wrap your legs around me," I order. I bite down on the tendon that runs along her neck beside the artery. Her nails dig into my sides.

"The feeling is mutual." Her greedy hands move to my belt.

"If you do that, this will be over quick," I tell her. She ignores me and, once the belt is loose, she pops the button on my jeans.

"We have all night," she tells me. "We can go slower with round two." As she tells me that, her skillful little hand finishes opening my pants, releasing my cock. She wraps her hand around it and strokes it while maintaining the tightest pressure she's ever dared with me. *Sweet Jesus.*

"What's gotten into you tonight, Beth?" I ask, even as my hands help to push my pants down.

"Are you complaining?"

"Fuck, no! Just wondering what made my *mujer* so bold. I'm thanking my lucky stars."

"Less talk, Skull. More action." She brings her tongue to my lips and curls it against my small lip ring. She sucks the ring into her mouth, playing with it just right... *so* fucking right, my balls are already tight.

"Point made," I tell her.

My hands go to her panties and I rip them. I push the ruined silk out of the way. Her body shudders as her hips thrust toward me with hunger.

"Hurry, Skull," she whispers, pushing my shirt up and latching her lips on my nipple, capturing the ring between her teeth and pulling on it, then drawing the nipple into her mouth, loving it with her tongue.

"I just... *Oh fuck...* Beth, let me make sure you're ready," I groan.

"I'm ready, I'm ready—I'm just empty," she responds, holding onto my dick again and positioning him at her pussy.

"*Fuck it!*" I growl, giving in and thrusting my cock into her without even seeing if she's ready. I didn't need to worry. She's so damn wet, I glide into her sweet pussy, her walls accepting my cock like they were made for it. They were. She's formed to fit my dick, and my dick alone. I don't stop until I'm balls-deep in her, and then I pull out. I balance her weight with my one hand and my right leg as I hold onto my cock just outside of her pussy. Our lips barely touch. Her sweet little pink tongue comes out and licks her bottom lip, teasing me. Her breathing is so ragged, her chest heaves. Her face is flushed and her hair is ruffled around it. Beautiful… and *mine*.

"I want your breast," I tell her, rubbing the head of my cock against her pussy. "Take it out, Beth. Feed it to me."

Her smoky eyes deepen in color at my command. She slides the straps of her dress over her shoulders so the top falls to her waist. She unlatches the silky white bra and pulls it from her body, never taking her eyes off of me. All the while, I just keep stroking the head of my cock over her firm little clit, up and down and then in half circles. She's so fucking wet and her body is trembling.

"Skull," she breathes.

"Feed me, *mi cielo*," I order again.

Her small hand slides under her breast, lifting it towards me. Her body leans and stretches. My mouth comes down on the nipple, sucking in as much of her breast as I can. At the same time, I slam my cock right back into her.

"Skull!" she cries out as my balls slap against her slick skin. My tongue teases her nipple. I suck so hard, it's plastered to the roof of my mouth and I can massage it with just the force of my mouth. I shift my hands so I'm holding onto her thighs. My cock sinks another inch inside of her, an inch neither of us knew I could go. The angle is different too, so I scrape against her inner wall, hitting that spot that makes her scream out my name again as her fingernails dig into my biceps. I suck her breast with more force, her nipple sliding against my tongue. I almost slide out of her pussy before pushing back in, riding her hard and showing her no mercy. Each time I sink all the way inside, I grind against her greedy little snatch.

"I'm close, baby," she gasps, but she didn't need to. I can feel the way her pussy is milking me, *needing me*. She just needs a little something to push her over the edge. I pull my mouth off her breast until the nipple is at my teeth, then bite into it, not letting go, and slide my tongue around it at the same time. I fuck her hard, giving her my cock without worrying about hurting her. I want her to feel my cock pumping her long after we're done. I want her body limp with exhaustion.

"Fuck, yes!" she hisses, and then I feel her teeth bite into my neck.

She's marking me. She's claiming me. That's what it feels like, and it's all I need to push me completely over the edge. I scream out her name and slam into her over and over, my cum rocketing inside of her with such force that her body quakes along with it. Then, I feel her whole body shake and her muscles clamp down on me as she comes apart and joins me, taking everything I can give her. When it's done, she releases my shoulder, letting her tongue slide along the imprint of her teeth.

"I love you, Skull," she whispers, tightening up on my cock again.

I move a hand to her clit and massage it slowly, gliding my cock in and out of her in a slow, steady pace.

"*Te amo, mi ceilo. Te amo,*" I whisper and continue until I push her over the edge again. This orgasm is gentle, and when she cries out, it's quiet, like a purr. Contented, a smile finds her lips.

CHAPTER 50
BETH

❝ *I will love him until my last breath.* **❞**

Skull's asleep. We're lying in bed and I've lost count of the orgasms he's given me, though I know it's at least five. I'm going to be sore tomorrow. The thought brings a smile to my lips... even while my heart feels like it's breaking.

I'm propped up on my pillow with a hand holding my head up. My leg is wrapped over Skull's body, watching him breathe and memorizing every mark of ink, every scar and curve of his body.

"How are you still awake, *querida?*"

His voice is whisper-soft and hoarse, and it sends delicious chills over my skin.

"I'm just watching you sleep."

"What on Earth for?" he asks.

I let my index finger slide down his chest, following a jagged scar.

"You're beautiful," I tell him honestly.

He turns to his side and props himself up much like I am, studying me.

"I think that last orgasm might have fried your brain. There's nothing beautiful about me, unless you count my woman," he says, his fingers trailing down my neck to my breast and kneading it before sliding his thumb over the nipple. Even sore and worn out, I can feel the answering moisture between my legs.

"Skull," I whisper, not even sure of what I want to say. He

216

must understand because he leans over and pushes me carefully on my back before taking my nipple into his mouth lovingly. My ass leaves the mattress as I strain to get closer to him.

He lets go of my breast to look at me. "Jesus, you want my cock again, *querida?*" he asks as his fingers brush through the sticky wetness of my pussy. I'm so sore there and he's taken me so hard and so much that it's almost painful. Still, the way he touches me and pets the swollen and tender area soothes me too.

"You, Skull. I just want you. I will always want you," I tell him, giving him honesty in those words that I can't with others. He positions himself over my body and looks down at me. I caress his face with a hand, my thumb brushing the contour of his nose and the fine wrinkles around his lips. He captures the tip of my thumb with his mouth, memorizing the feel and the shape, then kisses it gently.

"So sweet, so fucking sweet," he murmurs, his voice quiet.

He blows on the breast he'd sucked on. His breath causes tiny bumps of awareness to pop up across the skin, making the nipple pebble.

"Make love to me, Skull."

"Are you sure, *mi cielo?* I don't want to hurt you."

In response, I spread my legs wider, making room for him. "Please," I beg him.

He pulls his pillow underneath my hip and wedges it, then guides himself into me. I hiss from the sting, and when he tries to back out, I tighten my legs around him. "No, don't stop," I urge him. He's worried, I can tell, but he begins carefully pushing inside of me at my request. I can feel every wonderfully thick inch of him sink into me.

"Every time feels like the first," he whispers, and he's right. It does. "It just keeps getting better, *querida.* Every damn time I'm with you, it just keeps getting better and better."

"I love you, Skull," I whisper, his cock stretching me more than ever before.

"It's never close enough is it, *querida?* No matter how far I get inside your body, it's never enough."

His words break me because they echo what my heart is screaming. "It's never enough, Skull. It's never enough." My voice breaks. I can't hold the tears back—I don't even try. I let loose the slow-rolling tears, spiked with emotion.

"My sweet, tender Beth," Skull says, his thumb wiping a tear away.

"Love me, Skull," I plead. "Never let me go."

"Always, *mi cielo*," he moans. "Nothing will ever stop me."

I hold onto him as he takes my mouth, kissing me and possessing it as surely as he's possessing my body. I come just like that, surrounded and owned by him, my orgasm sweet and gentle and consuming. When he does too, I feel his heat fill me. I swear, I feel it all the way in my soul.

CHAPTER 51
BETH

" *It begins. God, please give me strength.* **"**

My palms are sticky from sweat and my heart beats out of my chest as I watch Skull talking to Beast. He's trying his best to get his brother to talk, but Beast only turns away and ignores him. I see the pain in Skull's eyes. I want to take it away. I'm mad at Beast for hurting him, but then remember that in just a few short hours I will be hurting him worse. Guilt churns in my stomach.

Skull finally gives up and moves to the window where I stand. It's a cloudy, rainy day and the drizzle of the water hits the windowpane. It matches my mood. He gathers me up in his arms and pulls me close. I can't resist touching the side of his face, wishing I could take away all his troubles.

"He'll be okay, Skull. He just needs to heal."

"I don't know, *querida*. The doctors say there's no reason he shouldn't at least be talking to us."

"Some wounds run so deep, it's hard to claw your way out. He'll talk when he's ready."

"How did you get so smart?"

I drink in his face. His eyes shine with love, his lips curving into a smile with the tiny laugh lines crinkling at the corners of his eyes. I love the way his dark hair falls in a beautiful mess that I can't resist touching. I commit all of it to memory, every bit of it.

"I met a man and fell in love."

"*Mi cielo*, you cannot be sweet now. I have to go oversee some shit so we can get this dark cloud off of us. We don't have time for me to fuck you. Besides, after last night, I think you broke my dick."

I smile despite my mood. I boldly rub my hand over his pants, finding his cock. He lied; he's semi-hard. I rub it, putting enough pressure so he can feel it through his jeans.

"He doesn't feel broke."

Skull groans, pulling my hand away.

"Enough, *mujer*. You wrung me dry last night. I don't even know how you're walking this morning."

I bite my lip as I remember the night we had. He's not wrong; every time I take a step, I feel the soreness in my stomach. There's bruises all over my body from his rough lovemaking and I relish every one of them. My body is tired and definitely well-used, but if he pulled me into the adjoining restroom right now, I'd gladly make love to him again. The thought of never again being able to get that close to him, to feel the heat of his body when he is holding me, to just be with him… is killing me.

"I can't help it. I want you again."

He kisses the back of my hand, but pulls away from me, not giving in. "I always want you, *mi cielo*, but I have to get to work. I will punish you later for torturing me."

I do my best to hide the pain that slashes through me at his words, because I know there won't be a later.

"Stay safe today, please?" I ask him.

"I will. I made Pistol and Latch promise to bring you home in an hour, *querida*. Do not argue with me. I don't even like you being here. I still don't know why I caved."

"Because you knew it would make me happy…?"

"I think it had more to do with your mouth on my cock, but your version makes me sound like a better man, so we will go with it. Promise me to keep Pistol and Latch with you, alright?"

"I promise."

"Give me your lips and let me get out of here before I weaken and give you my dick."

I kiss him, and maybe he can tell by the way I wrap my arms

around him tight and drag his lips down to mine. I'm not sure, but our kiss is more urgent, rougher, definitely more demanding than any we've shared in a long time. My tongue sweeps into his mouth, searching and finding every hidden spot that I can, dueling with his and coming out victorious. I drink in his taste, hoping I will still taste him on my tongue in the months and years to follow. Maybe I will get lucky and it won't be that long.

The truth is, I don't trust my father. There's a reason I've taken to calling him the Devil. He's pure evil. I don't know the real reason he's demanding this of me, but I figure he may kill me. If not on purpose, then he will when I grab Katie and break free, because I won't rest until my sister and I are free from that monster. I hope somehow I can get Katie from him and manage to kill him. I could die happily if I achieve that.

"*Wow!* That was a kiss, *mi cielo!* You are feeling needy today, aren't you?"

"I am always needy around you, Skull. You better get going before you're late," I tell him regretfully. I just caught a glance at the clock on the wall. I have twenty minutes to get down to my father. I don't want to risk being late; I don't know how he'll lash out at me.

"*Sí*," he says, kissing my forehead. "Pistol, Latch… you two, do not let her out of your sight. Keep her safe."

"Will do," Pistol says, and I wish I could kick him in the balls and stomp on him. I need to find a way to warn Skull further about Pistol. I just don't know how without risking my sister's life… or Skull's.

Skull leaves, and we are all sitting around Beast's bed. Pistol gives me the signal with his hand. I take a breath. Time to get started, I guess.

"Would one of you mind taking me to the cafeteria? I'm starved. I was running late this morning and didn't get any breakfast."

"I can—"

"Nah," interrupts Pistol. "Latch, you stay here with Beast. I need to stretch my legs, anyways. I had to ride a freaking cage over here."

"Only if you're sure," says Latch.

I try to smile reassuringly when he looks at me. "I'll be fine. I'll be back soon," I tell him, and that's just the first of many lies I'll be telling today.

CHAPTER 52
BETH

" Each step is harder than the one before. "

I hear the echo of footsteps. They seem abnormally loud, like what a man on death row might hear as he makes that final walk to his execution. I feel like that, like each step I take brings me closer to the end. I allow a few tears as I picture Skull's face when we said goodbye. I rub my hands down the sides of my pants, trying to calm the emotions inside of me. I need to be cold when I talk to my father. I can't let him see how much I'm hurting. Something tells me that will only bring him pleasure.

"You might as well dry it up. It must be really hard being filthy rich and having your father cart you off to the South of France to protect you."

South of France? I have a feeling Pistol wasn't supposed to let that escape. I can't imagine why my father would do that. That's where the Donahue family have a lot of holdings. I know if I wasn't so emotional, I might be able to piece it together better.

"Skull will kill you someday," I promise him quietly.

"He'll be destroyed when he loses you," Pistol responds. "He won't notice what's going on right under his nose."

"He might not. But his brothers will, and when you're found out, he'll kill you."

"Don't worry about it, doll face... You won't be around to see it."

"Maybe not, but I'll take comfort in knowing that it *will* happen, and Skull will spit on you when it's done."

Pistol slaps me hard across my face. His ring catches my lip and tears it open. The coppery taste of blood drips on my tongue. I would respond, but my father picks that moment to walk out of the room and meet us. I glare at him, not bothering to contain my hate.

"What happened?" my father asks right away, and the spark of anger in his eyes surprises me.

"Just a little love tap from your henchman," I answer sarcastically.

He turns to Pistol. "You hit her?"

"She was mouthing off," he says with a shrug.

That's when I see a side to my father I should have known was there, but somehow didn't.

"I told you she wasn't to be harmed."

"She's in one piece. I just decided to teach her that women should be *seen* and not—"

I scream. I can't help it. Before Pistol can finish that sentence, my father shoots him in the stomach. Pistol drops to the floor moaning and clutching his belly.

"W-We had a deal—" he moans.

"That didn't include you touching my daughter. Besides, you had to know your men would suspect you if you weren't injured. This way, you have the perfect cover... *if you live.*"

"Damn you!" Pistol gasps, his breathing turning hard.

"You should save your breath, unless you use it to pray that Devil's Blaze cares more about you than you obviously do them," my father says, then turns to me. "Elizabeth, hand me your locket."

My hand goes to it, grasping it tightly with refusal on my lips. My father shoots Pistol in his foot. I jump in response.

"Do it, or I'll just keep shooting, and then we'll move onto those men upstairs in room two hundred and three that you actually care about." I surrender the locket to him, doing my best not to cry. He puts it in Pistol's hands, then calmly looks back at me. "Come along, sunshine. We need to get out of here before people start looking for you."

He grabs my arm and doesn't give me a choice. He leads us away and into the room he came from. I look over my shoulder at Pistol before my father jerks me away, demanding my attention.

He walks me quickly through the back room, which appears to be a storage room for the hospital, then through a metal door which leads to the outside. I briefly consider running away, but the tight, bruising grip my father has on me doesn't give me the chance.

A limo waits for us at the corner. A man in a nondescript suit stands with the door open. My father pushes me in without a word. I stumble inside, managing to keep from face-planting into the seat. Just as I sit upright, my father joins me.

"Where's my sister? I want to see Katie!"

"Don't worry," he says. "I'll make sure you get to see her soon."

"Where are we going?" I ask, staring straight ahead at the privacy screen and thinking I've made the wrong decision. That phrase just keeps going over and over in my brain: *I've made the wrong decision... I've made the wrong decision...*

"To my yacht," he says, and I hear the tinge of pride in his voice.

"We can't! Skull—never mind."

My father laughs. It's a warm laugh, one I remember as a child. The same laugh he used when my sister Katie climbed up on the table for our fourth birthday. She saw the birthday cake and wouldn't stop until she got up on the big fancy dining room table that was my mother's pride and joy. The trouble was, she had on her muck boots that we had to wear to go to the barn. My mother freaked out and came running, screaming at Katie. It scared Katie. She scrambled to get away from mom and, in the process, dumped the cake all over my mother's dress. Dad laughed for ten minutes, infuriating my mother so much that she left for two days.

I had forgotten those memories. How? My father had doted

on both of us during that time. It had been good. We were happy, but now...

"Don't worry, sunshine. I already know your boyfriend is striking today and destroying my yacht. I told you before, I know it all. You don't have to fear spilling the beans. Interesting, though. You would be willing to kill me and yourself to guard his secrets? Such loyalty. I definitely kept the wrong daughter."

"If you know Skull is destroying it, why would you be heading straight there?" I ask, confused and hating the man in front of me at the same time.

"That is the question, isn't it? A question that will become all too clear, soon. For now, I suggest you lie back and rest. We have an exciting day in front of us."

I turn away from him, staring out the window.

CHAPTER 53
SKULL

" I cant lose her. "

We've got two hours until the charges are triggered. Two fucking hours, and Beth isn't back yet.

I ordered her and my men to be back early. Fucking hell, I don't need this added stress. Pistol, the fucker... He isn't answering his phone, and no one can seem to find Latch either. If they're alive when I find them, I'm going to kill them.

I climb off my bike, Briar and Sabre behind me. Shaft, a new recruit, stays behind to watch over the bikes and be on lookout. I push through the doors intent on finding my woman. When I feel my cellphone vibrate in my pocket, a small amount of panic leaves me. Finally, the fuckers are checking in. I'm going to take off their heads and turn Beth's ass red for worrying me. I look at the caller ID and notice it's Beast's room.

"Where the fuck have you been? I thought I told you to come home early?"

I expect to hear Beth's voice. When I don't, my stomach clenches and my heart lodges in my throat, fear choking me.

"Boss."

The voice is strained and hard to hear. It's gruffer and different from the way it used to be, but I instantly recognize it.

"Beast? Where the fuck's Beth? Or my men? Son of a bitch, are you okay?"

"Boss... A-Attack..."

"Motherfucker!" I growl, taking off running, ignoring the elevators and bolting up the stairs. I hear my brothers running

227

behind me, their steps echoing. I've got my gun drawn and I burst into Beast's room, unsure of what I'll find. Beast is lying on the bed, shaking as he tries to pull himself up. Latch lies on the floor, bleeding.

Pistol and Beth are nowhere to be seen.

"Where's Beth?" I ask Beast while Sabre checks on Latch.

"Caff... Caff-a... ear..." he struggles to say, and despite the broken words, I know what he's trying to say. Without waiting for him to finish, I take off running.

I glance over my shoulder. Torch and Briar are there, following. "Get a hold of Cade's men!" I order them, yelling. "Find out where the fuck they are! How in the fuck did this happen if they're watching the exits??"

I fucking expect someone to find me an answer. My gut tells me Cade's men and Pistol are behind this. That might seem unfair, but I'm kicking my fucking ass for letting my guard down with that motherfucker. I respected Cade though... *Fuck*. I hope my stupidity doesn't cost Beth her life. If something happens to her...

Fear threatens to overtake me, but I buckle that shit down; I don't have time for it. I slam open the doors to the cafeteria. People look up, startled by my sudden entrance. The place is pretty much deserted. Someone screams, which is understandable as I still have my fucking gun drawn. I ignore them, marching into the kitchen. There's a few people in there, but not one sign of Pistol or Beth. I go to the bathrooms, hoping to find them there.

"Boss! Down here!" I hear Torch yell.

I follow the sound of his voice. Through a small hall, there's a supply room to the right with its door left open. Torch leans over an unconscious Pistol at the doorway. Pistol has a bad-looking wound in his gut.

"Beth?" I ask him, and for a man who didn't used to feel fear, that shit is nearly strangling me now.

"No sign of her, boss, but—"

"But…?"

He holds up Beth's locket, covered in blood.

I tear it out of his grip. My hands are shaking as I pull it over my head, screaming with a mixture of fear and anger. Spotting the door through the supply room that leads to the outside, I move behind Torch and shove it open, desperate to drag air into my lungs. Off to the side of the door is one of Cade's men with a hole in his head. I look around hopelessly for Beth, but I know in my heart that I won't see her.

I'm too late. The motherfuckers have her.

"Boss? Six of Cade's men have been brought down. The others were watching the front exits. That means they came this way. Torch went to the security room to check the camera footage. We'll find her, boss. Torch will know something any minute now."

I can hear Briar in my ear, but it doesn't matter. Nothing matters right now. All that matters is the one fact I can't get away from.

I'm too fucking late.

CHAPTER 54
SKULL

I've buckled emotion down. I had to. I couldn't function, and that wouldn't get my woman back. Colin wants her. I know what he *wants*. I refuse to believe I can't get her back before that happens. I will get her, and then I will chop Colin up into fucking pieces and feed him to my dogs. The only thing I can do until Torch comes up with a lead as to where they took Beth is move full steam ahead.

"Is everything in place?"

"Yeah, boss. When do you want us to start letting off the discharges?"

"Thirty minutes. I want Diesel here."

"I can't figure it out. I thought the fuckers would up their security after our first round of attacks. This seems almost too easy," I grumble, raking my hand down the side of my face, losing my fingers in the stubble. I look like fucking hell. Losing your heart does that to a man. I have to get her back... *I have to.*

"I think the fuckers are just underestimating your fire power, *ese,*" Diesel says, strolling in like he owns the fucking world.

"Or maybe they realize what a fucking fool I was to concentrate on attacking them and not protecting my woman."

"No word?" Diesel says, kicking a chair out and straddling the back of it between his legs, propping his hands on the top of it.

"She was pushed into a limo right outside the hospital," I tell him. "It wasn't Colin with her. Fucker knew where the cameras

230

were, so his face was hidden. I have no idea who he is."

"Redmond?"

"I don't know."

I'm fishing in the fucking dark here and that's what drives me crazy. With Colin, I know what to worry about. If this is Redmond, then why is he making himself known now? What the fuck does he want with Beth? Is she going to be a pawn in a fucking play for power? The pencil I'm holding in my hand snaps. I throw the pieces at the table in frustration. I hate this fucking song and dance shit. Why can't the motherfucker just be a man and face me head on?

"How's Pistol and Latch?" asks Diesel.

"Pistol just got out of surgery," I tell him. "They say the fucker should be okay. Latch is fine, already trying to bang a nurse. Are we ready for fireworks?" I ask Torch. I'm fucking tired and need to concentrate on Beth.

"Yeah, boss. We upped the firepower. Because of the long range this time, I'll type the coordinates and codes into the computer and there will be about a one minute delay before the charges ignite."

"Let's hit Colin's pretties first. I'm in the mood to fuck up his playthings," I tell him while looking at the screen, which shows Colin's private garage that has over fifty cars housed in it. They range from the rarest of classic vehicles to state-of-the-art. These beauties are solely Colin's, especially the 1950's Ariel 650 Cyclone in the corner.

"Got it. Command code sent, boss," Torch says.

We sit back and watch. True to his word, in about a minute we watch as the explosion starts. We only get to see inside for one blast. Fire erupts and I get the joy of seeing the motorcycle destroyed before the building is toast, along with the camera. Torch switches to another view. This time, it's a camera across the street, and we watch as the building burns to the ground. Fire trucks come charging in, but they can't help save and contain what is already gone.

"Next, boss?"

"Take out his planes."

One by one we go down the line of precious things we're destroying until we arrive at the yacht that Colin and Matthew keep off the coast of Tybee Island. I smile because I know this one will hurt the most. This one, they use constantly. Word has it that Colin even lived on the yacht for a year. It's his favorite, though, if the intel Torch was getting holds true, Redmond is the one who controls the purse strings and is the actual owner. Doesn't matter; I'm taking all of them down. Colin, Matthew, Redmond... I don't fucking care. No one messes with my woman.

"Let's get this done. I have a woman to find."

"Got it, boss. Punching the last of the codes in now," Torch answers. I hear the beeps and the rattle of his keyboard.

"What the fuck?" I yell, jumping out of my seat to go to the monitor. "Jesus fucking Christ! Stop it, Torch! Stop the blast! Abort it!" I yell, standing in front of the screen. My heart pounds a million times a minute and my body feels like it's on fucking fire. There on the screen is my sweet Beth. I know it's her. She's wearing the same beautiful pink dress she had on this morning, and her hair is pulled back and clipped high on her head so the rest swings down. She's being held by two men and her hands are tied behind her back. They're all but dragging her up the wooden dock to the ship.

"*Torch!*" I scream. "Stop the motherfucking bombs!"

"Goddamn it, boss, I'm trying!"

"Jesus!" one of the men behind me exclaims. "Holy Mother of God!" shouts another. "Stop it, Torch!!" I scream myself, hearing the others, but they don't matter—nothing matters except stopping this bomb.

"I'm trying, boss! I'm trying!"

The screen blinks out once and my breath freezes in my fucking body because I know that's it. Then, it comes back on. She's at the top of the yacht now.

I'm fucking losing it.

"No. No. No. *No! Motherfucker!* Stall them, Beth!" I scream at the monitor. "*Torch!*"

"Boss, there's some kind of interference. I... I can't get the codes to go in. I'm almost there, just one more sec and—"

That's all he gets out before the middle of the ship explodes. A split second later, another charge goes off right in front of Beth. The explosion is gigantic, the biggest one yet, because I wanted this motherfucker in so many pieces that parts of him could be found in every ocean.

I drop to my knees, screaming as I watch the flames erupt all over the one woman I love more than anything in the world, devouring her. I cry out in agony, my arms wrapped tight over my head and pulling it down, trying to block what I just saw. It can't be true. *It can't.*

"Oh my God, I killed her. I killed my Beth. *No!*" I scream as loud and as long as I can, trying to make the Heavens hear me so they can fix this. "Oh, God, please don't let this be real... Oh, God! Baby... *mi cielo...* What have I done? W-What have I done??" I just keep repeating the words as the sobs rack my body. "What have I *done?*"

CHAPTER 55
SKULL

❝ *I feel her around me,*
but inside . . . I am empty. **❞**

Three Days Later

I sit on the pier, the same spot I've been sitting every day since I destroyed my world. Bottle in hand, I watch the water and try to decide if I shouldn't just jump in and join Beth. I feel so cold... so motherfucking cold that I could swear I'm dying, piece by fucking piece. Beth brought out the man I had forgotten I was, the man mi madre raised. She held the darkness, the beast down inside, at bay. Strangely enough, her death has silenced him. He's just another part of me that's rotted away.

I raise the bottle to my mouth to take another drink and find it's empty. I toss it into the water, then bring a hand to Beth's locket. I've cleaned it, but since then, I haven't taken it off. I never will. It's a reminder of what I had... *and destroyed.*

The area where the yacht was has been taped off with yellow and black caution tape that reads "Do Not Cross". It didn't stop me. I went through every inch of the remains, whatever was left. The rest had either disintegrated during the explosion or sank down to the bottom of the ocean. No bodies were found. The coroner said they may never find them. I wanted to believe that meant Beth was still alive, but that would be impossible. I saw the explosion. I saw the way it rocked her body and how the flames... ignited and swallowed her. I still see it. Every time I close my fucking eyes, I see it. It haunts me.

"Boss?"

"I'm nobody's boss," I tell Torch, not bothering to turn around and acknowledge him.

"The club needs you. There's... things we need to figure out."

"There's nothing to figure out anymore, Torch. Nothing matters. The only thing that ever mattered is gone and there's no one to blame but me."

"That's not true, boss. There's a person to blame. Redmond."

The name alone makes hate coil up inside of me, but I don't hate that bastard half as much as I hate myself. Colin either, for that matter. They weren't the ones who acted so carelessly with Beth's life. They weren't the ones who not only failed to protect her, but... killed her.

I killed her.

"Boss, something has happened," Torch tries again. He's ruining the numbness the alcohol has helpfully lent. I need to be numb right now. I need to be alone.

"I told you, I'm not your motherfucking boss. I'm done. Ask Pistol. He wanted the fucking job, he can have it." Shit, I should have given it to him sooner. I should have just grabbed Beth and left. I should have put her first above everything else. I was so fucking cocky, playing the big shot, bringing my club into a war, putting everyone's lives on the line...

I look down at my hands. They look the same; normal, even. But I know they're not. I may not be able to physically see it, but my hands are stained with so much blood that they will never be clean again. My club members, Cade's men, Diesel's men, Annabelle, and now my Beth... Everyone but the fucking people I was after. *I was a fucking fool.*

"Boss, Colin wants to meet."

"Colin can go fuck himself," I tell him, squinting against the sun that picks right *now* to glare off of the water.

"Boss, he wants our help."

"Will you just go the fuck away? Don't you get it? I don't give a fuck about the club anymore. I don't give a fuck about

Colin! I just don't give a fuck. I want to lie here on this damn pier and pass out. Then, when I wake up, I plan on drinking another bottle." *Rinse and repeat.*

"That's not what Beth would want from you. That's not what she deserves from you."

I hate him. I fucking hate him. His words dive through the alcohol haze and tear into the wounds inside that are still bleeding, the wounds that will never heal. Fueled by anger, I pull myself up with ease, which is surprising considering how drunk-off-my-ass I am. Remaining standing isn't quite as easy, but I grab both of Torch's shoulders to aid me. My hands bite into him cruelly as I force him to take my weight. He goes back a couple of steps, but manages to keep his balance.

"Beth isn't here!" I shout. "Beth's dead and *I killed her!* She deserved to never know me! I destroyed her! Don't tell me what she would want. *Don't tell me what I should do!* I *know* what she deserved... I know! Every fucking breath I take..."

"Boss, listen to me..."

"I killed her, Torch. I killed her. She was everything good in the world. She was my world and I was careless. *I was so fucking careless.*"

The tears fall then. You would think the rivers I've cried would have stopped them. I should be cried out, but I'm not. I never will be.

I pull away from Torch and let gravity have its way. Collapsing, my head slams back into the light post I had been leaning against. It throbs. I register the pain, but it doesn't matter. I'm lost to the misery, to the tears that are being torn from my very soul. My body quakes as I lose myself inside the hurt.

"I killed her... I killed her..." I just keep repeating it. When I wake up, I'm screaming it every fucking time, as if saying it will somehow make it untrue.

Torch leans down to pull on my collar and look at me. His face is blurry from the tears, but even I can see the pain and disappointment in his eyes. I turn away, jerking myself free. He doesn't understand. How could he? *How could anyone?*

"Skull, Colin wants our help to kill Redmond. If we can get rid of that fucker, then we can at least get revenge for Beth. Don't you want to have that, at least?"

My churning stomach, which hasn't had anything in it for days but alcohol, revolts. I cramp hard in my gut, so hard that I yell out with the pain. "I killed her," I whisper before I heave up bitter liquid that can't consist of anything other than alcohol and stomach acid.

"Jesus Christ, *ese*, you need to wake the fuck up here. Beth is gone, but you still have a purpose. You need to make those motherfuckers hurt. Honor your woman's memory. She sure as hell would be sorry she gave herself to a sorry fuck who can do nothing but wallow in his own vomit," Diesel says, kicking me.

I roll onto my back and stare at him. I wipe the tears out of my eyes, which doesn't do much good because more just take their place.

"Load him up, boys," I hear Torch say. "We're dragging his ass home and sobering him up whether he wants it or not." The blackness closes in. I try to fight it because therein lies the dreams and I'm not drunk enough yet to handle them, but I lose the battle.

CHAPTER 56
SKULL

> **When you hit rock bottom,**
> **you apparently join the scum.**

Beth stands in front of me. She fucking stands in front of me, taking my breath away.

"Beth, sweetheart? You're here? How... How is that possible? How are you here?" I want to approach her, but I cannot. I'm frozen in place, afraid to scare her off. She's wearing a white dress, much like the one she was wearing when I first met her. Her blonde hair is brushed until it shines and those gray eyes are beaming at me.

"I'm here, Skull. I had to see you."

"How is this possible?" I ask again. She doesn't answer, but that's okay. She walks over to me and wraps her arms around my body. I can't believe how good she feels, how right she feels in my arms.

"*Mi cielo.* I love you. Oh, God, baby, I never thought I'd see you again." I kiss the side of her face, wrapping my hands in her beautiful hair. For the first time in days, my heart feels as if it's beating again.

"I loved you, Skull. I did. Why did you do this?"

"What? No, *querida.* I didn't mean it. I tried to stop it. I did. I would never hurt you. How did you survive? Did the blast throw you into the water? I searched all day trying to find you. I could only find pieces of your clothes. What happened?"

"But you did hurt me," she says, pulling away from me suddenly. "You murdered me, Skull. Why? I loved you so much."

238

The white of her dress slowly has deep crimson red leaking from it.

"What? No, I didn't. What's happening? Beth? Sweetheart!" I look up into her eyes, only to find her face covered in blood.

"Why did you kill me, Skull? Why? I loved you!" she cries, backing away from me.

"No! Beth! Don't leave me! I can fix this! Don't go!"

"I loved you, Skull."

"Beth!" I scream.

"Boss? Wake up man! Wake up!"

My body jerks. When I open my eyes and sit up in the bed, I'm still screaming her name. Torch stands over me appearing worried, but for a minute it's not his face I see at all. It's Beth's.

I reach over, grab the opened bottle of scotch on my bedside table, then take a large gulp and hope the alcohol burns out my insides.

"What are you doing here?" I wipe my mouth with the back of my hand. "Fuck, what am *I* doing here?" I ask when I realize where I'm at.

"Little early for alcohol, boss."

"Fuck you. I asked why I'm here." I try to get my legs to cooperate. I want to go back to the dock, back to the last place my Beth was. That's where I need to be. I can't leave there. "*She might show up*," I whisper without realizing I'm saying that out loud.

"She's not going to show up, boss. No one could survive that blast."

I ignore him, he doesn't understand. He couldn't.

"*Ese*, Matthew wants to meet today. You need to get your ass out of this bed, shower, and get your ass in gear."

"What the fuck are you doing here?" I retort. "Shouldn't you be back in Tennessee?"

"I'm here to kick your ass in gear. We're going to meet with Matthew and see what the fucker has to say, and you're going if I have to kick your ass all the way."

"What the fuck for?"

"He and Colin want to bring Redmond down, and you're going to help the motherfuckers."

"Why the hell would I meet with them? Fuck them, and fuck you too. Get out and leave me alone."

Diesel pulls me off the bed, letting me fall to the floor.

"I never pictured you as a chump, *ese.* I thought you were made with more metal than that."

"Fuck you! You don't know shit."

"I know your Beth deserves vengeance, not a sad-ass fucker who smells like shit."

"How the fuck do I get vengeance? I'm the bastard who killed her!"

"You start by dragging your ass into the shower. Then, you gather up your sorry balls and go to the fucking meeting and work on ending that son of a bitch Redmond."

I stare from the floor up at Diesel. I'm about to tell him to go fuck himself yet again when he says something that stops me. He kneels down to get a closer look at me.

"Your woman died," he says. "I get that, motherfucker. But you have a chance to kill the man who kidnapped your woman, who is responsible for Beast losing his daughter... You have a chance to take his fucking blood. Your woman deserves that. *Beast* fucking deserves that."

I close my eyes. Diesel doesn't understand. The one person who needs to die for Beth... is *me.*

CHAPTER 57
SKULL

❚❚ The enemy of my enemy
is still my fucking enemy. ❚❚

"Where's Colin?" I ask Matthew. I'm at the fucking meeting just like Diesel wanted. This is the most sober I've been in days, and it's not a fucking joyride.

"He's not your concern," answers Matthew. "Let us just say, I had to make sure he understood some things. I go out of town for a month and come back to chaos and my sister dead, and that is just the beginning of the fucking shit storm that welcomed me back. It's time I get my house in order, and you can either be a part of that, or I'll look elsewhere."

"Why come to me?" I ask the question that's been bothering me since I sobered up.

"Because I figure the only person hating Redmond more than my brother or me right now... is you. If I'm wrong, then—"

"No," I say at once. "I want in. I'm just wondering what you could possibly want us for, since you obviously have your own resources."

"True, but word has it, Redmond's in France. While I'm chasing him down, I can't be worried about everything going to hell here."

"I'm not a damn babysitter for your brother Colin, and it isn't why I agreed to this meeting." I push away from the table. "I'm out of here."

"Redmond will be back in two weeks for a family meeting that Colin and I called. He thinks it's to welcome him back as ruler of the family."

CAPTURED

"And it's not?"

"It is, but it will also be Redmond's death."

"What do you want from me?"

"Extra firepower."

"What do I get in return?"

"When the time comes, I'll let you put a bullet in him."

"Why would I wait for you? Now that I know where he'll be, I'll just do it myself."

"Because I think, if anything, Beth's death has shown us that we will achieve more working together."

"You'll forgive me if I don't want to work with you. Let's get out of here, boys."

"You're making a mistake," Matthew says.

"It's mine to make. Load up, boys," I tell my crew, turning to leave.

"Okay, fine." Matthew sighs, giving in. "Redmond has complete power and family support. The only shot we have of taking control back is if we kill him. I need your help to accomplish that because, without my grandfather's approval, I have very limited resources."

"It must suck having to get approval for taking a shit," I prod him. Matthew's eyes flash and I know I've scored a direct hit.

"I'll do this without you," Matthew growls.

I go back to the table and lean down in front of him. I want eye contact. I want to see his reactions to what I'm about to say.

"You know what I think, Mattie-boy? I don't think you can. I think Colin got you into some hot water trying to overthrow Redmond, and now Granddaddy has frozen your assets, which means you can't afford a bottle of beer, let alone hire someone to help you take down your Uncle. In fact, I have to think this meeting isn't something you arranged. I think it's something Redmond called and has more to do with punishing you and Colin for your failed attempt at taking control." Matthew doesn't say anything, but I see the truth in his bitter eyes. "I think that's also the only reason Redmond would let his guard down enough to walk into your house on these terms. He thinks he's coming back to claim his home." Matthew avoids my eyes, which pretty much confirms what I've said. I was mostly guessing, but what little intel Torch had been able to gather before our meeting made the guessing easier.

"I thought you would be more reasonable, considering I was helping you to make Redmond pay. Apparently, I overestimated you," Matthew says, moving away from the table.

"Tell you what. I'm going to agree to this plan of yours. I'll help you take Redmond down, but I want it written in the pig's blood that you and your fucking brother won't bother my crew anymore. You don't even breathe in our territory."

"I can agree to that."

"So, we have a deal? I kill your Uncle, and you get control of the family again. In return, you leave me and my crew alone, forever."

"I'll get you the details of the meeting this week."

"Tell me, Matthew, what would your grandfather do if he knew you were plotting to kill his only remaining son?" Matthew pales, and that's the point I want to get across. "Fuck me over, Matthew, and he'll know everything. Everything, because this meeting... I have it on tape."

I pull open my cut, revealing a mic taped down and leading to the recording system.

"Let's roll boys," I say. "I'll give you a week to get me the info, Matthew. Don't make me wait," I warn him, then leave.

Diesel was right. I do owe Beast this. Not Beth, because I'm the fucker that hurt Beth. I can't fix that, but I can avenge my brother's daughter, and I will. It's the only thing keeping me moving right now.

CHAPTER 58
SKULL

Three Weeks Later

Three weeks, and every day is darker than the last. My light is gone. Warmth is gone. Beth is gone. Somewhere in the back of my mind, I've held out the hope that she somehow survived. It happens in the movies, right? She was thrown from the blast, hit her head and can't remember who she is, right? I'll have to convince her I'm her husband, make her remember and fall in love with me again. I can handle that.

This isn't the movies, though. All I have are memories, loneliness, and pain... so much pain, it hurts to breathe. I think I'm starting to understand what Beast is going through. Since Beth's attack, he's said very little, but at least he's acknowledging us. He and I are alike. He's blaming himself for the death of his daughter. If he hadn't left his keys there, hadn't fallen asleep, hadn't gotten drunk... Oh yeah, I fucking understand him because I play that fucking what-if game a million times a day with myself. I always lose, too.

"Everything's ready, boss," Torch says into the earpiece I wear.

I'm sitting at the conference table at Colin Donahue's mansion. To my right sits Matthew. Beside him, Colin, who has obviously been beat all to hell. His eye is black, his face swollen, and his nose has obviously been broken. He wears a cast on his arm as well as a back brace. I'm not sure Matthew's the one who delivered the punches, but I'm fairly certain he had it done. Surprisingly, I find myself respecting him a little, at least as much as I can possibly respect a Donahue. There are four others in the room. Sabre and Latch are standing behind me as my protection, and Matthew has two men with him.

"Redmond just pulled up. He has six men with him. Two stayed with the car, and that sends four up your way. Briar's showing them in, now."

"Showtime," I tell everyone out loud, mostly to notify my men. I could give less than a fuck about the others. I had Briar dress as the Donahue butler. Of all of us, he's the one with the least noticeable tattoos and piercings. I knew they would never buy me, but then again, I figured Redmond has had me investigated pretty damn thoroughly.

Sabre goes to stand behind the door and waits. It takes a few minutes, but Briar opens the door for them. I got a file on Redmond a couple of weeks ago. The bastard's picture was imprinted on my brain, but even so, when he walks through the door and looks at me, I'm still shocked. I don't know why. Maybe it's just too fucking easy, too anticlimactic. Or maybe I thought it would feel better to end him. I don't know.

His men start to back out of the door, but Briar's there to stop them, and this time, he has an AR-15 to do his talking for him.

"I got to say, I didn't see this one coming," says Redmond, staring straight at me. I don't bother answering. He looks at Matthew and Colin. "Well played, nephews. You apparently had more brains than I gave you credit for."

"We learned from our father," responds Matthew. "You know the man who defeated you before?"

"This family reunion is sweet and all, but I have better shit to do," I interrupt them. I put myself in front of Redmond. The cocky bastard doesn't even flinch. He stares right back at me. Matthew's men subdue the two men flanking Redmond, and still the bastard seems unruffled.

"You're the last person I expected to work with my

nephews," Redmond says, and he's smiling. I don't know what the fucker thinks he has to smile about. Shit, maybe he's fucking nuts. "Politics makes strange bedfellows, I suppose."

"Under no circumstances am I or would I ever get in bed with you sad fucks. This is about vengeance, plain and simple."

"I can almost see what my daughter saw in you."

My heart trips and it takes all I have not to react.

"Your daughter?"

"Didn't know that small tidbit, did you? Oh, the things I know that you don't. Your head would spin."

He's baiting me, I know it, but I can't resist asking again. "Beth... was your daughter?"

"Yes. I was trying to get her to come home. She, of course, didn't want to leave. It took some convincing. I told her you would hurt her, but I never knew just how much. Tell me, how does it feel to know you're responsible for killing the one person in this world who didn't realize what a waste of air you really are?"

My hand trembles, but I ignore it. He scored his point, but I'm fucking tired of it.

"Now, Sabre."

Sabre fires the rounds into Redmond's men after they are turned loose. Redmond does jump then, but the fucker still faces me head-on.

"This isn't about Beth," I say, my voice deadly cold. "I've already lost her, though if I'm to blame for that, you are too, aren't you, Redmond?"

He shrugs. "You'd be surprised the lengths a father would go to."

"I'm sure. Trouble is, I don't give a fuck to listen to your voice anymore. Latch? You got your phone?"

"Yeah, boss. Right here."

"Tape it."

He aims his phone at Redmond. The man looks confused for a minute.

"You see, Redmond, all this time I thought Colin had ordered one of my men's vehicles rigged. Imagine my surprise when Matthew told me the orders hadn't come from either of them."

Redmond glances at his nephews. I expect him to deny it. Honestly, I'm hoping he will. I'd like to kill all of them and be done with it. I really thought Matthew lied to me and Colin was the one that gave that order.

"All's fair in war," mutters Redmond, shrugging again.

"Your actions caused my brother to lose his daughter."

"Your actions caused the same for me. I'd say that makes us even."

Bastard. "There's only one problem with that. I'm not interested in being 'even'. I have something else I'd like more."

"What's that?"

"I want to be completely rid of all of you. Matthew and Colin here assure me that, with you dead, this is done and I will get just that."

"I could assure you the same. Besides, what's to stop them from going back on their word? Obviously they can't be trusted, or I would not be in the position I am."

"Nothing... except this tape, and a recording I have of them making the deal. They really want to be rid of you. Right, boys?"

"Absolutely," says Colin while Matthew just nods. That's enough confirmation for me; Sabre getting them on video is just one more thing I have for security.

"Ah, I get it. It wouldn't do for my father to see what his nephews did to his only remaining son, right? I'm impressed, boys. I did the same thing when I killed your father."

"You son of a bitch!" Matthew growls.

"Oh relax, you would have eventually done the same thing."

"Fuck this," I say. "I got better shit to do and I'm tired of breathing the same air as you."

"What would Beth think about you ending her father's life?" asks Redmond. "I could tell you something that'd make you think twice about your deal..."

I don't let him finish. I've had enough of games. I shoot Redmond's gut three times in quick succession. He drops to the floor.

I spit on him. "That's for Annabelle and for the hell you put Beth through. This last one is just because I think you smell," I tell him.

Then, I empty my gun into his chest.

I turn to Latch. "You get it?" The deal was for Beast and Latch to tape it while making sure I wasn't in the footage. That way, this couldn't be linked back to me, should something happen. Beast needed to see that revenge was achieved for his daughter.

"Got it, boss."

"Let's get the fuck out of here." I turn to Colin and Matthew. "I'm heading to Kentucky to start over. The crew that takes over here and mine, wherever we end up, are clear from you. Your shit does not enter into my territory, ever. If it does, your grandfather will know just what happened to his son."

"We're clear," answers Matthew. "Redmond's body will be loaded onto his private jet, which will crash into the Appalachian Mountains after having engine trouble. No one will know what took place here today."

I walk off. I really can't handle being in the same room with them anymore. *I'm done.*

CHAPTER 59
SKULL

❚❚ Saying goodbye is impossible. ❚❚

Two Weeks Later

"Beth, *mi cielo*. I don't want to leave you, but I can't stay here. You're everywhere. You're in my bed, in my club... my dreams. Hell baby, I even feel you on my bike. I can't breathe here. It's too much. I want to join you. I feel like I'm dead already. I've thought about it, but something stops me each time. Hell if I know, *querida*. Something inside me says you don't want that from me, so I'm going on. I know you wouldn't want me to blame myself for your death, but I do. The guilt chokes me. Fuck. It's because of me that all I could do was put another empty tombstone beside your sister's. I'm sorry for that the most, *querida*. God, there's so much I'm sorry for." I sigh, looking over top of the tombstone. "I don't want to be here. I couldn't leave without saying goodbye. I just couldn't."

I release a large breath, rub my hands together, then start again.

"I killed your father. I made a pact with Colin and Matthew. God, *mi cielo*, I hated doing that. I still feel like I let you down, but I'm fucking tired. There's been so much blood... *your blood*. It had to end. Without you, none of it matters anymore. None of it. Part of me wonders how you'd feel knowing I took your dad's life. Did you even know Redmond was your dad? Were you keeping secrets from me? I can't keep going like this. So... I'm leaving." My hand goes to her locket, still hanging around my neck. I hold it and close my eyes. It's almost as if I can feel her with me, like I can smell her. Jesus, I'm going insane. "I'll always love you, *mi cielo. Always.*" With that, I rise, placing the daisies I brought on top of the tombstone, then walk away. I know I'll see her tonight in my dreams.

I'll never let her go. *I can't.*

EPILOGUE
BETH

" Dreams die hard. "

Almost Eight Months Later

"I can't believe we're standing outside the theater like a couple of thieves casing the joint. You said he loves you? You... love him, or you wouldn't be carting your pregnant ass all this way. Why can't you just go up to him?" Katie asks.

She doesn't understand. I wish it was that simple.

"It's been almost nine months, Katie. What if he's moved on? He thought I was dead! I can't just walk up to him and say, 'Oh, hi. I'm not dead. Here I am and, by the way, I'm having your baby.'"

"Why not? It's the truth."

"You're really starting to annoy me."

"It's a gift," she says, and I regret saying it instantly.

"There they are," I whisper, my voice trembling.

I turn to watch as Skull's crew comes out of the theater. There's Sabre and Latch, Torch, and quite a few new guys I've never seen before.

"Oh, he's pretty," says my sister. "I wouldn't kick him out of my bed. Well, at least not until I was done with him." I can tell she's looking at Torch. She's probably not even kidding. My sister is nothing like me. I envy her sometimes.

"That's Torch. He's kind of a player," I warn her.

"He could play me like a deck of cards. Slam me down, flip me over and deal me all fucking night," she says. I can see her licking her lips.

The first one to really catch my eye is this huge man with a thick beard and so much hair that it's hard to tell if there's a face under it. "Beast. Oh, God... He's okay."

"*Beast?* Well, that's a good name for him, that's for sure," Katie responds.

She makes me want to giggle, and how that's possible when we're doing this, I don't know. If she hadn't been by my side all this time, especially after we escaped our grandfather, I'm not sure what would have happened.

I stop thinking about all of that at once, because I see Skull coming out of the theater. He hasn't changed much. He's still so beautiful, he hurts my eyes. His hair is shorter... a lot shorter. I mourn it. I want to move my fingers in it like I used to. He's lost weight too, though his muscles are still amazing, especially his arms. I want to take off running to him. Even being this heavily pregnant, I probably would.

Except for one small detail. He has a beautiful blonde standing beside him. She's got angles and curves I could never hope to achieve. She's laughing at him and you can tell she's enjoying being with him. He's got his hand on her back, just like he used to do with me. He has his club surrounding them, protecting her.

I know that's it, without a doubt. My heart feels as if it's being squeezed. *Has he moved on already?* I almost whimper at the pain that fills me with that thought. My hand goes to rub my stomach. I was so young and completely out of my element. What if what I thought was soul mates was nothing like that to Skull? It's only been months. Could I have meant so little? Oh, God... What if I have this all wrong?

"Beth, I'm sure it's not what it looks like. We're going to go over there and stick to the plan, right?"

"I don't know, Katie."

"Well, I do! We've been through too much not to do this. Where's your balls?"

"My balls?" I shake my head, snapping out of it. She's right. I'm just allowing all the things my grandfather said to fill me with doubt. Skull loves me. He's flirting, but he's not telling her he loves her. I can do this. "To the wall, right?" I look at her, trying to build up my courage.

"Exactly." She holds out her hand. I take a breath and grab it, rubbing my stomach. I've been on my feet too much; my daughter is protesting. I smile at the thought of the child I'm carrying. Hand-in-hand, Katie and I step away from the bushes and go to give my husband the shock of his life.

We get just behind them, and this big pain hits me in my back. It's so hard that I have to stop and catch my breath. I breathe through it and concentrate on the sound of Skull's voice. I can hear him now. Somehow, his voice is different. It doesn't have the same depth to it as it used to. He almost reminds me of Torch; laidback, always happy… *Is he happy?*

"A pity, but yet you have not seen what I have to offer. Perhaps I may yet entice you," Skull's saying, and that pain in my chest increases. *Entice her?* Oh God, has he really moved on?

"You get an A for effort, but don't bother, and save us both some trouble," the girl says, but she's laughing at him. They look good together. They look like they *fit.*

"I think I might be able to surprise you, *querida*," he tells her.

And with that one word, it feels as if he's destroyed me. I think, for a moment, my heart actually stops. The pain is so bad, I can't breathe. I feel it *everywhere.* Tears fill my eyes. I just hold my stomach and try to sort through this, trying to bear the pain.

"Bethie?" Katie looks worried. She should be. I think I'm dying. There's so much pain.

"He called her *queriaa*," I tell her. He called me several things, true. But, most of the time, he called me *querida. Dear one*, he told me. It sounds like something an elderly grandmother would say, but not when Skull said it. When he called me dear one, I felt like I was dear and precious to him. "That's what he called me…" I whisper.

I might have underestimated my sister because she gets such a look of anger on her when she looks at me. "Right. I got this, Bethie. Don't worry," she tells me. "I'm going to tear his balls off. We can put them on a chain and hang them in the baby's room as a mobile," she growls.

I want to yell at her—to either tell her to quit or to cheer her on—but right then, another pain hits my back and squeezes around my stomach. It's so strong it nearly brings me to my knees. Then, I feel it. Warmth spreads from my legs and, in an instant, Skull isn't on my mind.

"Katie!" I cry, my dress soaked. *"My water just broke!"*

The End.

Turn the page for an excerpt of Book 2 of the Devil's Blaze Trilogy, coming your way on February 25. I've also included the first story in the Devil's Blaze: Craved, a novella, right after it! Then, keep going for news on upcoming books and exciting excerpts of books from some of my favorite authors!

BURNED

TORCH

*"I like women. I like all women.
I like them more when they have
a little fire inside them."*

1

I kick my feet up in the seat across from me. The chair scoots on the wooden floor, tilts, then rights itself as I cross my legs. Sabre and Latch are going on about some damn trip Lucy wants to go on, a semester at sea or something. Annie is adamant that it's a great opportunity. Those two are like old married men now—even if it is to the same woman. I tune them out.

I *should* be tracking Beth and her sister Katie down. That's what I'm in this blink-and-you-miss-it town for, but hell, I needed a day off. I've been working with Diesel and his crew nonstop trying to find these bitches, but they were covering their tracks—and that's putting it lightly. I don't know who they're getting help from, but whoever it is, is damn good. Skull has me, Sabre, and Latch tracking down leads in Tennessee which, according to the latest intel we have, is where the Donahues have spotted Katie. Skull is looking at other states too and called in some markers. My brother is in bad shape at just the thought that Beth is still alive and has been lying to him this whole time. If it's true, and so far everything we're learning says it is, then I kind of pity her.

Skull will destroy her.

I'm not thinking about that shit. Right now, my eyes and attention are elsewhere. Specifically, on the woman sitting with her back turned to me at the bar. She's got curves to make men fall down on their knees and worship at her feet. Her ass is this perfect pear shape that draws a man's eye and makes him want to dig his hands in and hold on for the ride.

"I bet you a C-note you can't tap that," Sabre says, reclining back in his seat.

"You make it too easy. It's like taking candy from a baby," I tell him with an easy grin.

"I don't think so, Torch, brother. Something about that woman says back the fuck away," Latch warns me.

"You see *that*, and all I see is the warm pussy I'm going to bury myself in for a couple of hours," I tell him.

"Just a couple of hours?" Sabre teases.

"Yeah. After that, I'm coming back to collect your money." I get up and saunter over to the lady in question.

"Crash and burn, Torch!" he yells out, and I hold my hand over my shoulder and flip him off.

I lean against the bar, standing beside little Miss-make-my-dick-cry-mercy. She's the hottest thing I've seen in a while, which is good because I'd never admit it to those sad fucks back there who are basically sown up over one woman. I haven't found a woman my dick has been interested in for freaking months. Two, to be exact. That might not sound like a lot to some people, but for me, it's a freaking lifetime. My cock is all-in with this little number, though.

She's a gorgeous brunette. Hell, even with the smoke in the bar and the dim lights, the color glows. It falls in waves down her back and over her shoulders, and I literally ache to wrap my hands in it. Her skin is tanned, and I'd love to lick every inch and see if it tastes half as good as it looks. She's squeezed into tight jeans that hug that ass that I've been memorizing to jack-off to later.

The top is just as good as the bottom. She has the sexiest little black top I've ever laid eyes on. Small black straps caress her shoulders, and silky fabric hugs her breasts close and draws attention to them. Fuck me, they are easily a D-cup or bigger— years of experience makes me feel comfortable enough to say that. Still, what really makes my balls heat up is the way her tits keep trying to bust out of that top. Those breasts are made for a man's dick to slide in between. My eyes drink it all in. I have to move my hand down to stretch and shift my cock. *Sweet mother of God.* Yeah, he's more than standing at attention for that thick ass, fuck-me tits, and climb-me legs.

She's yet to notice me as she chats with the bartender. It's enough to give a man a complex. I'll have to punish her for that later. The bartender's eyes are glued to her breasts, and I think it's about time that stops. Those are *mine* tonight. He can try again tomorrow.

I lean down against the bar, look directly at her instead of him. "Jack and Coke," I order, waiting for her to say something.

She stops talking to what's-his-face and turns her attention to me. Green eyes. I don't ever remember having seen eyes this particular color before. I don't think I'll be able to ever forget them now. The color of a murky sea, they draw me in. She looks me up and down while sucking on a straw. She slowly puts her drink back down and tilts her head to the side to get a look at me.

I speak first. "Can I buy you a refill?"

She shrugs. "If you want, I won't stop you."

"What are you drinking?"

"White chocolate martini."

"That's not exactly a manly drink to order—"

"I'm not a man."

"Oh, I noticed, girl… I noticed."

"Here's your Jack and Coke," the bartender grumbles over my shoulder. He slams the drink down beside me in a thank-you-for-cock-blocking-me kind of way.

"The lady here will have another martini," I tell him while taking my drink and sliding onto the stool beside her.

She watches me drink and shakes her head.

"Something on your mind?" I ask, studying the look in her eyes.

"Just appreciating the fact that my drink wasn't manly

enough for a Jack-and-Coke kind of guy." She leans in, smirking.

She's more than a little drunk, which is kind of a shame, but not a deal breaker by a long shot. She has sass and, fuck, I can definitely appreciate that.

"Don't dis the Coke man. It lets me stay sober and still get a kick from the Jack so I can admire your fine ass longer."

"Did you just say *fine ass?*"

"Oh, yeah. You have one very fine ass."

She takes her drink from the bartender without acknowledging him. I can't help but shoot him a look of victory. Fucker wants to deck me right now.

"Do these lines actually work for you?"

"They've been known to," I answer honestly.

"Damn. I thought I was, but apparently I'm not drunk enough, because so far they're not working at all on my *fine ass.*"

"Ouch," I say with a smile, taking another gulp and enjoying this conversation way more than I would have thought.

"In fact," she adds, leaning in closer to me, and I can only hope her breasts come out to play as she leans further—surely another inch and nipples will be visible. "You could even say I'm kind of... *bored.*"

Those words would chill a lesser man, but the light in her eyes and the smile on her face tell me different. I put my drink down and move my finger along the side of her face.

"I sure wouldn't want to bore you. How about we leave this place and go play Barbie?"

She looks at me, genuinely confused.

"Barbie?"

I lean in close to her ear, inhaling her scent. Sweet and sugary like cookies. Damn... just *damn.*

"Yeah. I'll be Ken, and you can be the box I come in," I whisper against her ear. I mean, really, can I help it if my lips graze against it?

She grows still, then pulls away from me.

"Did you really go there just now?" she asks like she can't

quite believe it. She's shaking her head and laughing, and she does *not* look bored.

Score one for me. "Figured I better come at you with my A-game," I joke, taking another drink.

"Good plan, Romeo. Not sure this romance could survive your B-game."

"What's your name, pretty girl?"

"Oh man, you are cheesy."

"I do try. Come on, give me your name."

She stops and looks at me for a minute, and it's almost as if she's trying to place me, but then shrugs it off.

"We won't know each other long enough to have to worry about using names."

"Is that so?"

"That's a fact."

I lean in to whisper for her ears only. "My name's Hunter. You need to remember it so you can scream it out later," I tell her.

She leans in to me, and her sweet scent claims me. "I'll do that very thing, Hunter. I'll scream it so hard my landlord will think someone is killing me."

"Now, we're talking," I tell her, my dick rock hard as she gets up. She starts to walk around me and I grab her arm, unable to ignore the way her warm skin sends an electric current through my body. "Where are you going?"

"I figured I'd better hurry before the store closes."

"The store?"

"Yeah, Hunter. I'm all out of batteries. I'll need them tonight when I'm in bed alone, but don't worry, I'll remember your name when I make myself come."

BURNED

KATIE

*"I gave up on fairytales. They're always backwards.
In real life, Prince Charming might marry Snow White, but he's
busy boning Little Miss Muffet two nights a week."*

2

He's a player. I spotted him a mile away. I also remember him. He's with my sister's husband's crew. What was it she said his name was? Torch? I like Hunter better. I should be running away from him, and I started to. Then, he touched my arm. In that moment, I felt connected to him. I don't know how to describe it, but I did. My life hasn't been my own from the day my father took me away from my mom and sister, Bethie. I've learned to take my pleasure where I can find it. Something about Hunter, or Torch—whoever he is—calls to me, and I'm going throw caution to the wind. Still, I need to make sure I've protected Bethie and her daughter Gabriella.

"I'll bring you more pleasure than anything with batteries, sweetness."

I wonder if he really thinks these lines work? He's a man, so he probably does, when really it's that fucking body of his that's working for me. He's got that 'V', I just know it. You know the one; the finely chiseled indention that starts along the hip bone and runs lower into the promised land? The one that makes all women lose their minds? It's there and, by God, I want to see it.

I just need to do one thing first. "Well, I need to use the little girl's room. So, I'll think about it. In the meantime, you just sit there and look pretty."

"I'll sit here and admire the view, instead," he tells me.

That's just annoying. He doesn't realize that's the one thing he could say that would turn me off. Still, I know he's watching, and it kills me, but I wore the right shoes tonight to hide my limp, so I take all the energy and focus I have into making sure my steps don't falter. When I make it to the little foyer that leads to the bathrooms, I lean against the wall and breathe. After I make sure he didn't follow me, I head into the bathroom. Luckily, it's a single-stall bathroom, so I lock the door, pull myself up on the counter, and call Bethie.

"Bethie, we have problems," I tell her.

"What? Where are you? Are you in trouble? I told you, you need to stop running around. They can find us."

"Will you relax? I don't look anything like you anymore... or myself, for that matter. Between the hair dye, the colored contacts, and thirty pounds I've packed on my ass, I don't even recognize my damn self in the mirror."

"It's too dangerous. You know they will be hunting for us. Especially now that grandfather—"

"Don't call him that. Anyway, that's kind of why I'm calling. I'm at the Broke Spoke and... there's this guy hitting on me. He says his name is Hunter, but..."

"But?" she asks, her voice laced with fear.

"It's that same good-looking biker who was at the movie theater that night with Skull."

"Oh God! You have to run, Katie! If one of Skull's crew is there, that means he has to know. Colin's carried out on his threat."

"Bethie, have you ever thought... maybe, just maybe, it'd be best to come clean and let Skull know you're alive?"

"We tried that, remember? Three times. I can't risk it anymore, especially with the family out there looking for us. Do you really think they will let me, you, or Gabby live? After what we did?"

She's right. They wouldn't. They won't stop until we're six feet under. "Okay. Then you need to start our escape plan, tonight. Take Gabby and go. I'll meet you in the morning."

"What? No! You need to come home now. We can't chance that whoever is there might place our resemblance and start asking questions."

"That's not going to happen, Bethie. You worry too much."

"And you don't worry enough. Please, Katie, do this for me. Come home and let's head out together."

"I'll try my best, but—"

"But nothing! Just do!"

Before she can finish talking, there's a hard knock on the door.

"Sweetness? You in there? I'm getting lonely out here without you."

"Oh my God!" Beth hisses over the phone. "Is that Torch??"

Hmmm. I guess I did forget to mention which one was here, probably because Bethie knew that fine man starred in several of my hot dreams after I saw him that night.

"I'll be out in a minute," I call to him through the door. "Anyone ever tell you that you shouldn't crowd a woman, Romeo?"

"I'm too busy fucking them senseless to listen to advice," he counters.

"Bethie, I've got to go," I whisper. "Just follow the escape plan we set up when we moved here. If something happens and I don't show, move on to our next destination. I'll meet you there. I promise."

"No, I don't like this. I can call the cops or something, make a fake report and distract them, then—"

"I got this. Just get my niece safe."

"You and I are going to have words when you make it to our spot," she warns me.

"I'll look forward to it. Stay safe, Bethie. Love you bigger than outer space."

"Love you, too," she whispers.

I hang up, trying to swallow down my nerves. I walk to the door and open it. Sure enough, there's the object of my lusts leaning against the wall with a wicked smile on his lips. He holds out a hand to me.

"Dance with me, sweetness. I want to feel you in my arms."

I let him take my hand, and I know I'm going to ignore my sister's plea tonight. I just hope I don't live to regret it.

GLOSSARY OF TERMS

Amante dulce	Sweet lover
Bella	Beautiful
Cielo	Sky
Has ido a hermano ahora	You've gone too far, brother.
Hermano	Brother
Lo siento, amor	I'm sorry, honey.
Loca	Crazy
Madre	Mother
Mi	My
Mujer	Woman
Pendejos	Assholes
Nunca dejar ir	Never let go.
Querida	Dear one
Si	Yes
Soy todo tuyo	I'm all yours.
Te amo	I love you.
Tengo miedo han sido capturados	I am afraid I have been captured.
Tio	Uncle

FINAL NOTE FROM THE AUTHOR

I hope you guys enjoyed Skull and Beth's introduction. I hated making this book a cliffhanger, honestly I tried every way I could to prevent it. The more the characters began talking, I just couldn't. I had to give in completely. I promised I'd never do that and now I understand the struggle that an author has. You don't want to disappoint your readers. You love them, (all of you), but you struggle to stay true to the characters. My compromise is that I'm going to kick my ass to get the books out superfast. Burned will pick up with this one. Skull and Beth will be featured in it, but it will contain Katie and Torch's love story. I will have it to you next month (February 25th is the goal) and then Conquered, the final installment which is Skull and Beth's Happy Ending will come your way in March.

Thank you so much for everything you've done to support me this past year. It's been an amazing year and you have my undying gratitude. I love to hear from my readers! Please feel free to contact me!

Jordan Marie
www.jordanmarieauthor.com

Made in the USA
Columbia, SC
23 July 2019